ALGORITHM·323

Erasmus Cromwell-Smith II

Algorithm - 323
© Erasmus Cromwell-Smith II
© Erasmus Press

ISBN: 9781733028981
Publisher: Erasmus Press
Proofreading: D. Suster, Tracy-Ann Wynter, Janet Bartos
Cover Design: Alfredo Sainz
Interior Design: Elisa Arraiz Lucca
www.erasmuscromwellsmith.com
First edition
Printed in USA, 2025.

<u>**Books written by the author**</u>

In English,

En Español,

As Erasmus Cromwell-Smith II:

Como Erasmus Cromwell-Smith II:

The Equilibrist series,

La serie El Equilibrista,

(Inspirational/Philosophical)
-The Happiness Triangle (Vol.1).
-Geniality (Vol. 2).
-The Magic in Life (Vol. 3).
-Poetry in Equilibrium (Vol. 4).

(Inspiracional/Filosófico)
-El triángulo de la felicidad (Vol. 1).
-Genialidad (Vol. 2).
-La magia de la vida (Vol. 3).
-Poesía en equilibrio (Vol. 4).

(Young Adults)
-The Orloj of Prague (Vol.1).
-The Orloj of Venice (Vol. 2).
-The Orloj of Paris (Vol. 3).
-The Orloj of London (Vol. 4).
-Poetry in Balance (Vol. 5).

(Jóvenes Adultos)
-El Orloj de Praga (Vol.1).
-El Orloj de Venecia (Vol.2).
-El Orloj de Paris (Vol. 3).
-El Orloj de Londres (Vol. 4).
-Poesía en Balance (Vol. 5).

As Erasmus Cromwell-Smith

Como Erasmus Cromwell-Smith

The South Beach Conversational Method   *El Método Conversacional South Beach*
(Educational)   (Educacional)
- Spanish   - Inglés,
- German   - Alemán
- French   - Francés
- Italian   - Italiano
- Portuguese   - Portugués

The Nicolas Tosh Series, (Sci-fi)
- Algorithm-323 (Volume 1).
- Tosh (Volume 2).

As Nelson Hamel (*)

The Paradise Island Series, (Action/Thriller)
- Miami Beach, Paradise Island (Volume 1).
- Dangerous Liaisons: Miami Beach (Volume 2).
- The Rebel Hackers of Point Breeze (Volume 1), (Sci/fi).

(*) in collaboration with Charles Sibley.

All titles are or will be available in audiobooks

TABLE OF CONTENTS

Chapter 1   15
San Carlos de Bariloche, Argentina – Cerro Catedral, 1974
Chapter 2   19
Washington, D.C. – The White House, 2016 (Day 1, 10:00 P.M. ET
Chapter 3   22
San Carlos de Bariloche, Argentina – Nuclear Power Plant Lab (1974, One Month Later)
Epilogue to Chapter 3   25
Chapter 4   26
Zermatt, Switzerland – 1977
Chapter 5   28
Zurich, Switzerland – Office of Union National Des Banques (UNB) 1977, A Few Months Later – 9 A.M. Central European Time (CET)
Chapter 6   32
Miami, Florida, USA – 2015 (Five Months Before Day 1)
Chapter 7   36
Miami, Florida – Zaptec Headquarters (2015, Three Months Before Day 1)
Chapter 8   38
Miami, Florida – Bain & Associates Headquarters (2015, Three Months Before the Present Day)
Chapter 9   40
Canouan Island, The Caribbean – 2015 (Three Months Before Day 1)
Chapter 10   44
Miami, Florida – American Justice Center (2016, Day 2, 3:00 P.M. ET)
Chapter 11   46
Washington, D.C. – The White House / Miami, Florida – American Justice Center (2016, Day 2, 3:00 P.M. ET)
Chapter 12   50
Washington, D.C. – The White House (2016, Day 1, 11:00 P.M. ET)
Chapter 13   53
Washington, D.C. – The White House (2016, Day 1, 11:30 P.M. ET)
Chapter 14   58
Boston, Massachusetts – Harvard Business School (2016, Day 1, 8:00 A.M. ET)
Chapter 15   61
Telluride, Colorado – Black Eagle Ranch (2016, Day 2, 7:00 A.M. MT)
Chapter 16   64
Zurich, Switzerland – Office of the Union National des Banques (UNB), 1977, 8:00 A.M. CET
Chapter 17   68
Zermatt, Switzerland – Zermatt Data Center (2016, Day 2, 8:00 A.M. CET / 2:00 A.M. ET)

Chapter 18   70
Zermatt, Switzerland – Zermatt Data Center (2016, Day 2, 8:30 A.M. CET / 2:30 A.M. ET)
Chapter 19   72
Telluride, Colorado – Black Eagle Ranch (2016, Day 2, 7:15 A.M. MT)
Chapter 20   74
Washington, D.C. – Federal Courthouse (2016, Day 2, 2:30 P.M. ET)
Chapter 21   75
Washington, D.C. – The White House (2016, Day 2, 2:30 P.M. ET)
Chapter 22   78
Zurich, Switzerland – Tosh's Organization Headquarters (2016, Day 2)
Chapter 23   81
Zermatt, Switzerland – Zermatt Data Center (2016, Day 2, 6:30 P.M. CET / 12:30 P.M. ET)
Chapter 24   83
Buenos Aires, Argentina – Sarmiento Travel Agency (1984, 11:00 P.M. ART
Chapter 25   87
Miami & Washington, D.C. – Federal Courthouses (2016, Day 2, 4:00 P.M. ET)
Chapter 26   89
Washington, D.C. – Senate Office Building (2016, Day 2, 2:30 P.M. ET)
Chapter 27   92
San Carlos de Bariloche, Argentina – Professor Benjamín Borjes's Home (1984, 10:00 P.M. ART)
Chapter 28   95
San Carlos de Bariloche, Argentina – Professor Benjamín Borjes's Home (1984, Next Day, 9:15 A.M. ART)
Chapter 29   99
Zermatt, Switzerland – Zermatt Data Center (2016, Day 2, 6:30 P.M. CET / 12:30 P.M. ET)
Chapter 30   102
Miami, Florida – 2016, Day 2 (6:00 P.M. ET)
Chapter 31   106
Washington, D.C. – The White House / West Palm Beach, Florida (2016, Day 2, 8:30 P.M. ET)
Chapter 32   108
Washington, D.C. – The White House (2016, Day 2, 8:30 P.M. ET)
Chapter 33   112
Harlem, New York City – 2015 (Twelve Months Before Day 1)
Chapter 34   114
New York City – Starbucks Café, Midtown (2015, Twelve Months Before Day 1)
Chapter 35   117
Washington, D.C. – The White House (2016, Day 2, 9:00 P.M. ET
Chapter 36   119
Washington, D.C. – FBI Headquarters (2015, Twelve Months Before Day 1)
Chapter 37   122

Washington, D.C. – The White House (2016, Day 2, 10:00 P.M. ET)
Chapter 38   124
Miami, Florida – FBI North Miami Station (2015, Twelve Months Before Day 1)
Chapter 39   127
Miami, Florida – Livingstone, White & Stawskoski Law Office (2015, Twelve Months Before Day 1)
Chapter 40   129
Washington, D.C. – The White House (2016, Day 2, 10:30 P.M. ET)
Chapter 41   133
Washington, D.C. – The White House (2016, Day 3, 2:00 A.M. ET)
Chapter 42   136
Washington, D.C. – Emergency Federal Court Hearing (2016, Day 3, 8:52 A.M. ET)
Chapter 43   140
Washington, D.C. – The White House (2016, Day 3, 8:25 A.M. ET)
Chapter 44   143
San Carlos de Bariloche, Argentina – Cerro Catedral (1983)
Chapter 45   146
Emerald Coast, Sardinia, Italy (1954)
Chapter 46   148
San Carlos de Bariloche, Argentina – Cerro Catedral (1983)
Chapter 47   151
Buenos Aires, Argentina (1983 – Two Months Earlier)   151
Chapter 48   154
San Carlos de Bariloche, Argentina – Cerro Catedral (1983)   154
Chapter 49   157
Buenos Aires, Argentina – Bruno Buonarroti's Computer Store (Spring 1989)
Chapter 50   159
San Carlos de Bariloche, Argentina – University Lab (Spring 1989, Twenty-Four Hours Earlier)
Chapter 51   162
Buenos Aires, Argentina – Bruno Buonarroti's Computer Store (Spring, 1989)
Chapter 52   164
Las Vegas, Nevada – Caesars Palace Honeymoon Suite (Autumn, 1989)
Chapter 53   166
Buenos Aires, Argentina – Alejandra Martínez-López's Home (Autumn 1989)
Chapter 54   168
Zermatt, Switzerland – Christmas, 1989
Chapter 55   171
Miami, Florida – Day 3 (12:00 Noon)
Chapter 56   174
Washington, D.C. – The White House (2016, Day 3, 3:00 P.M. ET)
Chapter 57   177
Miami, Florida – The Tosh Home (2016, Day 3, 3:00 P.M. ET)
Chapter 58   181

Miami, Florida – The Tosh Home (2016, Day 3, 6:00 P.M. ET)
Chapter 59   184
Miami, Florida & Washington, D.C. – Day 3 (10:00 P.M. ET)
Chapter 60   187
Buenos Aires, Argentina (Day 3, 12:00 A.M. ET/ART)
Chapter 61   189
Washington, D.C. – The White House (2016, Day 4, 1:00 A.M. ET)
Chapter 62   191
Miami, Florida & Washington, D.C. – Day 4 (2:00 A.M. ET)
Chapter 63   193
Miami, Florida – Day 4 (3:00 A.M. ET)
Chapter 64   194
Miami, Florida (The Tosh Home) / Washington, D.C. (The White House) – Day 5 (10:30 P.M. ET)
Chapter 65   196
Shanghai, China / Zermatt, Switzerland (Data Center) – Day 5 (12:00 P.M. CST / 12:00 Noon CET)
Chapter 66   197
Shanghai, China – Day 6 (12:00 Noon CST / 12:00 Midnight ET / 6:00 A.M. CET)
Chapter 67   198
Zermatt, Switzerland (Zermatt Data Center) – Day 6 (7:00 A.M. CET / 1:00 P.M. ET / 1:00 P.M. CST Next Day)
Chapter 68   199
Washington, D.C. – The White House, 2016, Day 6 (2:00 P.M. ET)
Chapter 69   202
Langley, Virginia—CIA Headquarters, 2016, Day 6 (4:00 P.M. ET)
Chapter 70   204
Zermatt, Switzerland – Zermatt Data Center 2016– Day 7, 7:00 A.M. (CET)
Chapter 71   208
Shanghai, China – 2016, Day 7, 7:30 A.M. (CST)
Chapter 72   210
Zermatt, Switzerland – Zermatt Data Center 2016 – Day 7, 7:30 A.M. (CET)
Chapter 73   212
Palo Alto, California – 2016, Day 8, 3:00 A.M. (PT)
Chapter 74   214
Boston, Massachusetts – 2016, Day 8, 6:45 P.M. (ET)
Chapter 75   216
Miami, Florida – The Tosh Home 2016, Day 8, 7:00 A.M. (ET)
Chapter 76   219
Zermatt, Switzerland | Washington, D.C. | Miami, Florida 2016 – Day 8, 7:30 A.M. (CET) / 1:30 P.M. (ET)
Chapter 77   220
Shanghai, China – 2016, Day 8, 7:45 P.M. (CST)
Chapter 78   222

Zermatt, Switzerland | Washington, D.C. | Miami, Florida 2016 – Day 8, 8:00 A.M. (ET) / 2:00 P.M. (CET)
Chapter 79   224
Shanghai, China – 2016, Day 8, 8:30 P.M. (CST)
Chapter 80   226
Zermatt, Switzerland | Washington, D.C. | Miami, Florida 2016 – Day 8, 9:00 A.M. (ET) / 3:00 P.M. (CET)
Chapter 81   227
Boston, Massachusetts – 2016, Day 8, 9:00 A.M. (ET)
Chapter 82   228
Palo Alto, California – 2016, Day 8, 6:00 A.M. (PT)
Chapter 83   229
Zermatt, Switzerland | Washington, D.C. | Miami, Florida 2016 – Day 8, 11:00 A.M. (ET) / 5:00 P.M. (CET)
Chapter 84   231
San Antonio, Texas – 2016, Day 8, 12:00 P.M. (CT)   231
Chapter 85   233
Chicago, Illinois – 2016, Day 8, 12:00 P.M. (CT)
Chapter 86   234
Zermatt, Switzerland | Washington, D.C. | Miami, Florida 2016 – Day 8, 8:00 P.M. (CET) / 2:00 P.M. (ET)
Chapter 87   237
San Antonio, Texas – FBI Interrogation Room 2016 – Day 8, 5:00 P.M. (CT)
Chapter 88   239
Chicago, Illinois – FBI Office 2016 – Day 8, 6:00 P.M. (CT)
Chapter 89   240
Washington, D.C. – Dulles Airport/FBI Office 2016 – Day 8, 6:00 A.M. (ET)
Chapter 90   241
Zermatt, Switzerland – Zermatt Data Center 2016 – Day 8, 12:30 P.M. (CET)
Chapter 91   243
Washington, D.C. – Dulles Airport/FBI Office 2016 – Day 8, 7:00 A.M. (ET)
Chapter 92   245
Zermatt, Switzerland – Zermatt Data Center 2016 – Day 8, 2:30 P.M. (CET)
Chapter 93   247
Washington, D.C. – The White House Bunker 2016 – Day 8, 2:45 P.M. (ET)
Chapter 94   248
Zermatt, Switzerland – Zermatt Data Center 2016 – Day 8, 10:00 P.M. (CET)
Chapter 95   250
Zermatt, Switzerland | Washington, D.C. | Miami, Florida 2016 – Day 8, 11:00 P.M. (CET) / 5:00 P.M. (ET)
Chapter 96   251
Shanghai, China | Washington, D.C. – White House Bunker 2016 – Day 9, 6:00 A.M. (CST) / 6:00 P.M. (ET)
Chapter 97   253
Washington, D.C. – The White House 2016 – Day 9, 7:00 P.M. (ET)

Chapter 98   254
Washington, D.C. – The White House 2016 – Day 9, 11:00 P.M. (ET)
Chapter 99   256
Zermatt, Switzerland | The White House, Washington, D.C. | Miami, Florida
2016 – Day 10, 6:00 A.M. (CET) / 12:00 P.M. (ET)
Chapter 100   259
Shanghai, China – 2009 (Six Years Earlier)
Chapter 101   261
Island off the Coast of China – Aboard an Agusta Helicopter (2009)
Chapter 102   264
Hong Kong Island, China – 2016, Day 10, 3:00 P.M. (HKT)
Chapter 103   265
Zermatt, Switzerland – Zermatt Data Center 2016 – Day 10, 9:00 A.M. (CET)
Chapter 104   266
Zermatt, Switzerland – Zermatt Data Center 2016 – Day 10, 9:15 A.M. (CET)
Chapter 105   268
Hong Kong Island, China – 2016, Day 10, 3:30 P.M. (HKT)
Chapter 106   269
Zermatt, Switzerland – Zermatt Data Center 2016 – Day 10, 9:45 A.M. (CET)
Chapter 107   271
Shanghai, China – 2016, Day 10, 8:30 P.M. (CST)
Chapter 108   273
Washington, D.C. – The White House Bunker 2016 – Day 10, 8:00 A.M. (ET)
Chapter 109   274
Island off the Coast, China – 2016 – Day 10, 9:30 P.M. (CST)
Chapter 110   276
Washington, D.C. – The White House Bunker 2016 – Day 10 – 9:30 A.M. (ET)
Chapter 111   278
San Francisco, California – San Francisco International Airport 2016 – Day 11 –
6:30 A.M. (PT)
Chapter 112   284
Zermatt, Switzerland | Washington, D.C., USA | San Francisco, California, USA
Lingtao World Headquarters – Day 11 (2016) 5:00 P.M. CET / 11:00 A.M. ET /
8:00 A.M. PT

EPILOGUE TO ALGORITHM–323   295
Zermatt, Switzerland – Several Weeks Later

PROLOGUE TO ALGORITHM–325   298
One Year Later – Lingtao Campus, Bay Area

GLOSSARY OF MAJOR CHARACTERS

Below are the principal figures that recur throughout *Algorithm – 323*. (Some secondary roles, like local lawyers or minor conspirators, are omitted for brevity.)

1. **Nicolás Tosh**

   o **Role**: Protagonist, mathematical prodigy, creator of the Communicational Discrete Algorithms (CDA-319–324).

   o **Background**: Born in Bariloche, Argentina; lost his mother early. Developed a hidden quantum data center in Zermatt, Switzerland. Also established Walkyria (for-profit) and Experta (foundation).

   o **Key Traits**: Brilliant, morally torn between secrecy and serving the "greater good," revered by G-7 powers as a "strategic asset."

2. **Alejandra Martínez-López (Tosh)**

   o **Role**: Nicolás's wife, formidable in her own right with top-secret projects.

   o **Background**: Argentine software entrepreneur. Eventually learns part of Tosh's hidden identity.

   o **Key Traits**: Fiercely independent, deeply loyal, but unsettled by the moral costs of mind-reading tech.

3. **Rainer Sábato**

o   **Role**: Tosh's longtime partner and co-architect of the Zermatt Data Center.

o   **Background**: Met Nicolás while skiing in Bariloche. Oversees day-to-day operations, software expansions, quantum network security.

o   **Key Traits**: Practical, detail-oriented, Toby's "voice of reason." Feels a deep sense of ethical caution.

4. **President Kelly O'Sullivan**

o   **Role**: Current U.S. President who becomes Tosh's reluctant ally, using CDA for national security.

o   **Background**: Inherited the G-7 obligations to protect Tosh's algorithms but initially believed the smear campaign.

o   **Key Traits**: Pragmatic, wary of the technology's power, forced to cut hush-hush deals to preserve stability.

5. **General Collins**

o   **Role**: High-ranking Pentagon official, point person for CDA usage in the U.S.

o   **Background**: Coordinates with Tosh, orchestrates intelligence sweeps, authorized by G-7 to handle WMD-level algorithms.

o   **Key Traits**: Loyal, direct, but treads ethical lines in pushing for broader CDA

Author's Note

Dear Reader,

I have always been fascinated by the intersection of technology and society. As a computer scientist and mathematician, I have witnessed the extraordinary power of algorithms to transform our world—for better or worse. Yet with such power comes an unshakable responsibility, a duty to weigh the consequences of what we unleash. *Algorithm – 323* is born from that tension, a cautionary tale woven from threads of ambition, innovation, and betrayal.

This story follows a man whose brilliance crafts a tool of unimaginable potential, only to watch it slip from his grasp, twisted into purposes he never foresaw. It is a narrative of clashing ideals: security versus privacy, progress versus control, freedom versus order. My hope is that these pages stir you to question the machines we build and the hands that guide them. Thank you for stepping into this world with me.

Sincerely,

Erasmus Cromwell Smith

Prologue

San *Carlos de Bariloche, Argentina – 1968*

The classroom held its breath. Outside, the windswept hills loomed beneath the craggy Andes, but within these four walls, only the faint rasp of chalk on slate broke the silence. Ten-year-old **Nicolás Tosh** hunched over his desk, dark eyes fixed on the labyrinth of numbers that stretched across the blackboard. Around him, his classmates had surrendered, their own slates blank or marred by half-erased scribbles. Yet Nicolás pressed on, unruffled by their defeat.

He was different—everyone knew it. Where other children chased each other through Bariloche's brisk mountain air, Nicolás lost himself in books and the hidden rhythms of logic. His teachers whispered "prodigy" with equal parts wonder and unease, sensing the shadow cast by such brilliance. A mind so expansive in a boy so small—what burdens would it bring?

Nicolás noticed none of their hushed concern. For him, the world was a puzzle, and numbers were the key. The equation before him now was no gentle riddle—it was a *beast*, bristling with exponents and variables that defied even seasoned adults. His pencil flew, tracing paths his classmates had never dreamed of.

Suddenly, a jolt of clarity lit his gaze. The pattern snapped into focus, simple and inevitable. He scribbled his final line, grinned with triumph, and thrust his hand into the air.

"Señor Gomez," he called, voice bright with certainty. **"I have the answer."**

The teacher looked up, eyebrows rising. **"So soon? This is no ordinary problem, Nicolás. Are you sure?"**

"Yes, Señor Gomez. I'm sure."

Slowly, Señor Gomez crossed the room and peered at Nicolás's slate. His breath caught.

"This… this is correct. Perfectly so. How did you—?"

Nicolás shrugged, small shoulders buoyed by excitement. **"I saw the pattern. It was there all along."**

The teacher's voice softened to a near-whisper, a flicker of awe and warning mingling in his gaze. **"You have a gift, Nicolás. Great gifts can become great burdens—remember that. Use your talents wisely."**

The caution slipped past the boy like a gentle breeze. He was ten, after all, and numbers were a kind of magic. *Wisdom* and *burdens* were adult concerns.

But the years ahead would prove Señor Gomez right. Nicolás's extraordinary mind would build wonders—and witness them turn, sometimes, into nightmares. He would discover that power, once loosed, often takes on a will of its own, and that the gravest threats sometimes wear the most familiar faces.

For now, though, he was just a child in a hushed classroom, the solution shining before him like a promise. The future stretched out boundless and uncharted, waiting for the boy whose brilliance would one day rattle governments and reshape entire worlds.

Chapter 1

San Carlos de Bariloche, Argentina – Cerro Catedral, 1974

San Carlos de Bariloche sits along the shores of Lake Nahuel Huapi, high in Argentina's Cordillera de los Andes. A Bavarian influence runs through its architecture and cuisine—an outdoor paradise with Cerro Catedral as its winter playground. From a distance, its alpine charm seems lifted straight from Europe.

Today, **sixteen-year-old Nicolás Tosh** was determined to seize that alpine magic for himself. He had worked the night shift at Müller Bakery, longing for a full day of skiing on his one day off. By 8:15 A.M., he was already at the base of Cerro Catedral, skis on his shoulder and raring to go. That was when the bad news hit: the chairlifts wouldn't open on time due to a power shortage.

The sun had just begun to streak the sky orange, and the slopes looked flawless from last night's fresh snowfall. Nicolás refused to let a mechanical hiccup ruin his plan. Slipping on his skis and boots, he decided to climb up on foot.

It was every bit as hard as it sounded. With heavy boots and deep snow, he fell repeatedly, scrambling up with stubborn energy each time. One hour of grueling ascent brought him past the stalled lower lift. High above, the untouched upper slopes glistened, calling him higher. Another two hours passed before he reached the crest near the top. The climb was punishing, but the reward—an unbroken sea of white—was irresistible.

He had just caught his breath when a lanky young man came crunching over the snow.

"So, I'm not the only lunatic climbing up today," the stranger said with a grin.

"Apparently not," Nicolás replied, still beaming despite the exertion. His sandy hair and green eyes were bright against the snow.

"I'm heading beyond the summit, to the mountain's far side. There's more walking before the real payoff—pristine off-piste. Interested?"

"Count me in." Nicolás tucked his poles under one arm, then offered his hand. **"I'm Nicolás."**

"Rainer Sábato. Good to meet you."

They found a firmer path through the pines, making the final climb a little easier. Cresting the ridge, they gazed down into a valley cradling a frozen lake. It was nearly 11:30 A.M., and the morning sun glinted off the snow. A stunning panoramic view of the Cordillera de los Andes was right in front of them; 360-degree of nature at its best. Beautiful, rough and calm.

"You local?" Rainer asked.

"Born and raised in San Carlos," Nicolás answered. **"You?"**

"Buenos Aires originally, but spent my teens in Düsseldorf, Germany. Now I work at the nuclear power plant near here."

"So, you're a scientist?" asked Nicolás.

"A nuclear physicist, yes. And you? You're—what—sixteen?"

"I am," Nicolás said, adjusting his goggles. **"I'm finishing a doctorate in mathematics at the local university. I pay my bills at Müller's Bakery."**

Rainer laughed in disbelief. **"A PhD by sixteen? That's more than unusual."**

"My research is in discrete algorithms. The field's still new, so I'm keeping parts of it private."

A curious light sparked in Rainer's eyes. **"Commercial applications?"**

"Possibly. Applied math touches everything: finance, tech, even communication. Discrete algorithms might become central to business someday."

"Or maybe even to physics," Rainer offered. **"Imagine using math to decode photons—like revealing a 'mathematical DNA.'"**

The phrase lit a fuse in Nicolás's mind. He paused, eyes narrowing as if he'd just glimpsed a hidden doorway.

"Photons… or the brain," Nicolás said slowly. **"What if the human brain can be mapped like that—if each mind had a numeric blueprint?"**

"Sounds brilliant in theory," Rainer said. **"But in reality?"**

"Someday," Nicolás said, half to himself, **"this might be possible. If we can isolate how the brain processes information, we could read it, communicate with it—like hooking up two computers."**

"An interesting thought experiment," Rainer mused. **"If you ever make it more than theory, I'll want a front-row seat."**

Nicolás only smiled. He could already feel the idea fermenting—an invisible thread drawing him toward something vast and unexplored. They buckled their skis and glided into the valley, carving arcs in the untracked snow. The slope was a blank canvas, each turn a stroke of exhilaration. Neither spoke much on the descent, both lost in the private thrill of discovery.

Later, as they neared the base, Rainer slowed to a stop, chest heaving from the run.

"That was unreal," he said, pulling off his gloves. **"Maybe we'll see each other again."**

"Count on it," Nicolás replied, already replaying that phrase—*mathematical DNA*—in his thoughts.

He and Rainer parted ways, but neither could shake the feeling that something extraordinary had begun on Cerro Catedral. For Nicolás, the question wouldn't leave him: **What if the mind was simply another system to be mapped, coded, and unlocked?**

That idea would follow him for years to come, driving him to unlock algorithms so powerful they would eventually be classified as Weapons of Mass Destruction. But on that crisp morning in 1974, it was just a spark—a single match struck in the bright mountain air, hinting at the conflagration that lay ahead.

Chapter 2

Washington, D.C. – The White House, 2016 (Day 1, 10:00 P.M. ET)

Forty-two years had passed since a young genius in the Argentine Andes first dreamed of unlocking the human mind. In the hush of the Oval Office, the full weight of that dream—and its unforeseen consequences—now bore down on President **O'Sullivan**.

He was still at his desk, replaying in his mind the tense meeting with CIA Deputy Director Mark Thiel and several cabinet members. A familiar, unsettling hum interrupted his thoughts. Rising from his chair, he retrieved a small, locked case from a side drawer and keyed in a five-digit code.

Inside, three items waited: a slender instruction manual bearing a G-7 seal, a sealed envelope, and a razor-thin display no bigger than a smartphone. The screen pulsed with the words **CODE 321**—words that made President O'Sullivan's stomach clench every time.

He inhaled sharply, tapping the device. **Instantly**, he felt the presence of a voice he knew by sound but had never heard in person.

"Good evening, Mr. President."

The President's pulse ticked faster. **"Mr. Tosh… What brings you tonight?"**

"I'm in immediate danger, Mr. President. Clear and present threat."

That crisp voice resonated **inside** his head, though the Oval Office itself remained silent. According to the G-7 protocol, once the device confirmed the President's location, the communication linked directly to his neural activity. O'Sullivan hated how little anyone understood about *how* or *why* it worked—only that it did.

He flipped open the G-7 manual to the "Clear and Present Danger" section. The heading alone made his mouth go dry. He scanned the lines, dreading what would come next.

"Mr. President, I'm requesting authorization to deploy Algorithm 323."

O'Sullivan's throat tightened. **Algorithm 323.** Even the best minds at the NSA and MIT had failed to unravel its mechanisms fully. The G-7 partners treated it like a weapon of last resort—one with the power to infiltrate, or possibly override, human thought.

He forced himself to remain calm. **"Where are you right now, Mr. Tosh?"**

A sudden image flickered into his mind: a dimly lit cell, a figure hunched behind iron bars. The vision was murky, but the prisoner's desperate posture was unmistakable.

The President braced himself. He had known that Tosh was often off the grid—never in the same place for long. But *this* was something else entirely. Who had captured him, and why?

"Mr. President?" The voice prodded gently. **"Time is critical."**

O'Sullivan inhaled, turning the device in his hand. He loathed this helpless feeling, the sense of dancing to someone else's tune. Yet *someone* had to hold the line. If half the rumors about these Communicational Discrete Algorithms were true, even a slight misuse could set off global consequences.

Still, he couldn't deny Tosh might be the U.S. government's greatest asset. He closed his eyes, recalling the pledge each new president made after the G-7 briefing: *Protect the algorithms. Use them only if there is no other option.* And now, Tosh was asking to *activate* the deadliest one.

O'Sullivan exhaled slowly. **"I'll do what I can, Mr. Tosh. But you know what this means."**

Another silent pause stretched across the Oval Office. His mind raced with questions: *Who took Tosh prisoner? What forces would be unleashed if he granted this authorization?*

He glanced again at the sealed envelope in the case, stamped with the G-7 emblem. He had hoped never to open it. The next moments would decide if he could avoid that inevitability—or if Algorithm 323 was about to come crashing into the world.

Chapter 3

San Carlos de Bariloche, Argentina – Nuclear Power Plant Lab (1974, One Month Later)

Rainer **still** couldn't believe his eyes. In a cramped lab at the local nuclear power plant, he stood before two chalkboards crowded with equations—numbers, symbols, and arrows trailing off like constellations.

Opposite him, **sixteen-year-old Nicolás Tosh** rested a piece of chalk against his chin, deep in thought. One month ago, they had met by chance on Cerro Catedral. Now they were here, forging a plan that felt like science fiction brought to life.

"Are you certain this works on human brains?" Rainer asked, stepping closer to the boards.

Nicolás's eyes sparkled. **"The math suggests it. Computers each have a unique ID. If you know that ID and you know how the system processes data, they can communicate—even transfer files—through cables or airwaves. The same concept applies to the human mind, but with a twist."**

He tapped the first board, labeled **CDA-319 to CDA-324** in bold letters.

"We call it the *Communicational Discrete Set of Algorithms.*" Nicolás began, pointing to the neatly arranged bullet points. **"It does two things: it *calculates* each brain as a set of mathematical formulas and *assigns* a unique identifier number. Then, depending on which CDA we use, we can communicate in different ways."**

Rainer leaned in, scanning the descriptions.

1. **Algorithm 319**

• *Derives a 'mathematical DNA' for every unique brain.*

• *Generates the 'identifier number' that unlocks that brain's data.*

2. **Algorithm 320**

• *Enables one-way or two-way voice communication between a 'carrier' and any identified brain (via a small device).*

• *Carrier can speak out loud; subject's spoken words are converted into thoughts for the carrier.*

3. **Algorithm 321**

• *Allows silent, brain-to-brain communication between carrier and subject—or between carriers themselves.*

4. **Algorithm 322**

• *Lets a carrier observe and record the subject's live experiences: sights, thoughts, sounds.*

• *All data is transmitted and encrypted in a secure facility.*

5. **Algorithm 323**

• *Reconstructs a subject's entire life memory—from birth to present—separating real events from dreams.*

• *Records every sight, word, thought, or sensation as a searchable archive.*

6. **Algorithm 324**

• *Maps the memories of other people who intersect with already identified subjects.*

• *Potentially reconstructs entire networks of interconnected lives.*

"And how exactly do we... do *this*?" Rainer asked, slightly unnerved. He watched Nicolás produce a sleek handheld device that looked like a futuristic remote.

"**We call it the *identifier device.*"** Nicolás spoke with quiet excitement. **"A carrier—or an operator—points it toward the person whose mind we want to map, so long as they're within about a mile. Once the device locks on, the subject is assigned an identifier number. After that, we can talk to them, read or record their thoughts. All the raw data goes to a central data center—something I'm still planning."**

"**And we just... store everything?"** Rainer asked.

"**Yes, in a massive, encrypted node. Someday, the network will be global—wireless, powered by quantum computing. I'm hoping to build that in Switzerland."**

Rainer let out a low whistle. **"You realize the power in this? The risk?"**

"**That's why I'm keeping parts of it private,"** Nicolás said, chalk squeaking as he added final annotations. **"For now, it's just us. But imagine the possibilities—secure communication, mind-to-mind research, medical breakthroughs."**

Rainer exhaled, a blend of awe and trepidation. **"Still, it sounds like a weapon."**

Nicolás nodded slowly. **"I know. And that's exactly why we have to be careful."**

Epilogue to Chapter 3

In the months that followed, Nicolás refined his discrete algorithms, applying a separate system to financial markets and amassing a modest fortune—enough to finance larger ambitions. True to his word, he invited Rainer to join him full-time. By late 1974, they'd laid the groundwork for a secure data center in **Zermatt, Switzerland**, complete with a prototype **quantum computer**.

That autumn, they finished linking their "identifier" devices to the fledgling **Communicational Discrete Set of Algorithms**—CDA-319 through CDA-324. From the outside, it looked like the promise of a new era in computing. Rainer, however, couldn't shake the worry that once you opened the door to a human mind, there was no going back.

Chapter 4

Zermatt, Switzerland – 1977

The helicopter swooped low over the Alps, its rotors slicing the thin mountain air. As **Nicolás Tosh** peered through the window, he felt close enough to brush the rugged peaks with his fingertips. Below, the glacial valleys glistened in shifting hues of green and blue, courtesy of sunlight refracting off crevasses. Farther ahead rose Mont Blanc, its white crown shimmering. Off to one side loomed the massive Monte Rosa. But it was the Matterhorn, Zermatt's iconic rock pyramid, that dominated the skyline, a silent sentinel towering over the valley.

With a sharp dip, the helicopter descended toward the remote Swiss village. Zermatt lay nestled against vertical rock walls and glacier-fed streams, its single main street branching off into narrow alleys. The craft tilted, aiming for a newly built helipad atop a five-story structure at the town's southern edge. It had once been a family-run hotel—**Nicolás** had bought it a few months prior and overseen its extensive renovation.

He felt the helicopter lurch as it touched down. The pad was barely large enough for the cabin, leaving the tail suspended in open air. Cutting the engine, the pilot nodded, signaling Nicolás it was safe to exit.

Nicolás stepped out, boots crunching against the deck. He surveyed his newly refurbished building: the top floor now crowned with a discreet landing zone, while the lower levels adjoined a solid rock face that dwarfed the structure. An ingenious addition—a backless elevator shaft—had been drilled into the mountain itself, allowing him to descend straight into the stone.

He entered the elevator, pressing a button labeled **3**. Halfway down, the front doors didn't open. Instead, a soft click echoed through the compartment, and a section of the rock pivoted aside, revealing an inconspicuous entrance.

"I'm here," he said, voice carrying in the hush.

A second door materialized in the stone, gliding open. Nicolás stepped into a wide, high-ceilinged chamber carved into the mountain. The muted hum of electronics reverberated through the space. Racks of hardware lined the walls, forming the core of his secret data center—**the nerve center of the Communicational Discrete Algorithms.**

He paused to take it all in. **This** was the culmination of his vision: a hidden fortress of technology, powered by the latest computers and shielded by sheer rock. Soon, a quantum processor would anchor the operation. There, Nicolás and his team—Rainer included—would monitor and manage the "identifier" devices that made direct mind-to-mind communication possible.

"Next step," he murmured, **"is to secure the right banker and audit manager."**

Professor Bernard Schneiderman, his longtime mentor, had recommended Zurich for that search. Zürich's financial acumen would complement this clandestine enterprise. Here in Zermatt, nestled against the Matterhorn's shadow, Nicolás felt both exhilaration and weight. He was building something revolutionary—**and** potentially perilous.

But for now, the hum of the data center filled him with a fierce sense of purpose. The future he had imagined on a snowy Argentine mountaintop was beginning to take shape in the heart of the Swiss Alps.

Chapter 5

Zurich, Switzerland – Office of Union National Des Banques (UNB) 1977, A Few Months Later – 9 A.M. Central European Time (CET)

Zurich wore its winter garb with rigid perfection. Immaculate streets, tidy buildings—an orderly universe shaped by unyielding rules. Yet behind these grand facades, centuries-old financial institutions guarded the world's deepest secrets. For those who knew where to look, *flexibility* was just as common as **precision**.

On a gray morning, **Markus Wildi**, chairman of the Union National de Banques (UNB), stood at the wide window of his corner office. He sighed, longing for his chalet in Flims—a resort village barely ninety minutes away, where the alpine slopes offered fresh air and tranquility.

His intercom crackled. **"Herr Wildi, Mr. Donaldson is here,"** came his assistant's voice in a thick Swiss-German accent. **"Show him in, Ute."**

Moments later, **Patrick Donaldson** entered. He was head of **Ticino & Co.**, Zurich's oldest auditing and tax-advisory firm, and a longtime collaborator with UNB.

"Morning, Markus," Donaldson said, shaking snow off his coat. **"Daydreaming again about Flims?"**

"Always," Markus replied wryly. **"Come, sit. I asked you here because I've got a new client wanting both our services."**

Patrick brushed back his salt-and-pepper hair. **"Someone big, I presume?"**

"Yes, but quite young," Markus said, tapping a slender folder on his desk. **"In fact, I know almost nothing else—only that he's *wealthy* and not long out of short trousers."**

Donaldson snorted. **"Another spoiled heir, perhaps? We'll see."**

Before Markus could respond, his assistant's voice echoed through the intercom once more. **"Herr Wildi, your nine o'clock is here."**

"Right," Markus said. **"Show him in."**

Ute Behrenz opened the heavy door, face tinged with half-skeptical amusement. The visitor who stepped inside was, indeed, a teenager. He looked no more than seventeen yet exuded a poised confidence well beyond his years.

"Gentlemen," the young man said in a clear, direct voice. **"My name is Nicolás Tosh. I'd like both your firms to manage my assets."**

Markus exchanged a quick, startled glance with Donaldson. Then he extended his hand. **"N-Nice to meet you, Mr. Tosh. Shall we sit?"**

Once everyone was seated, Tosh's gaze flicked to Markus. **"I chose UNB for its discretion—and because you handle the accounts of Professor Bernard Schneiderman."**

A flicker of recognition crossed Markus's face. Schneiderman was a brilliant, if irascible, Nobel Prize–winning mathematician who had demanded the bank's best rates and near-impossible returns for years. He was equal parts genius and headache.

"Shall we call him?" Markus asked. **"As you wish,"** Nicolás said smoothly.

At Markus's nod, Ute dialed the professor. The call connected with a rustle of static.

"Yes?" The voice was impatient. **"Professor Schneiderman,"** Markus said politely, **"I have a young client here—"** "Nicolás Tosh?" the professor interrupted, voice warming. **"He's the finest mathematical mind I've met in decades. He's already years ahead of his contemporaries."** "I… see," Markus replied. **"What he does will be noble—and world-changing,"** Schneiderman added. **"Good day, gentlemen."**

The line went dead. Markus set down the phone, trying to mask his amazement. Donaldson's eyebrows rose, curiosity piqued. Meanwhile, Nicolás waited calmly, as though this was all perfectly routine.

"So, Mr. Tosh," Donaldson began, clearing his throat, **"you mentioned assets. Just how much are we talking about?"**

Nicolás glanced between them. **"One hundred million U.S. dollars."**

Silence draped the room. Outside, Zurich's bustling streets carried on, oblivious. But inside that polished office, Markus and Donaldson realized they were looking at far more than a privileged heir. This was *something* else—a new client who clearly wielded an uncanny brilliance and possessed a fortune of his own making.

Markus recovered first. **"Then let's talk specifics, Mr. Tosh. You have our attention."**

Nicolás nodded, confident but not arrogant. **"Good. I have a substantial project in mind—one that requires total privacy and expert management. We'll need to move quickly."**

He paused, letting them absorb the gravity of his request. On the polished wood desk lay Zurich's typical contract forms and account folders, but neither banker nor auditor could shake the feeling that whatever they were about to sign onto extended *far* beyond standard Swiss protocol.

Chapter 6

Miami, Florida, USA – 2015 (Five Months Before Day 1)

They called him **"the Handler."** Each week, he delivered twenty disposable phones—eight in D.C., twelve in Miami. Each phone came tucked inside a bland folder of legal papers, handed off in public places to people who knew to expect them: a federal judge here, an FBI agent there, a journalist, a lobbyist, a high-profile attorney. No words exchanged beyond a cursory greeting. Just a phone slid into a discreet plastic bag, then on to the next.

He never asked why. He had his instructions and a generous paycheck from **Bain & Associates**—where he'd worked most of his life. His job, like the phones, was disposable. But the Handler always kept his own records…just in case.

"A Situation"

Sitting in the back seat of his car on Biscayne Boulevard, **Ryan McNamee** checked his watch. Traffic was at a dead stop, and he was late. He sighed, stepped onto the sidewalk, and walked briskly to **Morton's**, where **General Robert L. Pinkus III (Ret.)** waited, glowering.

"McNamee, you were supposed to be early," the retired four-star snapped. **"Yes, sir."** McNamee slid into the booth, ignoring the glare.

Five years ago, Pinkus had founded **Zaptec**, a private security firm run with military precision. McNamee, his head of special operations, had served under him in the Middle East and knew better than to waste time on small talk.

"Sir, I requested this meeting because we've got a lead on the Klein & Co. surveillance job. During routine video checks, we caught something unusual." "Spit it out."

McNamee told him about **Rodney Ortega**, the client who'd hired Zaptec to watch his partner. Yet on the videos, Ortega himself appeared in the background—accepting folders with disposable phones, then discarding the folders.

"We followed the delivery man afterward. He made eleven more identical drops each day: federal judge, public prosecutor, FBI agent, journalists, business leaders…"

Pinkus frowned. **"Our client is part of a phone ring? So what?"**

"The Handler is your future in-law, sir. Jimmy Ocando—Jennifer's father."

The news landed like a punch. **Jennifer** was engaged to Pinkus's son, Robert IV. She was the bright, spirited center of the General's life since he'd lost his wife years back. If Ocando was tangled in some conspiracy, it threatened everything Pinkus held dear.

"I need to talk to Ocando," Pinkus said, rising. **"Now. You have his address?"**

McNamee nodded, sending the data to the General's driver. Minutes later, two tinted sedans slipped through the gates of a guarded community in Doral. An unsuspecting security guard waved them on, mistaking them for law enforcement. Pinkus, six-foot-two and well over two hundred pounds, loomed on Ocando's doorstep.

"General…this is unexpected," said Ocando, forcing a smile. **"We need to talk—inside."**

McNamee swept the home for bugs before Pinkus confronted Ocando:

"You've been handing out disposable phones every week to high-level officials. That looks like a conspiracy. Care to explain?"

Ocando, shoulders tense, hesitated. **"I…I just deliver them. It's Bain & Associates. They tell me who gets what. After each drop, I log every phone number and recipient. That's my insurance."**

Pinkus's brow furrowed. **"Insurance against what, exactly?"**

"I don't ask questions. But I keep records of every date, location, phone number—everything."

Pinkus nodded. **"Good. You're going to give those records to me. Then you and Jennifer are leaving town. Now."**

Within the hour, McNamee drove Ocando to the University of Miami, where Jennifer taught Urbanism. With quiet urgency, they persuaded her to come along, no luggage or phone calls allowed. McNamee dropped them at Miami-Opa Locka Executive Airport, where a private jet waited to whisk them to a remote Caribbean safe house.

"Follow the Trail"

Later that afternoon, McNamee navigated his sedan onto I-95, heading south. Downtown Miami's skyline gleamed in the distance. His phone buzzed—Pinkus.

"Report," came the General's voice. **"We have Ocando's records: who received the phones and when. But we need call logs—dates, times, tower pings—to see who they contacted and where." "You know what to do,"** Pinkus said briskly. **"Yes, sir."**

McNamee ended the call. Tucking the phone into his jacket pocket, he couldn't help but wonder how deep this operation went—and how far Bain & Associates would go to protect their secrets.

Chapter 7

Miami, Florida – Zaptec Headquarters (2015, Three Months Before Day 1)

General Robert L. Pinkus III (Ret.) had thought he'd found calm at last. His son, Robert Jr., had been relentless—demanding to know why his fiancée, **Jennifer**, had vanished without explanation. Their confrontations had escalated into shouts and threats. Finally, the General relented, letting Robert Jr. join her in the Caribbean safe house. Once his son was gone, Pinkus breathed easier—until his phone rang.

"General, it's McNamee. I've got something. We should talk in private."

They arranged to meet aboard Zaptec's Challenger jet, lifting off just before sunset. As the plane banked out over the Miami skyline, the sky glowed in fiery shades of orange and crimson.

"We Have a Lead"

Settling into a leather seat across from the General, **Ryan McNamee** flipped open a tablet with a series of data overlays.

"Sir, the phone ring we've been tracking is bigger than we suspected. Eight key players in D.C. manage another twelve targets in Miami. One user coordinate with *all* of them—the mastermind."

Pinkus's brow furrowed. **"We know who's involved, but not what they're plotting?"**

"Correct. Through cell tower triangulation, we matched each disposable phone to the same individuals who originally received them. They make calls in public places—restaurants, parks, jogs, dog walks, even one on a sailboat. We've captured video and

recovered some of the discarded phones. It's definitely a conspiracy—corruption and influence at high levels—but we can't tell the endgame."

McNamee tapped a folder labeled **Ocando**.

"That's why we need to talk to Jimmy again. He may not realize what he knows, but he's been at the center of it for months."

Pinkus nodded grimly. **"Have we kept Ocando's cover intact?"**

"Yes, sir. He claimed a terminal illness and resigned from Bain & Associates. His calls were routed through secure lines, so as far as Bain's concerned, he quietly disappeared. A new handler took over, delivering the phones to the same group."

The General exhaled. **"All right. We find out everything Jimmy can tell us, and we keep him, Jennifer, and my son safe until we know who's pulling the strings."**

Touchdown

As the jet descended, a small runway shimmered at the water's edge. The pilot leveled off, wheels hitting the tarmac with a jarring thud. Brakes squealed, wrestling the aircraft to a stop just yards from the runway's end. McNamee gripped his seat, heart pounding.

Pinkus only grimaced. **"You sure you want to bring Jimmy back stateside? Might be safer to talk in the Caribbean."**

"He'll agree to meet wherever you say, sir," McNamee replied. **"He owes you—big time."**

Pinkus glanced out the window. The last sliver of sun dipped below the horizon. **"Let's hope what he tells us breaks this wide open. Then maybe I can finally have some honest peace."**

Chapter 8

Miami, Florida – Bain & Associates Headquarters (2015, Three Months Before the Present Day)

John Hill, a former Secret Service agent built like a linebacker, stepped into **Mark Bain's** office and closed the door quietly.

"It's been four weeks, Mark. We've had three operatives watching the new handler around the clock—no sign of trouble. Nobody's trailing him, nobody's asking questions."

Bain, seated at a sleek steel desk, tapped a pencil against a file stamped **CONFIDENTIAL**. His mouth tightened.

"I still can't believe Ocando's daughter is engaged to General Pinkus's son." He tossed the pencil aside with a sigh. **"How did we not catch that before?"**

Hill shrugged. **"He's been with us twenty years. We don't typically run background checks on long-standing employees—not until something goes sideways, like this mess with Ocando."**

A muscle in Bain's jaw twitched. He ran a hand through his thinning hair. **"Well, keep following the new handler. If Pinkus is sniffing around, I want to know *before* it becomes a problem. I might have to meet the General… for old rivalries' sake."**

Hill nodded and started for the door. **"Understood."**

The Smoker's Itch

Left alone, Bain felt the urge claw at him again. Ever since he'd quit smoking a year ago, stress made his skin prickle, and his mouth go dry. His once-heavy habit still showed in the yellowish stains on his fingers and the ash-gray pallor of his face. At fifty-nine, he looked older—like a man who'd lived off nerves and nicotine for too long.

His eyes flicked to a photo on his desk: Bain, younger and healthier, in an official CIA portrait. That was before he resigned suddenly, two decades ago, to found **Bain & Associates**. Everyone in the intelligence community knew the firm operated in the shadows, skirting the edges of legality for high-paying clients. Some missions, like this phone-delivery conspiracy, were simply too big—and too lucrative—to fail.

Bain clenched his fists and forced a slow breath. **Ocando's disappearance** gnawed at him. If the man truly was dying, that was one thing. But if he'd turned or cut a deal with someone—**Pinkus**, for instance—Bain needed to know. Loose ends were unacceptable.

He pushed away from the desk and stood, gaze drifting toward the window that overlooked the Miami skyline.

"You won't slip away from me that easily, Ocando," he muttered under his breath.

Just then, the door opened again, and Hill poked his head inside. **"Anything else?"**

Bain's grim expression answered for him. **"No. That's all."**

But his mind was already calculating. With Pinkus in the mix, old grudges threatened to resurface. And if Ocando's exit spelled betrayal, Bain was prepared to ensure he never lived to regret it.

Chapter 9

Canouan Island, The Caribbean – 2015 (Three Months Before Day 1)

For **Jennifer Ocando** and **Robert Pinkus IV**, the first weeks on Canouan Island felt like a honeymoon. They basked in the turquoise waters, strolled quiet beaches, and tried to forget Miami's swirling conflicts. But as time dragged on, frustrations surfaced—most of them aimed at Jennifer's father, **Jimmy "the Handler" Ocando**.

"You're the one who got us into this, Dad."

The bitterness had festered for years, Jennifer's love colliding with her father's murky work. Now the pressure-cooker atmosphere pushed her to vent decades of unresolved hurt.

"Your life's been one gamble after another, Dad. Mom couldn't handle it—and you let her die."

Her voice cracked with anger, echoing heartbreak she'd tried to bury. Jimmy stood speechless, guilt twisting in his gut. *He* knew the cost of his shadowy jobs, but hearing his daughter's pain laid bare was a fresh wound.

Meanwhile, Robert IV kept in discreet contact with his father, **General Robert L. Pinkus III (Ret.)**, by secure satellite phone. He'd chosen to stay hidden with Jennifer, but the General's sudden arrival signaled fresh developments—likely concerning Jimmy.

The General Arrives

A small jet glided onto the narrow island airstrip at dusk. Jennifer clutched Robert's hand, anxiety flaring.

"**Are we leaving? Did your dad come to take us home?**" she whispered.

"**I don't think so,**" Robert answered, peering through the window. "**He's here for your father.**"

Minutes later, the plane stopped and the General emerged, inhaling warm tropical air. **Ryan McNamee**, Zaptec's head of special operations, trailed him. Robert hurried forward for a firm embrace.

"**Dad, welcome to paradise,**" Robert said, forcing a smile.

The General's gaze shifted to Jennifer, who stood a few paces back, eyes downcast.

"**C'mon, beautiful,**" he beckoned, pulling her into a hug. "**You're practically my daughter already. None of this is your fault—and I won't let anything happen to Jimmy, either.**"

Relief flickered across her face. "**Thank you…**" she murmured.

In silence, they drove along the narrow roads to the **Pinkus estate**— a spacious, Caribbean-style house with wide porches and ocean views. Standing on the veranda, Jimmy Ocando watched the SUV approach, tension coiling in his shoulders as he realized who had come.

"**Jimmy,**" the General called out, stepping from the vehicle. "**Let's walk. McNamee, give us a few minutes, then follow.**"

Confrontation and Confession

With slow strides along the beach, Pinkus laid out what he knew:

"**We've identified the ring using those disposable phones. We know *how* they communicate. But we don't know *why*. And we suspect Bain & Associates is pulling the strings.**"

"I only delivered phones," Jimmy insisted. "I never spoke to the recipients. I have no idea what else they're up to."

Pinkus's jaw tightened. "Jimmy, you realize Bain doesn't leave loose ends. Jennifer's at risk if we don't uncover the whole truth."

Jimmy's expression twisted with regret. "I swear, General, my job was just to hand things off. I handled a few *other* cases—exchanging documents, videos, maybe incriminating evidence. Nothing to do with the phone deliveries, far as I know."

"Tell me everything."

Jimmy explained how, for six months, he'd also been passing sealed envelopes—sometimes damaged—containing court filings, spreadsheets, bank statements, even corporate PowerPoints. He delivered them to two local newspaper editors, possibly fueling investigative stories. But he never looked too deeply into specifics.

"All that ended abruptly last month," he finished.

Pinkus exhaled, scanning the shoreline. The sun dipped below the horizon, painting the sky in fiery swaths of orange and purple.

"McNamee!" he called, waving his lieutenant over. "We need every article from the local press for the past year—business, politics, high-profile figures. If those deliveries fueled any exposés, we'll find the link. Jimmy, stay here."

The General clapped a firm hand on the Handler's shoulder.

"We'll keep you and Jennifer safe. But I need the missing piece—*why* Bain is orchestrating all this."

As McNamee pulled out his phone to relay orders, Jimmy's gaze drifted to the ocean. He felt the weight of Jennifer's accusations pressing on him, but also the faint stirrings of hope. Perhaps, with the General's help, they'd finally unearth the truth—and free themselves from the shadows he'd helped create.

Chapter 10

Miami, Florida – American Justice Center (2016, Day 2, 3:00 P.M. ET)

The large courtroom at the American Justice Center in downtown Miami, designed to seat up to two hundred spectators, was nearly empty. Quiet echoes bounced off paneled walls. Only a handful of reporters and curious onlookers occupied the rows, waiting.

Outside, the skyline gleamed—testament to decades of ambition and reinvention. Miami had long been shaped by the surge of Cuban exiles arriving in the early 1960s, fleeing Castro's regime. Their artistic, entrepreneurial, and intellectual firepower jump-started an era of explosive growth. Determined to reclaim the country they had lost, these newcomers poured energy into building businesses, forging political influence, and transforming Miami into a thriving gateway for Latin America.

That success, though, came with hazards. During the '80s and '90s, the city's reliance on regional markets made it ride the waves of economic booms and busts. Miami also earned a reputation for drug trafficking and money laundering—stains on a place striving to prove itself an international metropolis.

By 2016, a different Miami had emerged: safer, less dependent on Latin American markets, and fueled by tourism from Europe and North America. Yet beneath the modern skyline and bustling downtown, a sense of fragility lingered. Memories of chaos and corruption were never far away. Now, with rumors of high-profile arrests set to shake the city's elite, the tension felt almost tangible.

And so, in a starkly vacant courtroom—where only a scattering of observers whispered behind half-raised hands—Miami's next chapter was about to unfold.

Chapter 11

Washington, D.C. – The White House / Miami, Florida – American Justice Center (2016, Day 2, 3:00 P.M. ET)

President Kelly O'Sullivan sat at his Oval Office desk, staring at the live video feed from a nearly empty Miami courtroom. Outwardly, his expression was calm. Inwardly, tension crackled. Just yesterday, **Nicolás Tosh** had pressed him to "purge the system," and O'Sullivan had agreed. Now, as he watched the screen, he realized how quickly that choice had triggered a chain of irreversible events.

"Mr. President," a staffer said quietly, **"we're linking you in. The hearing starts in five minutes."**

He nodded. The camera panned over a handful of recognizable faces—federal judge, prosecutor, FBI agent, journalists, attorneys, powerful business leaders. All summoned under presidential orders to witness the sentencing of a **convicted felon** in an orange jumpsuit.

In the courtroom, a bailiff announced, **"All rise." Judge Amanda Beltran** entered. Across the screen, O'Sullivan watched her cast a confused glance at the unusual gathering. Then she addressed the monitor directly:

"Mr. President, welcome to my courtroom. Are you ready?"

"Thank you, Judge," O'Sullivan said. **"I appreciate your cooperation."**

Beltran turned to the defendant—**Nicolás Tosh**—shackled at the defense table.

"If there's nothing further…" she began.

Juliette Stevens, the U.S. Federal Prosecutor, abruptly stood. **"Your Honor, the government moves to withdraw all charges against Mr. Tosh."**

A roar of disbelief surged through the small crowd. **FBI Agent Louis Tomassi** leapt to his feet. **"What the—?"** Judge Beltran slammed her gavel, demanding silence. She glanced at Tosh, then back at the screen.

"On what grounds?" she asked, her confusion echoing the onlookers' shock.

"Per direct order of the President," Stevens said, looking unsettled herself. **"And in the interest of…national security."**

The judge hesitated, then spoke with measured authority. **"Motion granted. Mr. Tosh, the court overturns your guilty verdict. You are free to go."**

Cheers and curses collided in a wild clamor. O'Sullivan's voice cut through the chaos, booming:

"No—he isn't leaving. Judge Beltran, Ms. Stevens, you will both join the rest of the attendees in the gallery. Defense counsel, court personnel, U.S. Marshals—leave now. Marshals, unshackle the prisoner before you go."

Secret Service agents entered, swiftly clearing the courtroom as directed. Tomassi and the other onlookers watched in stunned silence. Once the doors were sealed, Tosh—still in orange but no longer cuffed—remained at the defense table under the White House's watchful gaze.

Declaration from the White House

O'Sullivan inhaled slowly. **"You are all here,"** he said, **"because earlier today, a G-7 *strategic military asset* came under imminent**

threat. We invoked a resolution to deploy Communication Discrete Algorithm 323—a WMD-level technology—to protect that asset."

A ripple of bafflement crossed the audience. Almost none of them knew what CDA-323 was, or why the President would personally orchestrate such an extraordinary scene.

Only **Nicolás Tosh** appeared unsurprised—still seated, eyes steady. Far away in Zermatt, **Rainer Sábato** watched all of this unfold through Tosh's direct neural feed, relief flooding him. Their entire network—ever cautious about the G-7 partnership—now saw that at least one world government was intervening to protect Tosh rather than destroy him.

But O'Sullivan's next words stiffened Rainer's spine:

"I've freed Mr. Tosh to help expose a conspiracy that threatens us at the highest levels of law enforcement, business, and government. Each of you in this courtroom is potentially implicated—or else you wouldn't be here. Make no mistake: we will uncover the truth."

A solemn hush fell over the room. Even the judge and prosecutor, now relegated to the spectator seats, looked unsettled.

High above the Florida skyline, thousands of miles from Swiss mountains and secret data centers, the stage was set. Tosh, newly freed, locked eyes with the President's image on the large screen. Agent Tomassi swallowed hard, certain that any illusions of normalcy had just dissolved.

Watching from Zermatt

Back in Switzerland, Rainer exhaled in a swirl of relief and apprehension. At least Tosh was no longer in chains. But their cautionary line—keeping CDA as far from government entanglements as possible—was blurred as never before.

We've never actively partnered with G-7 on a full-blown operation, Rainer thought, eyes on the data streams. *And now we're knee-deep in it.*

Yet for all the tensions to come, one truth lit his mind: **Tosh was safe.** They could now focus on revealing the conspirators who had threatened him—and protect the algorithms that just might reshape the world.

Chapter 12

Washington, D.C. – The White House (2016, Day 1, 11:00 P.M. ET)

President Kelly O'Sullivan sat rigidly at his desk, eyes flicking over a thin document labeled **1977 Resolution – G-7**. His aide had left moments ago, after delivering emergency summons for an overnight meeting with Congressional leaders. Now O'Sullivan had to face the man at the other end of this clandestine connection: **Nicolás Tosh**.

"Tosh," the President said, pressing a button on his comm device. **"I've read the G-7 resolution. I'm prepared to bring Congress into the loop first thing in the morning. Now I need you to explain why you requested we invoke it. Tell me everything—especially how these algorithms work."**

A clear, calm voice resonated in O'Sullivan's mind, though the Oval Office was silent.

"Yes, sir. I'll start with the basics. The Communicational Discrete Algorithms—CDA-319 through 324—connect a target brain to a global neural network via a device we call an *identifier*. Some of the CDAs are considered safe enough for future public use, while the rest have been classified as Weapons of Mass Destruction."

The Basics of the "Identifier"

Tosh explained how the *identifier* picks up a subject's brainwaves if it's within a mile and pointed in their direction—much like a router detecting a Wi-Fi signal.

"The neural network itself runs on data centers and quantum-based computers. When we connect a brain, the *identifier* downloads

the relevant CDA from the network. We always apply them in ascending order: 319 first, then 320, and so on."

O'Sullivan's expression tightened. "And *I* have one of these devices, correct? That's how you're speaking directly into my mind?"

"Yes, Mr. President. G-7 leaders are authorized to carry *identifiers* for communication with us, even though you aren't what we call *carriers*. A *carrier* is an operator trained to use these devices for broader applications."

CDA-319 through 321

"CDA-319," Tosh continued, "assigns a unique number to each brain—think of it like a digital ID. Once a subject is registered, *any* carrier with an *identifier* can reconnect to that subject's brain."

"All right," O'Sullivan said. "Then CDA-320 is how you're talking to me telepathically?"

"Precisely. CDA-320 lets the carrier transmit thoughts to a registered subject. The subject replies by speaking normally, and the *identifier* converts their spoken words back into thoughts for the carrier."

"What about carriers talking to each other?"

"That's CDA-321. It allows pure, two-way thought communication between carriers, no spoken words at all."

The President rubbed his temple. "So you're *not* licensing any of these to anyone yet?"

"No, sir. Even 319 through 321 would give unfair advantages to whoever used them—governments, businesses, intelligence agencies.

Society isn't ready for mass adoption. We're a nonprofit, so we don't profit from licensing these algorithms anyway."

The WMDs: CDA-322, 323, 324

"That brings me to your so-called 'weapons'," O'Sullivan said, flipping through the resolution in front of him.

"CDA-322," Tosh explained, **"allows *live* monitoring of someone's mind. You see what they see, hear what they hear, and even capture their thoughts in real time. CDA-323 is essentially total memory access—reconstructing someone's entire life experiences. CDA-324 extends that ability to anyone who's interacted with the subject, creating a vast, interconnected web of data."**

The President's grip on his pen tightened. **"And all that is automatically stored in your data center?"**

"Yes, though it remains heavily encrypted. G-7 mandated that certain key officials, including data-center workers and designated government posts, be subject to these WMD-level CDAs for life— allowing mutual oversight."

Why Tosh Is in Jail

O'Sullivan sighed, leaning forward. **"All right, Tosh—so how did you end up behind bars in the first place? You called me claiming you were under 'clear and present danger.' Speak plainly."**

Tosh hesitated for a beat, then his voice emerged with a note of grim resignation.

"I was waiting for you to ask that, sir. It starts with a conspiracy that reached deeper into government and corporate institutions than I ever imagined..."

Chapter 13

Washington, D.C. – The White House (2016, Day 1, 11:30 P.M. ET)

President Kelly O'Sullivan leaned forward at his desk, rubbing weary eyes. Across the neural link, **Nicolás Tosh** spoke to him from a prison cell—yet also from a secret vantage of formidable technological power.

"First, Mr. President," Tosh said calmly, **"I want you to know who I am."**

O'Sullivan nodded. **"Go on."**

Tosh's Triad of Identities

Tosh began: as a teenager in the mid-1970s, he'd resolved to reinvest his mathematical earnings back into society. By 1977, he'd established a foundation called **Experta** in Switzerland, funneling **100%** of his income—derived from proprietary algorithms—into global charitable work. Experta, in turn, donated those funds to every country on a per-capita basis. The foundation ran with **less than 1%** administrative costs. He protected his own anonymity by splitting into three roles:

1. **Secret Identity**:
- The neural data center (codenamed Zermatt) and algorithms.
- *Experta* itself, a foundation with near-mythic secrecy.

2. **Public Identity**:
- A mathematics professor with a colorful past, known publicly as *Nicolás Tosh.*

- O'Sullivan recognized him from a few fundraising events—an Argentine-born academic with a dubious reputation and multiple business stumbles.

3. **Private/For-Profit Identity**:

- *Walkyria*, a multinational entity that licenses Tosh's vast software catalog.

- All proceeds flow to Experta—none remain with Tosh personally.

Tosh explained how Experta had quietly supported the U.S. for decades, regularly purchasing T-Bills and injecting emergency liquidity at the Treasury's request. O'Sullivan felt his pulse quicken. *Experta* was rumored to control well over a trillion dollars in assets—no other nongovernmental entity came close. It funded American education and poverty-reduction programs to the tune of fifty billion dollars a year.

"Are you saying Experta and *you* are one and the same?" O'Sullivan pressed.

"I founded and fund it," Tosh confirmed. **"Everything we earn— via my algorithms—goes back into Experta."**

The President let out a slow breath. **"And your *Walkyria* business?"**

"Licenses advanced algorithms to government agencies, corporations—even Wall Street. Thousands of them. All profit is transferred straight to Experta."

O'Sullivan glanced at his notes. **"So, the U.S. is dependent on your math tools, yet you're in prison on terrorism charges. How did that happen?"**

Why Tosh Is in Jail

Tosh paused. **"Sir, I was framed by a powerful conspiracy involving high-level officials and business interests. I let it happen to protect *Experta*'s secrecy and the data center's location. We hoped to uncover the plot through conventional means, but that took longer than expected."**

O'Sullivan recalled the blitz of negative press labeling Tosh an extremist, plus the swiftness of his trial and conviction. Over a hectic few weeks, Tosh's public identity had been systematically dismantled. Even the President had tacitly believed it—until tonight.

"You could have invoked diplomatic immunity under G-7 guidelines," O'Sullivan said, tapping a paragraph in the 1977 Resolution. **"Why not do it sooner?"**

"Because stepping forward would expose my role as the data-center founder—and possibly jeopardize everything we've built," Tosh replied. **"We wanted to root out the conspirators from within."**

General Pinkus & The Conspiracy

Tosh signaled to an unseen operator, and **General Robert L. Pinkus III (Ret.)** appeared in a split-screen feed. Pinkus believed he was on a standard videoconference, unaware of the neural technology bridging them.

"General," O'Sullivan greeted him wearily, **"I hear you've uncovered quite a conspiracy."**

Pinkus recounted his findings: a clandestine phone-delivery operation that roped in judges, FBI personnel, prosecutors, business moguls, and lobbyists. All had received burner phones weekly, using them for covert communications. At first, Pinkus's team had intended to ignore the pattern—until they realized the "Handler" behind those deliveries was Pinkus's own future in-law. The deeper they dug, the more the conspiracy implicated powerful insiders who had orchestrated Tosh's downfall.

"It looks like at least twenty individuals," Pinkus said. **"Possibly more. We suspect one U.S. senator's tangential involvement, though we lack direct proof."**

O'Sullivan felt his chest tighten. The pieces were falling into place. Tosh—once demonized—was actually a G-7 strategic asset. Pinkus's mention of a potential senator among the conspirators added another explosive layer.

"Thank you, General," O'Sullivan said quietly. **"That's all I need for now."**

Pinkus vanished from the feed, leaving the President alone with Tosh once more.

Deploying CDA-322, 323, and 324

O'Sullivan steepled his fingers. **"What do you propose, Tosh?"**

"To exonerate me the *right* way—by proving the charges were illegitimately obtained. We already have each conspirator's unique brain ID, so with G-7 clearance, I can deploy CDA-322, 323, and 324. In three to four hours, we'll have a comprehensive record of their memories—every detail of this plot, and whomever else was involved."

The President frowned. **"So you want to broadcast their entire lives into your data center?"**

"Yes, sir. Then the U.S. Attorney General can see the evidence, force the state prosecutors to dismiss the case, and hold the conspirators accountable. It won't rely on my diplomatic immunity, so my secret stays safe."

O'Sullivan shifted in his chair, imagining the political blowback. *But then*, he thought, *Tosh has saved the U.S. from countless crises—his algorithms, his T-bill infusions, his philanthropic billions.* If Tosh was truly a G-7 "weapon," O'Sullivan had an obligation to protect him.

"All right," the President said at last. **"I'll get G-7 approval and Congressional buy-in. By tomorrow morning, you'll have legal cover for the algorithmic deployment. Once we see what you uncover, we can nullify your conviction."**

Tosh's voice was calm, but O'Sullivan sensed the relief behind it. **"Thank you, Mr. President. I appreciate your willingness to 'purge the system.' The conspirators won't expect what comes next."**

O'Sullivan ended the link and stared at the clock—past midnight. In a few hours, he'd be on a classified conference call with the leaders of the world's most powerful nations. Then would come the real fight: pushing a reluctant Congress to sign off on unleashing a technology that laid bare human minds.

Exhaustion tugged at him, but there was no stopping now. **He** had triggered this cascade. For the sake of national security—and a man who might be the greatest benefactor in American history—he had to see it through.

Chapter 14

Boston, Massachusetts – Harvard Business School (2016, Day 1, 8:00 A.M. ET)

Professor Christopher Musial surveyed the packed lecture hall. Today's topic: *global employment shifts and politics.*

"A few years ago," Musial began, **"the President asked Steve Jobs if Apple would ever bring manufacturing jobs back from China. Jobs's response was: *Those jobs aren't coming back.* Was he right?"**

A low murmur rippled through the students.

"Raise your hand if you think *yes*," Musial said.

All but one hand shot up. He nodded at the lone holdout, a poised woman in the front row.

"Mrs. Chambers, why not?"

"He never actually answered the question," she said. **"He could've suggested incentives—like a repatriation tax holiday—to make it worthwhile."**

Musial tapped the podium. **"Incentives matter, sure, but Apple's real barrier is a shortage of skilled U.S. workers. According to their internal study, we don't have enough engineers and specialized labor to staff a Shenzhen-scale factory. It'd take months just to *find* enough qualified people, let alone relocate them. Wages would skyrocket."**

He paused, letting the point sink in. **"That's not just about Apple. It's about *education.* China's cities have dozens of universities. The pipeline of trained workers there dwarfs ours, and they can ramp up overnight."**

A hush settled as he concluded. **"We can debate taxes, but the real issue is whether we're graduating enough skilled talent."**

A Shift in Topic

Musial checked the clock, impatience flickering in his gaze—he needed to finish fast. Events unfolding in Miami tugged at him.

"Let's pivot quickly to politics. Our outgoing President's reelection—what clinched it?"

Hands shot up. Students cited the African American and Latino vote, plus support from women, youth, and independents. Musial offered a small smile.

"Those were crucial demographics. But he still needed more than thirty-nine percent of *white* voters. That group made up seventy-two percent of the electorate. Without a decent chunk of them, none of those other blocs would've carried the day."

He glanced at his watch. **"That's all for now. Dismissed."**

A Carrier's Call

In the hallway, Musial—tall, bearded, and forever compared to TV's Dr. House—was known for his blunt, *no-holds-barred* style. His *Current Affairs* class had become a coveted forum for fearless debate. But he barely acknowledged the flock of students lingering to ask questions; he had somewhere to be.

He jogged across campus to his car, when a familiar **buzz** from his pocket startled him. **The "identifier."** Musial was one of **Nicolás Tosh's** earliest "carriers"—and an active recruiter for new carriers from among his most promising MBA students.

He pressed a button on the small device. A voice resonated in his mind—**Rainer Sábato**.

"Chris, we need you in D.C. ASAP."

"Understood," Musial answered silently, slipping behind the wheel. **"I'll catch the next Acela."**

"Wait near the White House until Tosh contacts you."

Musial's pulse kicked up. **"What's going on?"**

"We're about to get G-7, U.S. Congress, and the President to approve deploying CDA-323 and 324 on civilians—for the first time ever." Rainer's tone held controlled excitement. **"If all goes well, Tosh's conviction gets overturned *today*."**

Musial grinned, gripping the steering wheel. **"That's incredible."**

"Your first assignment: once you have the official resolution in hand, register and apply CDA-319 to that senator you've been tailing."

Musial's smile faded. **"So he's possibly part of the conspiracy?"**

"We're not certain," Rainer said. **"Find out. Good luck."**

The connection cut. Musial took a steadying breath. *So it's really happening.* He glanced at the stately red-brick buildings of Harvard Business School one last time, then turned the ignition. By the day's end, he might help exonerate one of the most powerful men alive—and expose a senator's role in a conspiracy that could rock the nation.

He pulled onto the highway, adrenaline humming. The next Acela to Washington left in an hour. After that, the real work would begin.

Chapter 15

Telluride, Colorado – Black Eagle Ranch (2016, Day 2, 7:00 A.M. MT)

High in the **San Juan Mountains**, the old mining town of **Telluride** huddled beneath 14,000-foot peaks. At nearly 9,000 feet, its tiny airport perched on a bluff like a remote aircraft carrier, surrounded by sheer drop-offs and thin air that tested even veteran pilots. In the distance, the **Bridal Veil** waterfall cascaded through the valley, a picturesque backdrop that felt closer to a hidden paradise than a modern city.

When the **Learjet 60** banked hard around a red-clay ridge, **Senator Gilbert Molina** stiffened in his seat, hands gripping the armrests. He despised flying into Telluride—the updrafts and narrow approach always left his stomach churning. But this trip wasn't optional. He'd received the call at dawn while sipping coffee at a French bakery near the Senate Office Building. The message was blunt: *Get on the plane at Manassas— immediately.*

He complied. *No questions. No choice.*

A Silent Arrival

The jet touched down with a heavy thud, brakes squealing as the pilot wrestled the plane to a halt. Molina stepped onto the windswept tarmac and sucked in a lungful of cold mountain air. His eyes darted across the stunning scenery—the pine-capped peaks, the frothy waterfall—trying to steady the knot in his gut.

A waiting SUV rolled up, driven by a silent, stone-faced bodyguard sporting dark sunglasses. Molina slid into the back seat without comment, letting the tension settle in. They descended the winding road toward town, only to turn off onto a rutted dirt track beneath a wooden arch reading **BLACK EAGLE RANCH**. After climbing a final stretch of rugged terrain, they arrived at a sprawling two-story log house.

Familiar Faces, New Fears

Inside, **four familiar figures** greeted Molina in a library paneled with dark wood. Their expressions were grim. One stepped forward, arms folded.

"Gilbert, we have a serious problem. The President summoned all our Miami operatives to Judge Beltran's courtroom today at three o'clock—for the *sentencing* of Nicolás Tosh."

Molina felt heat flush his cheeks. **"They're forcing them to attend? No public allowed—just our people? That can't be a coincidence."**

His contact nodded. **"It's worse than that. If the President knows exactly who to summon, he must have uncovered our entire network."**

Molina swallowed hard. He'd only just secured reelection in Florida, riding high on support from the Hispanic community. Now, he was summoned to this secluded ranch—**ordered** to come—while the entire ring of conspirators faced exposure in Miami. The name **Nicolás Tosh** flickered in his mind, accompanied by a sinking sense that the day's events could blow everything wide open.

"So the question," Molina muttered, **"is how much the government actually knows. And who else they plan to haul in next."**

No one answered, but the silence spoke volumes. Outside, the whistling wind and dramatic peaks framed the group's sudden, undeniable panic. They might have picked this remote hideout for secrecy, but the clock was ticking—and it looked like the President had beaten them to the punch.

Chapter 16

Zurich, Switzerland – Office of the Union National des Banques (UNB), 1977, 8:00 A.M. CET

Markus Wildi and **Patrick Donaldson** exchanged curious looks as **Nicolás Tosh** entered the conference room. He appeared even younger than his nineteen years, yet his gaze conveyed a calm self-assurance beyond his age.

"Gentlemen," Tosh began, **"Professor Schneiderman persuaded me to meet you. His endorsement alone tells me you're the right team for this job."**

Wildi nodded. **"We trust the professor implicitly. So, how can we help?"**

Tosh took a seat, leaning forward. **"I'm in the *mathematics* business—a concept not yet widespread, but highly profitable. Specifically, I develop *discrete algorithms* that spot market inefficiencies in finance, commodities, and precious metals. They've netted me over a hundred million dollars so far."**

Patrick Donaldson arched an eyebrow. **"I've never heard of anyone using math like that—at least not on this scale."**

"I intend to place all my current and future earnings from these algorithms into a structure separate from my everyday life," Tosh said. **"I want a robust system of treasury, accounting, and auditing processes. And I want *you two* to run it, ensuring utmost transparency."**

He let the words sink in, then continued.

Walkyria, Experta, and Zermatt

"First, we'll form a for-profit company called Walkyria—to handle all math-related business. It currently pulls in around fifty million a year, debt-free, with only a few staff scattered worldwide."

Tosh explained that Walkyria would soon license algorithms to financial markets and governments, causing revenue to skyrocket. **Markus** would oversee global accounts and ensure funds were readily available for stocks, futures, and commodities trading in any major jurisdiction.

"Second," Tosh said, **"Walkyria will donate *all* of its earnings— minus one small budget line—to Experta, a not-for-profit foundation. I'll lead it personally, and it must remain private and anonymous."**

"All of it?" Wildi asked in surprise.

"Every cent," Tosh confirmed, **"apart from running costs for the third entity."**

Donaldson leaned forward. **"What about *you*, Mr. Tosh?"**

"I plan to earn a living from pursuits that *don't* involve my algorithms. My focus here is philanthropy—what I call *social entrepreneurship*. Experta will invest worldwide, but it'll never engage in profit-making. It can't exceed one percent in operating expenses, and it must disburse every year's donations by year's end. Always anonymously."

Markus and **Patrick** exchanged amazed glances. Few clients had such grand—and strict—plans.

"The third organization," Tosh went on, **"will be Zermatt: a confidential data center and advanced math lab powered by a quantum supercomputer. We've already built it in a cave on donated Swiss mountain land. It remains fully secret, with your government's blessing, given the possibility of future military applications."**

Ambitious Deadlines

Tosh stood, pacing with quiet energy.

"I'll wire you fifty million dollars to start. I expect all three entities—Walkyria, Experta, and Zermatt—structured and operational as soon as possible. How long will it take?"

Wildi shrugged. **"Sixty days, minimum—international regulations and all."**

Donaldson nodded in agreement, but **Markus** raised a hand. **"We can push for thirty if we mobilize teams around the globe first thing tomorrow."**

Tosh smiled. **"Excellent. I'll handle final approvals for hiring. You'll each serve as fiduciaries: Mr. Wildi as treasurer, Mr. Donaldson as head of accounting and internal auditing. Protect our privacy at all costs."**

They stood to shake on it. Tosh's grip was steady; his tone cool yet earnest.

"Thank you, gentlemen. I look forward to working together."

When Tosh had gone, **Wildi** and **Donaldson** sank into their chairs, reeling at the audacity of what they'd just agreed to.

"**All these mathematical tools going to philanthropic causes,**" Donaldson murmured. **"I've never seen anything like it."**

"He's like a modern Robin Hood," Wildi mused. **"Taking from the markets, giving it all back through that Experta foundation."**

"But legally," Donaldson added with a half-smile. **"He's not stealing—just redistributing wealth in a radical new way."**

Wildi nodded, mind already racing with logistical challenges. **"If he pulls this off, it could change the world. God help us keep pace."**

"God bless," Donaldson agreed softly.

Even as they anticipated hefty fees, both men sensed they'd stepped into uncharted territory—perhaps the start of a financial juggernaut that would leave an indelible mark on the global stage.

Chapter 17

Zermatt, Switzerland – Zermatt Data Center (2016, Day 2, 8:00 A.M. CET / 2:00 A.M. ET)

A section of rock slid aside with a low rumble as **Rainer Sábato** pressed his palm to its hidden sensor. In an instant, the **neural network** verified his identity and authorized entry. The camouflaged door was solid as a bank vault, matching the mountain's craggy texture so perfectly that any outsider would assume it was just another stretch of stone.

Beyond it lay a short passage that opened onto a **five-story atrium** carved from the heart of the mountain. At the rear stood a towering glass wall, overlooking the **Quantum supercomputer** that dominated much of the ground floor. Around it clustered racks of **neural network servers**, router arrays, and two massive backup generators. Four maintenance specialists bustled among the hardware, checking readouts and securing cables.

In the upper floors, tiered workspaces circled the atrium's open core:

- **Fifth Floor – Math Lab** A team of eight, mostly software engineers, refined **CDA visualization** tools and government/industry algorithms.

- **Fourth Floor – Monitoring Station** Forty operators tracked every active *identifier*, *carrier*, and registered subject—verifying connections, archiving data, and flagging anomalies.

- **Third Floor – Data Security & Integrity** Ten analysts combed through gigabytes of new logs, patched vulnerabilities, and ensured no data corruption threatened the global system.

- **Second Floor – Database Management** Thirty programmers, network architects, and troubleshooters updated the software that kept the entire neural infrastructure humming.

- **First Floor – Quantum Supercomputer Team** Five specialists monitored server loads, performed calibrations, and watched for any sign of performance lag in the system's powerful core.

Rainer checked the digital clock perched above the atrium: **8:00 A.M. CET**, meaning it was **2:00 A.M.** on the U.S. East Coast. **Five more hours** until sunlight broke in Miami—five hours until the court convened to decide **Nicolás Tosh's** fate.

He paused in the hush of the cavernous chamber. The hum of cooling fans and the faint buzz of servers underscored the sense of *waiting*. In this hidden fortress, every second was recorded and archived—a testament to the power Tosh had built. Rainer closed his eyes, inhaling the chilled mountain air, and **prayed silently** for the outcome that might save Tosh from the conspirators who wanted him silenced.

Chapter 18

Zermatt, Switzerland – Zermatt Data Center (2016, Day 2, 8:30 A.M. CET / 2:30 A.M. ET)

Compared to modern cloud-computing giants, the **Zermatt Data Center** was relatively small. Yet at its core pulsed a **trinary-based quantum supercomputer**—a state-of-the-art system required to handle the monumental processing behind mind-to-mind communication. Through it ran a **worldwide neural network** encompassing over a hundred *carriers* and ten thousand *identifier* devices, each linking directly to human brains.

All data collected by these devices was categorized by **Communicational Discrete Algorithms** (CDAs). Three of them—**322, 323**, and **324**—were designated as **Weapons of Mass Destruction** and placed under the strictest security. Unlocking their records required a **unanimous G-7 resolution**, plus written authorization from the **U.S. President** and **Congress**, and final execution rights lay with the **Pentagon**. This arrangement had been self-imposed by **Nicolás Tosh** and **Rainer Sábato**, who, upon seeing the algorithms' terrifying potential, insisted on measures to prevent abuse.

Since 1977, these high-level CDAs had only been used on *carriers* and Tosh's immediate team, along with select G-7 officials for transparency. But two days ago, Tosh requested **full deployment**—for the first time ever—on civilian targets, citing a **"clear and present danger"** to himself. No one doubted the gravity of that plea. Yet, once governments gain unprecedented means to peer into private minds, it rarely ends with a single crisis. *After all, when the dam breaks, there's no going back.*

Chapter 19

Telluride, Colorado – Black Eagle Ranch (2016, Day 2, 7:15 A.M. MT)

"Why has the President summoned our entire local power circle?" demanded **Leroy Sinclair**, pacing the length of his log-framed living room.

Senator Gilbert Molina glanced at his phone. **"I've asked around, but no one knows. You should call the White House and demand answers."**

Sinclair jabbed a finger at him. **"No, *you* call. You've got the connections, Senator."**

Reluctantly, Molina dialed. A curt female voice answered.

"Office of the President."

"Good morning, this is Senator Gilbert Molina. I need to speak with the chief of staff."

A minute of silence passed before the woman returned. **"He's unavailable, but the President wants to speak with you."**

A beep, another tense pause. Molina felt his heart hammer in his chest. Finally, the President's voice came on.

"Senator Molina, stay out of this."

Then the line went dead.

Sudden Departure

Molina's gut twisted. He relayed the cryptic warning to the others—Leroy Sinclair and two colleagues—who all fell silent. In Molina's mind, one thing was clear: *He needed to leave.*

"I have to get back to Washington," Molina muttered, already heading for the door.

He was gone in minutes, whisked to the small airstrip where a waiting jet took off into the crisp mountain air. *A wise move*, as it turned out—because moments later, a convoy of black SUVs roared onto Black Eagle Ranch.

The FBI Arrives

From the window, **Sinclair** watched in disbelief as **FBI agents** fanned out across his driveway. The knock on the door was brusque, followed by the flash of badges and a swift wave of **handcuffs**.

"What is this?" Sinclair shouted, but no one bothered to answer. Within minutes, he and his three companions were loaded into an unmarked **Falcon** jet under federal guard.

Just as abruptly, once airborne, the agents unlocked their cuffs and stepped back.

"You're not under arrest," explained the lead agent. **"We're here to ensure compliance with a direct presidential order. You'll be attending a federal hearing in D.C. at three o'clock this afternoon."**

Sinclair glared, rubbing his wrists. **"Why rough us up like that?"**

"We didn't have time to debate. Any lawyer could have stalled your travel, and we have strict orders that *all* of you appear in that courtroom."

Shaken but uncuffed, Sinclair and his associates exchanged uneasy glances. None of them knew what awaited them in Washington—or whether they'd leave that courthouse still free men.

Chapter 20

Washington, D.C. – Federal Courthouse (2016, Day 2, 2:30 P.M. ET)

A row of SUVs pulled into the Justice Department building, and four uneasy figures stepped out, escorted by **federal agents. Leroy Sinclair** and the others from Telluride were hustled down a hallway to a **nearly empty courtroom**, where they sank into the audience pews without a word.

Sinclair's mind churned. *Why the rush? Why involve the President?* Something told him this had spiraled well beyond any routine legal matter.

Moments later, the doors swung open again, admitting four more equally tense individuals—*women* he and his group recognized all too well. No one spoke. One glance confirmed they were on the same dark page. *Now we know why we're here,* Sinclair thought grimly.

He bowed his head, recalling how many in the current administration and Congress owed him favors. *Political capital*—that was supposed to be his shield. Yet the "how" of it all gnawed at him. *How did they discover our conspiracy?*

A hush fell over the courtroom. Outside, the buzz of the city continued as if nothing unusual were happening. But inside, eight people sat in silent dread, each wondering if this was the day their hidden empire would collapse—and how harshly the government would choose to bury the truth.

Chapter 21

Washington, D.C. – The White House (2016, Day 2, 2:30 P.M. ET)

For **President Kelly O'Sullivan**, the past twenty-four hours had been a sleep-deprived whirlwind. At **3:00 A.M.** he'd convened a **G-7** video call, bridging multiple time zones, to reveal the truth about **Nicolás Tosh**—the elusive data-center founder and hidden benefactor behind the **Experta Foundation**. The numbers spoke for themselves: Experta's donations to G-7 nations were colossal, and Tosh's request to deploy **CDA-322, 323, and 324** on civilians demanded unanimous approval. By **6:00 A.M.**, the President had the resolution in hand.

Congress Before Dawn

Next came the **trickier** part: winning over a **skeptical Congress** at an unnaturally early hour. Gathering the majority and minority leaders by **7:00 A.M.** was a feat in itself; persuading them to endorse "mathematical formulas" as *weapons of mass destruction* seemed ludicrous on its face. But O'Sullivan hammered home that no physical harm or economic meltdown would result—only data analysis. The G-7 resolution's near-completion left Congress little choice, and by **9:30 A.M.** they'd unanimously voted to authorize the algorithms' use, in exchange for various funding concessions for pet projects. It was an ugly compromise, but it worked.

A Call to Tosh

At **11:00 A.M.**, O'Sullivan grabbed his *identifier* and tapped the screen. **"Tosh, I've got the approval."**

"**Excellent,**" Tosh replied, voice emanating from the President's small device. **"I'm bringing a carrier onto the line now."**

Christopher Musial appeared in a split-screen view. The President offered a rueful smile.

"Christopher—I should've suspected your 'extracurriculars' when you turned down that cabinet post." **"Now you know, sir,"** Musial said cheerfully.

The President cleared the line for a moment, allowing Tosh and Christopher to exchange a quiet burst of excitement. Then he returned.

"All right, Christopher. Come by the White House. I'll have your pass waiting."

Delivering the Resolution

An hour later, Musial strode into the **Oval Office**, picked up the official G-7/US resolution, and confirmed it via the *identifier*. He turned to the President.

"We'll contact the Pentagon for the unlocking codes next."

O'Sullivan nodded. **"They're on standby. I understand the neural network remains under G-7 oversight?"**

"Yes, sir," Musial said. **"Any data from civilians goes straight to your designated server, with Pentagon specialists monitoring every step."**

The President exhaled. **"Once we confirm the evidence, we'll instruct the Florida Attorney General to drop all charges against Tosh."**

"Thank you, Mr. President," came Tosh's voice over the link. **"We appreciate your help."**

Musial excused himself. The moment he left, Tosh's **Zermatt Data Center** began exchanging final signals with the Pentagon. Two sets of codes—one from the U.S. government, one from Zermatt—had to match **precisely**. A message flashed across Rainer Sábato's console: **CODE ACCEPTED**.

Unmasking the Conspiracy

Instantly, the **lives** of the twenty suspected conspirators began downloading into the Pentagon's supercomputers, courtesy of **CDA-322, 323, and 324**. Their calls, memories, and mental footprints flowed through the neural network, unstoppable. Zermatt's role ended there; from that point on, the **Pentagon** had total visibility. By **2:30 P.M.**, O'Sullivan and the **Attorney General** were already poring over the damning data.

Amid that frantic review, O'Sullivan insisted on being on the phone as the Attorney General reached out to Florida's legal team—particularly **Juliette Stevens**, the federal prosecutor overseeing Tosh's case. She was to drop all charges with *no delay* and *no outside contact* before the hearing. The President wanted zero chance for the conspirators to stall their fate.

Within the hour, the directive was given, and the last barrier to Tosh's freedom began to crumble. Meanwhile, the conspirators—unaware of how deeply they were compromised—waited in separate courtrooms, certain their well-laid secrets might yet be salvaged. They had no idea *every second* of their guilt was now streaming through the Pentagon's servers.

Chapter 22

Zurich, Switzerland – Tosh's Organization Headquarters (2016, Day 2)

On a quiet cobblestone street in Zurich, a nondescript **twenty-story** office building served as the operational core for **Nicolás Tosh**'s global ventures—both **for-profit** and **philanthropic**. Inside, teams managed vast networks of clients, technologies, and charitable initiatives that spanned continents.

The Administrative Hub (Floors 1–8)

Patrick Donaldson and **Markus Wildi** had spent four decades shaping Tosh's empire. Originally Swiss bankers persuaded to join Tosh, they now held key executive roles. Donaldson, as **Chief Financial Officer**, oversaw accounts, contracts, and complex taxation structures; Wildi, as **Treasurer**, handled treasury operations and the flow of funds across global markets.

They and their administrative staff filled the first eight floors—handling everything from **accounting** to **legal reviews**, ensuring that both Tosh's innovative business and his ambitious philanthropy ran smoothly.

The Walkyria Business Team (Floor 9)

Walkyria, Tosh's for-profit entity, licensed advanced **mathematical algorithms** to governments, militaries, and corporations worldwide. A tight-knit group of ten executives—each with at least 25 years of experience—managed these high-stakes relationships. Only **Rainer**

Sábato and **Tosh** could finalize deals, reflecting the delicate balance between secrecy and innovation at the heart of their enterprise.

Zermatt & Experta HR (Floors 9–10)

Within the same level that housed Walkyria's executives, a section of Floor 9—and all of Floor 10—supported the **Zermatt Data Center** and the **Experta Foundation** from a human-resources standpoint. **Miko Pakkinen**, a meticulous recruiter, profiled and vetted each potential hire—whether they'd become an Experta employee, a Zermatt tech specialist, or a "carrier" trained to operate Tosh's neural network devices.

Rainer and **Tosh** personally interviewed final candidates. Those who passed found themselves inside a hidden world of quantum computing and philanthropic reach. Pakkinen's HR team then handled orientation and training.

The Experta Foundation (Floors 11–20)

Spanning ten floors above, the **Experta Foundation** employed more than five hundred staff. Groups were organized by **country** and by **cause**—everything from educational programs in Latin America to agricultural initiatives in Africa. Funds for these projects flowed from Tosh's math-driven profits, channeled through tight financial controls set by Donaldson and Wildi.

While some of Experta's strategic decisions were made here, **software development** for philanthropic tools still took place exclusively at the **Zermatt Data Center**, the real heartbeat of Tosh's organization. That secluded alpine facility remained the epicenter of

algorithmic breakthroughs—and the hidden nerve center for Tosh's global operations.

Chapter 23

Zermatt, Switzerland – Zermatt Data Center (2016, Day 2, 6:30 P.M. CET / 12:30 P.M. ET)

Rainer Sábato headed straight to the **neural network** station on the first floor. Rows of monitors flickered with real-time data streams, and the faint hum of servers filled the enclosed space.

"Status?" he asked quietly.

Dieter Jürgen, one of the lead technicians, glanced up from his console.

"All data from the twenty suspects was downloaded without incident. The Pentagon remains connected, verifying that the CDA-322, 323, and 324 links stay open. No further data is flowing in or out."

Rainer exhaled. **"So we're standing by for their order to shut down those communications, correct?"**

Dieter nodded. **"Exactly. Once they confirm they have everything, they'll instruct us to terminate."**

Touching Base with Tosh

Rainer tapped the earpiece linked to his **identifier**.

"Nicolás, you still on?"

Tosh's voice came through, calm but laced with tension:

"Yes, I'm in the courtroom, waiting for the President to return with some video evidence. We're all on hold."

"Got it. I'll keep our line open."

"Thanks."

Rainer ended the call and let his gaze drift to the data center's glass wall overlooking the quantum supercomputer floors below. *Nicolás's ordeal* sparked an old memory of **Argentina**, pulling Rainer's mind back three decades to **another** time he'd stood by Tosh under dangerous circumstances.

Chapter 24

Buenos Aires, Argentina – Sarmiento Travel Agency (1984, 11:00 P.M. ART)

Rainer Sábato ran through the damp, fog-choked streets of Buenos Aires, shoes sliding on slick cobblestones. In the moonless dark, the few streetlamps felt like lifelines. He was gasping by the time he ducked onto the narrow pedestrian lane called **La Valle**.

Hours earlier, he and **Nicolás Tosh** had landed in Argentina for a quick trip: exchange a few U.S. dollars on the black market (the official rate was absurdly low) and buy plane tickets to **Bariloche**. A friend back in Zurich, **Markus Wildi**, had given them the address of **Sarmiento Travel Agency**—supposedly a discreet place to handle both currency conversion and travel arrangements. They never expected to walk into a **police sting**.

The Trap

Argentina was still reeling from its economic collapse after the Falklands War. Hard currencies were confiscated, black-market trades declared illegal. Yet foreigners kept selling dollars under the table, and unscrupulous agencies lured them in. That evening, **Sarmiento Travel** was crawling with **plainclothes officers**—the dreaded "Black Leather Jackets" known for disappearing or torturing citizens. Rainer and Tosh were ushered into a cramped office, faced by a grim policeman in a worn leather jacket.

"**Names?**" barked **Captain Ruben Borjes**, flipping open a notebook. "**Nicolás Tosh. Rainer Sábato.**" "**You're exchanging five hundred dollars? And you're carrying more?**"

They surrendered every last bill—fifteen hundred additional dollars. Borjes accused them of **violating foreign currency laws**. In a country where thousands had vanished under military rule, that charge could mean years in prison. They were ordered to sit in a waiting area with a crowd of frightened tourists. Women wept; children clung to their parents. **Tosh, inexplicably, fell asleep.**

Meanwhile, Rainer couldn't rest. He remembered how Tosh insisted on "living like any regular person," traveling in coach, buying local currency on the cheap. *This is the price we pay,* Rainer thought bitterly.

A Desperate Communication

When Tosh finally stirred, Rainer nudged him to activate the small pager-like device in his jacket: an "identifier," loaded with **CDA-319, 320, and 321** to allow silent, thought-based communication between "carriers."

"**Tosh, we're in danger,**" Rainer urged in his mind. "**Yes, let's contact Patrick and Markus,**" Tosh replied telepathically.

They explained the predicament. **CDA-322, 323, and 324**—the advanced mind-reading algorithms—were still incomplete. The best they could do was gather intel from the data center back in Switzerland. **Patrick Donaldson** advised them to shift from "pure anonymity" to using their philanthropic muscle if it could secure their release.

Captain Borjes

Suddenly, a policeman shouted. He'd discovered a hidden stash of **gold bars** and **U.S. bills** under loose floor tiles. The agency owner, **Sarmiento**, was handcuffed immediately, unleashing new panic among the detainees. Tosh seized the moment—he pointed his identifier at **Captain Borjes**, registering the man's brain signature.

"Peter, run a limited CDA-323 query—just references to the Experta Foundation," Tosh thought to the data center. **"Nicolás,"** responded the voice of **Peter Friedli, "these modules aren't fully tested. And Borjes isn't a data-center employee." "I'm recruiting him right now,"** Tosh insisted.

He crossed to Borjes, who sat at a desk, smoking triumphantly.

"What do you want?" the captain growled. **"I heard your passion for this country,"** Tosh began quietly. **"I have an organization—one that donated over a hundred million dollars here last year. We need someone like you."**

Borjes blinked, torn between suspicion and curiosity. Tosh pressed on, describing how his group financed major **social projects**, albeit in secret.

"If I can prove it, would you consider working for us part-time?" Tosh asked.

Meanwhile, the crowd was being herded downstairs. Time was running out. The captain was on the fence—could this "rich tourist" be legit, or was it all a hoax?

The Phone Call

Tosh eyed an antique rotary phone on the desk. He telepathically signaled **Patrick** for help.

"Patrick, call this number, speak to me. The captain will be listening," Tosh thought.

Seconds later, the phone rang. Borjes answered, then passed it to Tosh. **Patrick** rattled off a list of **Argentine** projects the **Experta Foundation** funded—big agricultural co-ops, youth training programs—asking Borjes if he recognized any. Suddenly, the captain's eyes widened.

"That last one—that's my uncle's farm project," he breathed.

In that instant, Tosh saw the final puzzle piece click. The policeman realized this "illegal currency exchanger" might actually be a *massive benefactor* to his own family's livelihood.

Chapter 25

Miami & Washington, D.C. – Federal Courthouses (2016, Day 2, 4:00 P.M. ET)

A hush fell over the Miami courtroom as **President O'Sullivan** appeared on the large video screen. Meanwhile, the Washington, D.C. court displayed the same feed to its eight attendees. Together, they formed the **twenty** individuals who had been summoned—plus **Nicolás Tosh**, standing off to one side in his orange jumpsuit.

"Ladies and gentlemen," the President began, **"earlier today, the G-7 unanimously approved deploying CDA-322, 323, and 324. These are *mathematical military weapons*—classified as WMDs—and Mr. Tosh is a G-7 *strategic military asset.* A few hours later, the U.S. Congress and I granted final authorization."**

A flicker of unease rippled through the courtroom. **Leroy Sinclair**, seated among the other "guests," repeated the phrase *mathematical military weapon* in his head. The President continued:

"We used these algorithms to process and store data from each of you, and in minutes, we found sufficient evidence to overturn Mr. Tosh's guilty verdict. Before we proceed, we'd like to show you certain images—footage, actually—relevant to everyone present. Please bear with us a moment while we set it up."

As technicians switched the video feed, the Miami group saw the eight conspirators in D.C., then the perspective flipped: the D.C. attendees observed the twelve in Miami. A tremor swept through the entire gathering. Each recognized they shared a singular connection: **Nicolás Tosh**.

Sinclair swallowed hard. Hearing the words *strategic military asset* and *WMD* made it clear no political favors or behind-the-scenes dealings would protect them now. *They had* to know everything. And if they'd gleaned it from a direct link to his mind, no secret remained safe.

He pressed clammy palms to his knees, realizing a cold, inevitable truth: *They were all going down.*

Chapter 26

Washington, D.C. – Senate Office Building (2016, Day 2, 2:30 P.M. ET)

The **carrier** sipped a grande macchiato at a small café table, eyes fixed on a tiny device resembling an old pager. An on-screen prompt read: **BRAIN SIGNAL DETECTED**. Then: **CONFIRM SUBJECT**. He pressed **YES** on the left button.

SUBJECT ENGAGED. APPLYING CDA-319. BRAIN SCAN IN PROCESS...

In the distance, **Senator Gilbert Molina** emerged from a limo, hurrying up the steps. The carrier tracked him calmly, letting the neural link establish as the senator drew closer. The device displayed:

SCAN COMPLETED. ID # 374x14p00312. SENDING INFO TO DATA CENTER... INFORMATION ACCEPTED.

Rising from his seat, the carrier strolled into the building, following Molina into a nearly empty elevator.

"What floor, sir?" asked Molina. **"Third, thanks,"** replied the carrier.

The senator tapped the panel. **"Same for me."** He glanced curiously at the device in the carrier's hands.

"I didn't know pagers were still a thing," Molina remarked. **"They have their uses,"** the carrier said quietly.

The carrier looked down at the menu, selecting: **APPLY CDA-320.** Then:

IS THE SUBJECT PRESENT? —YES— ENGAGING... ENGAGED USING CDA-320 (SUBJECT) AND CDA-321 (CARRIER).

Once the doors opened, Molina headed left; the carrier turned right.

Suddenly, the senator froze in the corridor. A voice sounded—*inside* his head.

"Senator Molina."

He spun around, expecting someone to be there, but the hallway was empty.

"Who's calling me?" he muttered aloud. **"We're connected via thought,"** came the silent reply, the tone clear in his mind. **"You should find a private space. People might wonder why you're talking to yourself."**

An aide passed by, blinking at Molina's confusion. The senator mumbled an apology and ducked into his office, slamming the door.

"This is illegal—violates my privacy. Who the hell are you?"

"We're part of a government-sanctioned, not-for-profit organization. We communicate on behalf of official channels," the voice answered. **"You were in Telluride this morning—spoke to the President, yes?"**

Molina's pulse raced. **"And the men I met were arrested. Am I next?"**

"We don't know. But we do know the government wants your cooperation. For now, you'll talk only through me."

"You're just a—beeper?" Molina asked aloud, half in disbelief.

"Yes, Senator." And then: **"Communication has ended."**

Silence. Molina gripped his desk, shaken. He hadn't realized that, behind the scenes, the team at **Zermatt** was waiting on approval to run **CDA-323** on him—an act that would expose his entire life to the Pentagon's servers. But for now, he was treated as a *potential ally*, or at least a *tool*, while final decisions about his fate were made at the highest levels of power.

Chapter 27

San Carlos de Bariloche, Argentina – Professor Benjamín Borjes's Home (1984, 10:00 P.M. ART)

Professor **Benjamín Borjes** lived simply in a compact chalet perched on the shore of **Lake Nahuel Huapi**. Though barely a thousand square feet, the house boasted a breathtaking view of the massive mountain range and the famous **Llao-Llao Hotel** across the way. A small kayak bobbed at the dock—his companion for long, meditative rows along the lake's edge.

Now *semi-retired*, math had been Borjes's great passion. He'd recently received a surprise windfall: a **five-million-dollar grant** for preserving the lake's pristine shores, arranged by an elusive donor through a Buenos Aires attorney named **Luis Puerta**. Borjes hadn't learned the benefactor's identity, only that other recipient existed throughout Argentina—together forming the largest philanthropic initiative he'd ever encountered.

An Unexpected Call

That evening, Borjes returned from a **moonlit** kayak trip, frost still clinging to his jacket. As he stepped into his cozy living room, the **phone rang**—a sturdy 1960s rotary model that seldom chimed so late.

"Hello?" "Uncle, it's Rubén," came the voice on the other end.

Captain Rubén Borjes, an officer in Argentina's intelligence police—and the professor's nephew—rarely phoned at this hour. Borjes's heart tightened.

"**Rubencito, how are you?**" "Busy, Uncle. Listen, do you recall your attorney, Puerta, and that big donation?" "Yes…"

Nicolás Tosh listened in via the captain's telephone extension, then spoke up, startling the professor.

"**Professor, it's me.**" "*You?* **So you did this.**" Borjes's voice caught with emotion.

For **Tosh**, hearing the warm acceptance in his mentor's words was overwhelming. Borjes had always been his greatest inspiration, the one who nurtured his mathematical brilliance and taught him to use it for good.

"**I'm so proud,**" the professor said, "**of what you've become—helping our country. Rubén, you've met someone extraordinary.**" "**I see that,**" Captain Borjes conceded.

A Welcome Release

A few moments later, the captain ended the call and turned to Tosh, still in the travel-agency office. Rubbing his temples, he asked:

"**Why come here for a mere five-hundred-dollar exchange on the black market?**"

Tosh shrugged. "**My *public* identity is an ordinary traveler—my philanthropic earnings go to the foundation. I try to keep them separate.**"

The captain's eyes shone with a sudden reverence. "**In that case, *Señor* Tosh, it'll be my honor to work for you.**"

"**Then start by interviewing each detainee,**" Tosh requested, "**and release those who are just regular tourists, like us.**"

Though unaccustomed to civilian orders, **Borjes** recognized Tosh's logic. The real profiteers were smugglers and black-market barons—not naive travelers. He complied, questioning each detainee. Soon, he returned passports and money to the harmless bunch, including **Rainer Sábato** and **Nicolás Tosh**. Only seven genuine racketeers were arrested.

Out in the chilly midnight air, Tosh decided to walk, pondering everything that had happened; Rainer jogged to clear his head. Looking back years later, Rainer realized that this night changed **Tosh's** approach to security forever—and recruited **Captain Borjes** into the fold. It also reminded them both that trust and vigilance went hand in hand.

And there was still another incident to come…

Chapter 28

*San Carlos de Bariloche, Argentina – Professor Benjamín
Borjes's Home (1984, Next Day, 9:15 A.M. ART)*

A **DC-9** from Austral Airlines touched down smoothly amid the frosty slopes of **San Carlos de Bariloche**. **Nicolás Tosh** and **Rainer Sábato** disembarked, reveling in the crisp mountain air. Neither had visited in years, and for security reasons, they seldom traveled together—so it had to be important.

Return to Bariloche

Their rented **Ford Cortina** wound through narrow, snow-edged streets before heading west along the lake. Rainer gazed at the quiet town, recalling that Tosh rarely spoke of his childhood here.

"I never even met your parents," Rainer murmured. **"They weren't around much,"** Tosh said gently. **"My aunt Camila raised me, but we've been out of touch."**

As they drove, Tosh admitted he also had a second reason for returning: a tip from an old family friend that his father, **Bruno**, had gone missing—again.

"I suspect he's hiding out in my mother's house," Tosh confided, **"but that's private. Right now, we have to see Professor Borjes."**

A Warm Welcome

By **10:00 A.M.**, they arrived at the professor's small chalet along **Lake Nahuel Huapi**. Though compact, it boasted a stunning lakeside view and a well-worn kayak beside a rickety dock. Spotting Tosh, **Benjamín Borjes** dropped the firewood in his arms and hurried forward.

"Nicolás—what a joy!" he exclaimed, voice catching as they embraced. **"Professor, I'm sorry it's been so long,"** Tosh said, fighting his own emotion.

Tosh introduced Rainer, reminding the professor that it was thanks to Rainer's off-piste skiing adventure decades ago that Tosh had first unlocked the spark of his **CDA** research.

"I remember," Borjes said with a grin. **"Viktor Frankl would call that the moment you found meaning. Come in; we'll have some mate and catch up."**

Inside, the chalet's single large room served as a living area, kitchen, and library. Stacks of reference books and a battered blackboard lined the walls. A half-finished arithmetic proof gleamed in chalk.

"I only have half an hour," Borjes apologized, **"then I'm off to teach. We can meet again at noon."**

A New Collaboration

Before they left, Tosh got straight to the point:

"Professor, I'd like you to join our organization. You can stay at this university and keep your schedule, but we need your help on a *major* problem with our CDA-324. You'd work remotely, plus occasional trips to Switzerland. One catch: you won't be able to accept further grants from the foundation, to avoid conflict of interest. However, you can appoint a team to continue your conservation project while you focus on our math lab."

Borjes's eyes lit up, though a hint of anxiety lingered. **"I'm honored, Nicolás. I'll try—but if it's beyond me, you'll have to let me go back."**

"If you truly want out, the project reverts to you," Tosh promised. **"But I doubt you'll quit."**

Rainer pulled out a small "identifier," scanning Borjes's brain signals using **CDA-319** to register him. When he finished, Borjes blinked, uncertain what had just happened. Tosh explained that within minutes, the professor would be able to *hear* the team's thoughts—an introduction to **CDA-320**.

"Rainer and I must head to Zurich—virtually—to recruit Professor Schneiderman, but Edgahar Preller, our data-lab head, will start explaining these algorithms to you."

Indeed, while Borjes blinked, disoriented, Tosh and Rainer slipped out into the corridor. With a quick mental command, they connected to **Patrick Donaldson** in Switzerland, repeating the same offer to **Schneiderman**—who also had to relinquish direct philanthropic grants in exchange for joining the lab team. By late morning, both revered professors had been brought fully on board.

A Mathematical Breakthrough

In a borrowed conference room, Tosh and Rainer then initiated a multi-party session with Borjes and Schneiderman. Via **CDA-320**, they demonstrated high-level formula flowcharts for the Communicational Discrete Algorithms—**319 to 324**—emphasizing the two key challenges:

1. **Batch vs. Single-Pass Memory Access**

- Currently, *CDA-323* could only download a person's life memories in slow "batches." The team needed a method to gather it all at once—*instantly*.

2. **Safeguarding Free Will**

- They wanted strong "blocker" protocols that would detect and block any unauthorized attempt to *upload* data into a subject's brain, preventing mind-control or manipulation.

Borjes and Schneiderman lit up with excitement, brainstorming potential solutions. That day launched a **two-decade collaboration** that brought new rigor to the CDAs, culminating in single-pass memory retrieval for *CDA-323* and *CDA-324*, plus advanced "blocker" algorithms ensuring no one could hijack a registered mind.

Quietly, **Tosh** reflected on how, in just two days, his life had pivoted from near-disaster in Buenos Aires to forging a bold new step in mind-communication technology. And beyond it all, he knew soon he must face his missing father—a private quest overshadowed by the demands of a technology that could reshape humanity itself.

Chapter 29

Zermatt, Switzerland – Zermatt Data Center (2016, Day 2, 6:30 P.M. CET / 12:30 P.M. ET)

Rainer Sábato jolted from his memories when **Nicolás Tosh**'s voice resounded in his mind:

"Don't you think the President is taking too long?"

"How long has it been?" Rainer asked. **"Long enough. Ping his ID number."**

Rainer tapped a command on his *identifier*, and moments later **President O'Sullivan** came online, sounding tense:

"Tosh, we have a problem."

A Sudden Crisis

The President explained that the Pentagon claimed the *downloaded data*—the evidence exonerating Tosh and incriminating the twenty conspirators—had become *corrupted* and **unreadable**. Military officials suspected sabotage by Tosh's team. Tosh denied it vehemently:

"Why would I destroy data that proves my innocence?"

General suspicion lingered, so **Tosh** and **Rainer** proposed a direct conversation with the Pentagon's data analysts. The President patched them in. **General Collins** from the DOD walked through an investigation showing no tampering during the neural-network transfer. Rainer mused aloud:

"If it wasn't altered in transit, the issue must lie elsewhere."

Suddenly Rainer remembered an older precaution: the **"blocker"** algorithms embedded in every CDA. He asked the Pentagon team to check the **blocker logs**—software designed to destroy any illicit data *incoming* to a target's brain. Within minutes, they found evidence that someone at the Pentagon had tried sending a cryptic message— *"Government scanning your brain. End inevitable, take the pill."*—to four conspirators after the memory downloads. That triggered the blockers, erasing both the conspiracy data *and* the invasive message.

"Whoever did this sabotage was on your end," Tosh said quietly.

The Saboteur Unmasked

A quick trace revealed the culprit: **Corporal Dan Gilbert, Jr.**— nephew to the **Secretary of Defense**, *Prescott Gilbert*. Security apprehended the corporal at the Pentagon as he tried to leave. The President and General Collins realized this likely connected to a higher conspiracy.

"Mr. President," Tosh suggested, **"re-run CDA-322 and 323 on all twenty suspects, gather fresh data."**

The President agreed. He also discovered that the Secretary of Defense himself *should* have been under perpetual CDA surveillance per G-7 rules, given his government post. Yet no one had enforced it. As details emerged, O'Sullivan ordered the Secret Service to watch the Secretary of Defense closely—and his suspicion proved right: waiting in the Oval Office lobby, **Gilbert** attempted to swallow a cyanide capsule. Agents forcibly subdued him, removing the pill.

Meanwhile, the same suicide instructions had gone to four conspirators in the DC and Miami courtrooms. Alerted by CIA and Secret Service teams, security discreetly removed them, confiscating hidden pills. O'Sullivan had them held overnight under *suicide watch,* while the remaining suspects in both courtrooms were told to return the next day.

A New Day Dawns

By **5:00 P.M. ET**, the President reconvened with General Collins, confirming the second data sweep was underway. Satisfied that everything was under control, he turned to Tosh:

"Nicolás, you need to come to Washington. Air Force Two is ready at MIA. Tomorrow, the country will recognize what you've done."

Exhausted but resolute, the President hung up. An empty Oval Office surrounded him in dusk's quiet. In the space between phone calls and crisis management, he wondered just how high the conspiracy might reach—and who else had slipped under the radar while an entire nation waited for the truth.

Chapter 30

Miami, Florida – 2016, Day 2 (6:00 P.M. ET)

FBI Agent Louis Tomassi steered his government SUV east along the **MacArthur Causeway**, red sunset flames glowing in his rearview mirror. On his right, the **Port of Miami** stood silent—no cruise ships docked midweek. As he neared **Fisher Island**, Tomassi swung right toward the ferry entrance, then immediately turned left into a **Coast Guard** parking lot. He parked in a designated government space, slipped his phone into the glove compartment, and moved toward a covered canvas.

Beneath it lay a sleek black **Kawasaki** motorcycle. Tomassi unzipped a duffel bag on the seat, withdrew a black leather suit, and hopped into it with practiced ease. He grabbed a helmet from the rear seat, snapped it on, and within seconds thundered westbound onto the causeway. In Miami's rush-hour muddle, he melted into the traffic—exactly as he'd planned.

Monitored by the White House

From the **Oval Office**, **President O'Sullivan** and **General Collins** tracked Tomassi's every movement—*and* his thoughts—via the recently deployed **CDA** link.

"Mr. President," said Collins, **"here's the transcript of his last few minutes. We're streaming his point-of-view feed now."**

At first, Tomassi's mental chatter revealed frustration. The conspirators' grand plan was unraveling: **Nicolás Tosh** had been exonerated, and the indicted courtroom audience had been there for only one reason—to see Tosh destroyed. Now it was all in jeopardy.

Tomassi raced north on **I-95**, exiting near **West Palm Beach**. He took a winding route eastward until he reached a private oceanfront golf club—opulent and exclusive, belonging to billionaire **Curtis L. Smith**. A guard at the gate paused before granting entry. Tomassi parked near the clubhouse.

"Is Mr. Smith expecting you?" asked the general manager. **"No." "He's in a private gathering."**

A helicopter's rotor blades rumbled overhead—someone was leaving in a hurry. Tomassi silently cursed his timing, uncertain if that was Smith or another VIP. The manager led him to the **locker room** and asked him to wait until the current high-stakes poker hand finished. Tomassi sat alone, tension bristling.

A Sudden Blackout

Back at the White House, **O'Sullivan** frowned. The live feed from Tomassi's viewpoint abruptly cut out.

"General Collins—why did the link drop?" the President demanded. **"We still have a signal, sir, but it's scrambled. Our system shows:** *LINK BLOCKED AS PER G-7 RESOLUTION, Code 535US.***"**

O'Sullivan stiffened. **"Which means?"** **"That code designates an individual who cannot, under any circumstances, be monitored by a CDA—like you, Mr. President, or certain other heads of state."**

Alarm slithered through O'Sullivan. Could that mean Tomassi was now with someone on that **off-limits** list?

A Bigger Threat Emerges

Elsewhere, Tomassi found himself pulled into a brief, tense conversation with **former President Layton Thomas**—the same man he had once served. Emerging from a sauna in a plush towel, Thomas listened grimly to Tomassi's frantic update:

"Tosh is free. The plan collapsed. Everyone in those courtrooms was waiting for the President's final verdict. Something about *mathematical weapons*—**some G-7 resolution."**

Thomas's phone buzzed. He answered, tension etched across his face.

"Layton, we're sending a helicopter. A private plane's waiting at West Palm Beach. You need to come to the White House."

The line went dead before Thomas could argue. He exhaled slowly, aware that the current President—O'Sullivan—was onto him. Moments later, the golf club manager discreetly announced that the building had been cleared for security, and a helicopter awaited him outside. In the hush, Thomas realized there would be no evading this: the confrontation in Washington loomed.

"Agent Tomassi," Thomas said quietly, **"You're coming with me or not?"**

But the manager shook his head. **"Sir, the agent already departed in your car."**

Thomas gave a short nod. Typical Tomassi—always operating on his own timetable. With no further pretense, the former President dressed, stepped outside, and boarded **Curtis Smith's** private Agusta helicopter. Within minutes, he landed at a small airstrip near an **FBI Falcon** jet, waiting to ferry him to D.C.

A seasoned politician, Thomas had weathered storms before. But as he settled into the Falcon's leather seat, he couldn't ignore the fear knotted in his chest. *CDAs, G-7 weapon... Tosh a "strategic asset."* He wondered how deeply he'd miscalculated. Now he was on a collision course with President O'Sullivan—one that might cost him everything.

Chapter 31

Washington, D.C. – The White House / West Palm Beach, Florida (2016, Day 2, 8:30 P.M. ET)

O'Sullivan's Dilemma

President Kelly O'Sullivan paced the Oval Office floor, phone silent at his side. The emerging truth—**former President Layton Thomas** might be tied to the conspiracy—warped every strategy for damage control. He could purge the system, sure, but publicizing a plot involving a former commander-in-chief could undermine the presidency itself. *How to protect the Office without suppressing justice?* he wondered.

In the hush, he replayed the day's events: the sabotage at the Pentagon, the near-suicides in court, the Secretary of Defense's betrayal, and now a **former president** en route to Washington under suspicion. The swirl of revelations threatened not just Tosh's future but the country's faith in its highest institutions.

Tomassi in West Palm

Meanwhile, **FBI Agent Louis Tomassi** sat in a small holding room at the **FBI West Palm Beach office**, fear coursing through his veins. He had arrived with minimal electronic footprints, certain nobody had tracked him to Layton Thomas. Yet somehow, the Secret Service had snatched him up anyway—bypassing official charges entirely.

A young, impassive Secret Service agent opened the door:

"Agent Tomassi, you're being held by direct order of the President, on the grounds of national security. You may be needed

for questioning in the next few hours. If so, we'll bring you a secure phone. Until then, please remain here."

Tomassi's stomach twisted. *National security* meant the usual rules didn't apply; they had near-limitless authority to detain him. The charges he might face—treason, espionage, conspiracy—carried staggering penalties. All because he'd landed on the wrong side of **Nicolás Tosh** and the G-7's so-called "mathematical weapons."

He eyed the austere room: two chairs, a table, and a glass wall reminiscent of an interrogation booth. No restraints, but he was effectively caged. *No electronics, no communication… no way out.*

"Am I being charged with a crime?" he asked quietly.

The agent's expression offered no reassurance.

"We're not authorized to discuss that. Just wait."

Tomassi sank into the hard plastic chair. The day's events weighed on him—Tosh exonerated, major conspirators imprisoned, the Secretary of Defense unconscious under sedation. Now he was trapped in the President's net, powerless. And if Layton Thomas really was a conspirator, Tomassi's role in bridging them might land him at the heart of a national scandal.

He bowed his head, wishing he could vanish as easily as he'd appeared. But it was too late for that. The noose of **national security** had already tightened.

Chapter 32

Washington, D.C. – The White House (2016, Day 2, 8:30 P.M. ET)

A Man Without an Exit

Secretary of Defense Prescott Gilbert woke in a small, windowless White House storage room. Two Secret Service agents guarded the door, offering neither explanation nor mercy. He reflexively checked the empty cavity in his molar—where he'd hidden a cyanide capsule. Gone. **No escape** if he wanted one. Now that the Pentagon was picking through every second of his life, there was little hope left.

Meanwhile, in the same building, **Nicolás Tosh** experienced the White House for the first time in person. Ushered into the **Lincoln Bedroom** as a special VIP, he couldn't help wondering about President O'Sullivan's next move. News that **former President Layton Thomas** might be part of the conspiracy changed everything, potentially implicating the entire Oval Office. Exhausted, Tosh dozed off with that grim thought in mind.

A Late Arrival

Ninety minutes later, **Layton Thomas**—who had served as U.S. President over a decade earlier—landed at **Andrews Air Force Base**. A short ride by **Marine One** brought him to the White House. Expecting a private huddle with O'Sullivan, he instead found himself face-to-face with the **Secretary of State,** the **Attorney General,** and the **Chief of Staff.**

"**Layton, have a seat,**" President O'Sullivan said, voice tight. "**We have everything on HD video from your co-conspirators, courtesy of CDA-323. Only you are missing—because CDAs are blocked from current and former presidents. I'm giving you a chance to come clean.**"

"**In exchange for what?**" Thomas asked warily. "**Nothing.**" "**Then why would I cooperate?**"

O'Sullivan's eyes flickered with resolve.

"**Otherwise, I'll petition the G-7 to revoke *all* blocks on heads of state for national security. I can have that approved within the hour. Then your life goes fully on record.**"

A High-Stakes Bargain

Thomas's mind churned. If O'Sullivan truly exposed him via CDA scans, **every** personal secret, every mistake—spanning decades—would come to light. Yet if Thomas did nothing, the entire scandal risked tarnishing the presidency itself. Sensing Thomas hesitate, O'Sullivan pressed:

"**Don't pretend I won't do it. I'll sacrifice my own immunity if necessary. There's too much at stake.**"

Thomas tried to call his bluff:

"**You'd open yourself to the same intrusion. *That* is a risk.**"

"**Secretary Kientz,**" O'Sullivan snapped, "**proceed with the G-7 resolution to drop the presidential restriction.**"

"**Wait!**" Thomas said quickly. "**I haven't refused.**"

O'Sullivan nodded, summoning the **Chief of Staff** to fetch **Nicolás Tosh** from the Lincoln Bedroom. Ten minutes later, Tosh entered the Oval Office.

"Mr. President, an honor to meet you in person," Tosh said calmly. **"We've met in passing,"** O'Sullivan replied. **"But indeed, we have _much_ to discuss."**

Tosh glanced at **Layton Thomas**, once an ally he had privately admired. But now, learning Thomas had orchestrated a campaign to destroy him—pushing Tosh's near-imprisonment—left him cold.

A Private Conversation

O'Sullivan sent the Secretary of State, the Attorney General, and the Chief of Staff out, leaving only himself, Thomas, and Tosh in the Oval Office.

"Layton, meet the _real_ Nicolás Tosh—the voice behind the 'identifier' devices and the founder of the entire data center behind CDA."

Thomas's jaw dropped. He realized the "businessman" he had attacked and the quiet genius behind the G-7 "military asset" were the same person.

"I...didn't know," Thomas stammered. **"I never suspected your ties to the G-7."**

O'Sullivan cut in, **"He's also the sole contributor to the Experta Foundation—yes, that mysterious global benefactor. You tried to obliterate him. Now, it's time to talk."**

Thomas's gaze shifted to Tosh, whom he once courted for donations. Tosh returned his stare with icy detachment.

"We're waiting," O'Sullivan prompted.

Thomas inhaled deeply. **"It started with a late-night call from a key donor—our party's biggest contributor—who was on the brink of financial collapse…"**

He paused, scanning Tosh's expression and the President's unyielding posture. If he told the entire story, perhaps he could salvage something. If he held back, they might unleash the G-7's full scanning power on him, exposing far more than mere political deals.

With dread coiling in his gut, Thomas began to speak, unveiling how a single phone call had drawn him into a conspiracy that threatened not only Tosh, but possibly the presidency itself.

Chapter 33

Harlem, New York City – 2015 (Twelve Months Before Day 1)

Jonathan Stanza—one of Washington's most influential lobbyists—rarely asked for favors. So when he dialed **former President Layton Thomas** late that evening, it meant a serious crisis was brewing.

"Mr. President," Stanza began, **"our client, *Newton, Fisher & Lorie*, is hemorrhaging contracts. They used to dominate 90% of the market for high-level financial modeling software, but they've slid to under 50% in two years—and might drop to 22.5% soon."**

Thomas tapped a pen against his desk. **"They build the tools banks use to hedge risk, right? Complex derivative modeling?"**

"Yes—*the* go-to suite for top financial institutions. Now there's a single competitor scooping up those contracts. We have *no* idea who they are or how they're winning."

Thomas frowned. **"No leads, no angle?"**

"We suspect bribes, but we lack proof." **"Are they foreign?"** Thomas asked, eyes narrowing. **"Likely, yes."** **"All right. If they're overseas, we can fuel negative PR. Let me see which CEOs might talk."**

Calling in Favors

Thomas knew exactly whom to call first: **Lawrence S. Green**, Chairman and CEO of the **New York Bank Corporation** (NYBC), the nation's third-largest bank and a longtime political ally.

"Layton!" Green greeted warmly. **"Been a while since Pebble Beach… Remember you threatened golf revenge."**

Thomas forced a laugh. **"I'll get you next time. Listen, I need a quick favor: are you still using Newton, Fisher & Lorie's risk-modeling software?"**

Green hesitated. **"We… changed providers a few days ago."**

"To whom?" Thomas pressed. **"Confidential. Contractual obligations. I'm sorry, Mr. President—business is business."**

Thomas hung up, frustration mounting. He phoned half a dozen other major-bank CEOs. All said the same: *they'd switched to a secret new vendor offering 'better service, better price.'* None would disclose the competitor's name.

Meeting the Operatives

Disgruntled, Thomas summoned two trusted operatives to **Manhattan's SoHo** district for coffee the next day—one traveling from Boston, the other from D.C. The plan was to meet them separately, glean their insights, and dispatch them discreetly.

FBI Special Agent Louis Tomassi, typically based in Miami, happened to be in D.C. that morning. Thomas gave him an urgent call:

"Lou, I need you in Manhattan—*today*. Acela train. I'll meet you at the usual spot."

Tomassi didn't hesitate. Half an hour later, he was on board, weaving north up the East Coast. He understood one thing clearly: whenever former President Thomas said he had a "problem," it usually meant high-stakes maneuvering—and serious trouble for anyone who stood in the way.

Chapter 34

New York City – Starbucks Café, Midtown (2015, Twelve Months Before Day 1)

"Agent Tomassi, thanks for coming on such short notice." Former President **Layton Thomas** greeted him with the same polite yet commanding tone that once resonated from the Oval Office. They sat at a bustling Starbucks inside a Barnes & Noble, the noise of espresso machines and chatty patrons providing perfect cover.

"Always available for you, Mr. President," Tomassi replied.

Years ago, Tomassi had dreamed of joining the Secret Service but never qualified. Thomas knew it—exploited it, even—but Tomassi ignored the fact. Serving a *former* president was the closest he'd get to that elusive badge.

"I need you to investigate a company—its registration, its directors, its ownership." "What's the catch?" Tomassi asked warily. **"They've cornered the market for complex financial-modeling software, effectively crippling one of our party's biggest donors, Newton, Fisher & Lorie. Find out who they are."**

Tomassi paused, noting the urgency in Thomas's eyes. **"All right, I'll tap my contacts. I'll be quick."**

Thomas nodded his thanks. They shook hands, and Tomassi headed off into the Manhattan crowds.

Calling Helen Bloom

His first call went to **FBI Special Agent Helen Bloom**, an MIT math genius who led Specialized Information Systems. They agreed to meet at **Giovanni's**, an old-school Italian spot near Penn Station, that evening.

He hopped a taxi to Penn Station and caught the next **Acela** southbound to D.C., scanning his watch—the train would arrive by 7:45 P.M., giving him just enough time.

Shortly after 8:00, Tomassi walked into Giovanni's and spotted Bloom—a tall, brilliant woman with an ironic sense of humor. She rose to greet him.

"Helen, do we develop or subcontract the Bureau's software for advanced risk-modeling?" "We subcontract," she replied, arching an eyebrow. **"Why the sudden math interest, Louis?"**

He gave a half-smile, then divulged the situation: a top-tier software competitor, hush-hush operations, *possibly foreign.* Her expression turned serious.

"I've encountered them. They're unbelievably advanced, but they demand ironclad secrecy. Even *we* can't investigate them. We've tried."

"A neural network?" Tomassi pressed. **"Exactly. Their own proprietary channel, untraceable. 'Radio silence' is part of every contract."**

She shrugged. **"They're multinational. No single nationality—and apparently some Americans, too."**

When they finished dinner, Bloom excused herself. **"See you later,"** she said softly, leaving Tomassi to his next meeting.

Stan Levitz & a Dead End

Stan Levitz led the FBI's Monetary Crimes Unit and arrived at Giovanni's around 9:00 P.M. The two men embraced like the old friends they were—both had joined the Bureau with big dreams.

"Louis, what's up?" Stan asked as they settled into a corner booth.

Tomassi explained the swirl around Newton, Fisher & Lorie losing two-thirds of their market share to a shadowy rival. **"I need your help checking the NYBC bank accounts—who replaced N, F & L as a payee, and for how much."**

Stan frowned. **"I'll try. But be careful, Louis—this is bigger than you think."**

He stepped outside to send an encrypted request. Ten minutes later, he returned, looking unsettled.

"We found a new payee—ten percent cheaper than what the bank used to pay Newton, Fisher & Lorie. But the beneficiary's name is literally *blank*. A note says, 'We must keep this vendor's name confidential.' That's it. No leads."

Tomassi exhaled in frustration. **"All right. Thanks, Stan."**

They parted ways, each weighed down by the futility of the search. Tomassi made a quick call to Thomas— **"Nothing yet."** The former president, meanwhile, had just wrapped up a similar request to a **CIA** contact in Boston. Both men realized they'd need deeper, more clandestine methods if they were to unmask the mysterious software giant.

Chapter 35

Washington, D.C. – The White House (2016, Day 2, 9:00 P.M. ET)

As **former President Layton Thomas** finished recounting how he'd tracked and sabotaged the secret software competitor, **Nicolás Tosh** felt a knot tighten in his chest. It confirmed the chink in his armor—**Walkyria**, his for-profit operation, had relied on private contracts and NDAs for secrecy, a veil that was infinitely more fragile than the ironclad G-7 protections around the **Zermatt Data Center**.

"So that's how you found us…" Tosh said quietly.

Thomas shrugged, looking weary. **"I didn't know it was *you*, Nicolás. Only that your operation undercut one of my biggest donors. I owed them a rescue, so my associates—Tomassi, Stanza, others—went digging."**

Tosh exhaled. He pictured the painstaking clauses, NDAs, financial disbursement rules—thousands of hours forging a labyrinth of secrecy around **Walkyria** and **Experta**. Yet it had all nearly unraveled under the pressure of money, bribes, or hacking attempts by those determined to unmask his organization.

"In Zermatt," he mused aloud, **"the data center's secrecy is enforced by governments. Unassailable. But Walkyria and Experta rely on *private* clients and beneficiaries—people who can be strong-armed or bribed. It was only a matter of time."**

Thomas nodded, a flicker of guilt shading his gaze. **"Yes, well. The more success your software had, the more contracts they lost, the more pressure landed on me to fix it. We never imagined…"** He trailed off, glancing at President O'Sullivan, who stood nearby in grim silence.

A hush settled in the Oval Office. **Tosh** understood now. The system he had built—**Walkyria** fueling **Experta** with philanthropic funds, all behind layers of anonymity—had been exposed by raw political necessity. And once a powerful figure like Thomas set his sights on it, *no* contract or penalty clause could stand in the way.

At length, Tosh cleared his throat. **"So, you attacked me on behalf of Newton, Fisher & Lorie. And nearly destroyed everything I'd built."**

Thomas looked away. **"I regret it, Nicolás—but it's done."**

"Not entirely," President O'Sullivan cut in softly, arms folded. **"We still have the matter of your formal confession, Layton—along with the rest of the conspirators. Let's settle that before we put any illusions of secrecy behind us."**

Tosh nodded, his mind already racing with new strategies. Whatever came next, the old illusions of an impenetrable private veil were gone. *Time for a different kind of shield,* he thought, *one that blends Zermatt's government-level protection with Walkyria's commercial reach—so that no single political favor or targeted bribe could ever topple it again.*

Chapter 36

Washington, D.C. – FBI Headquarters (2015, Twelve Months Before Day 1)

FBI Agent Louis Tomassi sat at his desk, scanning a file that seemed to lead nowhere. He'd been investigating an extraordinarily secretive organization—a top-tier supplier of advanced mathematical software used by governments, militaries, and the biggest financial firms. Their cloak of anonymity was nearly flawless. Yet Tomassi refused to believe they were *untouchable*.

"If they won't show themselves," he muttered, **"maybe we make them come to us."**

He dialed **former President Layton Thomas**:

"Sir, I have an idea. Could your foundation *become* a customer?"

Thomas paused, then agreed. **"Yes. We'll post an R.F.Q. for risk-modeling software on our website. Whoever this competitor is, they'll likely respond."**

The Thomas Foundation Bait

Within a week, the **Thomas Foundation**—a massive philanthropic entity known for global projects—announced it wanted scenario-modeling tools for donation fluctuations. Sure enough, a wave of quotes poured in. Among them was an offer from a Californian reseller calling itself **AMTFB—Advanced Mathematical Tools for Business**.

Working alongside the Foundation's tech team, Tomassi recognized the hallmark secrecy: the reseller demanded a rigid **NDA** before revealing its actual supplier. After a cursory check by in-house counsel showed no severe financial risk, the Foundation signed. Soon, the official documents arrived—but the vendor's name was only **"Tillman, Ltd."** in the **Cook Islands**, a shell corporation with zero traceable ownership.

Thomas vented his frustration:

"We tried. That's all we got—*Tillman, Ltd.* Where do we go from here?"

Parallel Pursuits & Dead Ends

Meanwhile, Thomas tapped another operative—**CIA officer Leonard Toms**—to probe overseas. Yet Toms soon encountered a "national security" shutdown within his own agency. Attempts to follow the money trail hit offshore shells and banks refusing to divulge client data. Even the CIA's own records on these software providers were sealed tight.

"It's a unique group," Toms later reported to Thomas in a Boston café. **"They embed confidentiality in every contract. They're rumored to have a proprietary *neural network* for communications. And they pay taxes diligently, so no legal leverage. According to our profilers, they're older mathematicians funneling profits into philanthropic causes, likely non-American nationals. Very hush-hush."**

Tomassi, for his part, ran into the same stone wall. He and Toms regrouped, but then Toms dropped a bombshell:

"I'm ordered to stand down. 'National security.' Sorry."

Thomas, seething, relayed the news to **Jonathan Stanza**, his go-to lobbyist:

"We can't touch this—it's 'national security.' It's over."

A Quiet Stand-Down

When **Tomassi** landed back in Miami, a final call from Thomas echoed the same message: *Walk away.* A "wild-goose chase," Tomassi thought in relief. He assumed he'd never hear from the former president again.

He couldn't have been more wrong.

Chapter 37

Washington, D.C. – The White House (2016, Day 2, 10:00 P.M. ET)

Former President Layton Thomas gave a resigned shrug as he finished describing the dead end he and his operatives hit in their quest to identify the elusive **Walkyria** software group.

"We got nowhere," Thomas admitted. **"I never realized I was up against *Nicolás Tosh*—until tonight."**

President **O'Sullivan** sat behind the Resolute Desk, arms folded, gaze steely.

"Layton," he said, **"this isn't the time for excuses. You orchestrated a hunt that nearly destroyed Tosh, and you knew it was all to protect a political donor. Now he's sitting right here in the White House."**

Thomas suppressed a grimace. He'd once felt the moral high ground, justifying his actions to rescue a major campaign backer. But the revelation that Tosh himself commanded **Walkyria**—and, worse, was a classified G-7 strategic asset—left Thomas cornered.

"I truly had no idea, Mr. President," Thomas murmured. **"If I had—"**

O'Sullivan cut him off with a curt wave.

"It's too late for that. We'll see how you handle the truth under oath."

Silence enveloped the Oval Office, weighted by the knowledge that the next steps would decide more than just **Thomas's** fate—they'd test the core of American political and legal institutions. And Nicolás Tosh, the man whose identity Thomas had tried so hard to uncover, held more power now than ever.

Chapter 38

Miami, Florida – FBI North Miami Station (2015, Twelve Months Before Day 1)

Former President Layton Thomas's first marriage had ended in bitter scandal—years of affairs, including one with a White House aide, publicly humiliating the late First Lady. Even after **Nancy Thomas** earned her own political victories (eventually becoming Secretary of Labor under President O'Sullivan), he'd left her for a much younger Argentine cabaret dancer named **Emanuella**. Polls showed **85%** of Americans disliked the new Mrs. Thomas. His personal ratings plunged by double digits.

Tomassi's New Briefing

Back in **Miami, FBI Agent Louis Tomassi** had just returned from the airport when he was diverted to a surveillance op—tied to an ongoing investigation into Professor **Nicolás Tosh**. Tomassi doubted Layton Thomas would continue any "big donor" software scheme, so he focused on his fresh assignment.

"We've got a live feed," a colleague told Tomassi, handing him a tablet. **"We were tailing Tosh for possible money-laundering leads, and we caught…this."**

On-screen, a hidden camera panned across a hotel bedroom. A man and woman were engaged in a passionate encounter. Tomassi froze when he recognized the woman's face:

"That's…Emanuella Thomas?" "Yes, live. President Thomas's new wife." "And the guy?" "A well-regarded economics professor at UM's Business School. *Nicolás Tosh,* married, and father of two."

Tomassi frowned. "His wife is well-known. A real pillar of society. Why would he be hooking up with a onetime cabaret dancer? Something doesn't add up."

The colleague shrugged. "We didn't expect this. Our official angle is that Tosh might be laundering money or evading taxes—he travels constantly, funded by unknown overseas sources. But tonight, we stumbled on this affair."

A Furious Call to Thomas

Tomassi stepped aside and rang **Layton Thomas**:

"Sir, there's a situation regarding your wife. She's in Miami at this very moment with…Nicolás Tosh." "That's impossible. She told me she's in Manhattan with friends," Thomas retorted, checking a 'Find My Phone' app. "Her phone's in Manhattan, all right. Must be a glitch on your end."

"We have live surveillance, sir," Tomassi insisted. "There's no doubt."

A long silence followed before Thomas quietly seethed:

"Get me the hotel's number, Tomassi." "We're in the middle of an operation—can't release details. We're here all night."

Finally, Thomas spat a command:

"I want Tosh ruined—locked up for life if possible."

The line went dead.

The Wheels in Motion

Moments later, **Thomas** dialed his longtime fixer, lobbyist **Jonathan Stanza**:

"Stanza, you're from Miami, right? I need a local taken down. He's sleeping with my wife." "Who?" "Nicolás Tosh."

Stanza hesitated. **"Sir, the Tosh family has been generous donors. They support the party. His wife is on my team."**

Thomas snorted. **"I don't care. Tomassi says they're together now, so forget party loyalty. I want Tosh wrecked—on a silver platter."**

Stanza drew a breath. He owed Thomas favors, and the ex-President had always come through for him. **"Understood, sir."**

"Focus on him alone. Leave his family out of it," Thomas snapped. **"Collaborate with Tomassi. Tosh is already under FBI scrutiny. Build your case from that."**

He hung up. Within the hour, **Stanza** met with a corrupt associate to coordinate the takedown. They agreed: if Tosh had dared cross a former President, he'd either end up dead or in prison for a long time. Stanza knew exactly which strings to pull—and he started pulling them right away.

Chapter 39

Miami, Florida – Livingstone, White & Stawskoski Law Office (2015, Twelve Months Before Day 1)

Mark Bain, CEO of the private security outfit **Bain & Co.**, entered the polished lobby of **Livingstone, White & Stawskoski**. He spotted **Kenneth Livingstone**—pale-faced, with a mortician's aura. The man's firm was famous for crushing adversaries through threats of criminal prosecution. Clients hired them not merely to win cases but to **ruin** foes.

"Mark, thanks for coming," Livingstone said, leading him down a corridor to a large conference room.

Inside, **Jonathan Stanza** stood up—short, bald, and famously volatile. Bain loathed him but forced a polite nod. He knew Stanza wielded enormous political clout through his role as a top **Liberal Democratic Party** lobbyist. After a call from **former President Layton Thomas**, Stanza had convened this meeting to plot a takedown.

Setting the Plan

"We need you," Livingstone began, **"to deliver disposable cell phones weekly to a list of individuals in Miami and D.C. They'll discard the old phones when they get the new ones. Each drop happens in public, part of their daily routine."**

Bain did the mental math. **"That's twenty people total—eight in D.C., twelve here."** He broke down costs. **"Expect twenty to twenty-five grand a week for man-hours and equipment."**

"Money's no issue," Livingstone assured him. **"We'll wire you ninety days in advance."**

They added a second request: discreetly delivering documents to targeted media outlets to smear **Nicolás Tosh**. Bain shook his head. He despised **Livingstone** and **Stanza**, but they were his biggest clients. The job promised up to a million dollars in revenue over the next year.

Once Bain left, **Stanza** and **Livingstone** huddled over the next phase.

"We'll bury Tosh in negative press," Stanza said, eyes gleaming. **"Start small—local papers, radio, then escalate to major TV stations. We have party members who spend big on ads; they'll ensure coverage."**

Livingstone nodded. **"Then I'll unleash *civil litigation*, enlisting twenty 'cooperating' plaintiffs to feed the Justice Department whatever we want. My friends at the Federal District Attorney's office and on the bench will guarantee not just an indictment, but the harshest sentence."**

They exchanged a grim smile. The decision was made: They would destroy **Nicolás Tosh**, an enemy who had dared cross the ex-President. And with Stanza's cunning, Livingstone's legal aggression, and Bain's covert ops, their target would soon face a storm of ruin he might not survive.

Chapter 40

Washington, D.C. – The White House (2016, Day 2, 10:30 P.M. ET)

Former President Layton Thomas spoke with resignation:

"Mr. President, it all started with a front-page headline—*UM Professor Involved in Terrorism Plot*—scandalizing the public. Media outlets painted him guilty from day one. Livingstone's firm launched bogus accusations, buttressed by 'informers' no one could verify. Civil lawsuits piled on; Tosh was deposed a dozen times, forced to produce thousands of pages of documents. In under a year, he lost multiple cases and faced federal charges for terrorism, money laundering, and tax evasion."

He exhaled, eyes downcast. **"Twenty people—judges, prosecutors, business leaders—colluded to bring him down. He never had a chance."**

President **O'Sullivan** turned to **Nicolás Tosh**:

"You could have stopped this early, invoking *clear and present danger* to reveal your true identity. Why wait?"

Tosh's gaze hardened. **"I underestimated them. I wanted to keep my philanthropic and business work separate from my university life—and spare my family the truth. By the time I realized how far it would go, it was too late. As for the alleged 'affair,' I have a video to show you."**

He hooked a small connector to a **TV monitor** emerging from beneath a panel in the Oval Office. A brief recording played: *Emanuella*

Thomas—whom Tosh only knew as "Natalia Barrios"—bumping into him at an airport café, both acting surprised.

"I didn't know who she'd become," Tosh said quietly. **"It was a single encounter—no idea she was married to a former President. I never heard from her again, never suspected the legal onslaught tied back to that."**

Thomas made a face. **"Regardless, you *did* cheat on your wife."**

Tosh bristled. **"That's not your business. Nothing excuses the corrupt warp of our legal system to ruin me. The saddest part is you never realized *she* manipulated both of us."**

Thomas opened his mouth to respond, but President **O'Sullivan** cut in:

"Enough. Everyone out but President Thomas. I need a private word."

A Private Ultimatum

Once the room cleared, **O'Sullivan** glared at Thomas:

"Layton, you put me in a nightmare. I endorsed your push to indict Tosh, believing he was a genuine threat. I had no clue you influenced judges, prosecutors, the FBI, even the media. Worse, he's a G-7 *strategic asset*—and probably our country's greatest benefactor."

Thomas's tone turned defiant. **"You want a deal, Kevin?"**

Anger flared in O'Sullivan's eyes. **"Spare me. I need to bring all these conspirators—including you—to justice with minimal damage to the presidency. Our institutions can't take another blow."**

Thomas smirked. **"You can't do it discreetly. It's all or nothing."**

O'Sullivan let out a slow breath. **"For once, you're correct. Let me finalize the plan. Meanwhile, stay in the building, or I'll have Secret Service confine you."**

The Midnight Crackdown

Once alone, O'Sullivan made a series of rapid calls. First to **General Collins** at the Pentagon:

"General, convene an emergency federal court hearing overnight—so it ends before sunrise. In half an hour, be ready to feed the entire body of evidence to the Attorney General."

Then to the **Secret Service** chief on duty:

"Transfer all detainees—Secretary Gilbert, his nephew, and others—to Federal Court by 4:00 A.M. We'll arrest the remaining sixteen suspects immediately. Get them on a plane to D.C. We start no later than 4:30 A.M."

Finally, he dialed **Attorney General Gene Cartwright** and **Judge Advocate General Colonel James Williams**:

"Colonel, I suspect *high treason*. Gene and I spent hours examining the data. He suggests a standard criminal process, but I note Tosh is a *military* asset for the G-7. I want your take."

Cartwright reeled at how many party insiders would face ruin, but O'Sullivan was adamant.

"I'm taking a brief rest—back by 2:00 A.M. for a second all-nighter. Gentlemen, go over the final proof with Collins. We'll reconvene in four hours."

Rounded Up

In the next ninety minutes, **U.S. Marshals** fanned out. They took each conspirator by surprise—**Judge Amanda Beltran** at home, **Mark Bain** and his lieutenant asleep, **Jonathan Stanza** leaving a late-night meeting, **Kenneth Livingstone** dragged from a fundraiser. **FBI Agent Louis Tomassi** realized the game was over when agents cuffed him. **Secretary of Defense Gilbert** was similarly taken into custody.

By **12:30 A.M.**, they were all in transport—some to a waiting FBI **MD-80** at **Opa-locka Airport** in Miami, others from various D.C. addresses. Estimated arrival: **3:15 A.M.** Then, as President O'Sullivan had ordered, they'd be ushered into a secret **federal court** session at dawn to face the avalanche of evidence that might change the course of American politics forever.

Chapter 41

Washington, D.C. – The White House (2016, Day 3, 2:00 A.M. ET)

President **Kelly O'Sullivan** emerged from a brief nap, resolved about how to handle **former President Layton Thomas**. After a quick shave and a quiet hour with his wife, he hurried back to the **Oval Office** and got **Attorney General Gene Cartwright** and **Judge Advocate General Colonel James Williams** on the phone.

"**Colonel,**" O'Sullivan said, "**do these charges qualify for military jurisdiction?**"

Williams answered promptly. "**No, sir. It falls under civilian courts. This is the Attorney General's domain.**"

Cartwright chimed in next:

"**I'm ready to indict all twenty conspirators on high treason. I've also prepared separate charges for the Secretary of Defense and his nephew. As for Senator Molina, there's no evidence linking him.**"

O'Sullivan nodded. "**Good. We'll convene an emergency federal court at four. A judge is on standby. How long to finalize the indictment brief?**"

"**Ninety minutes for a bare-bones version,**" Cartwright replied. "**Then I'll file the motion for a hearing.**"

"**All detainees** are already in custody," O'Sullivan assured. "**We'll have them at the designated court by four.**"

Explaining the Plan

O'Sullivan summoned **Nicolás Tosh**, his Chief of Staff, and Secretary of State into the Oval Office. They'd showered, rested, and were bracing for the intense night ahead.

"Only you three, plus the conspirators and Layton Thomas, will attend the hearing," he informed them.

Suddenly, a soft *buzz* from the President's "identifier" signaled Tosh was speaking to his mind:

'Mr. President, under the G-7 resolution, we should run CDAs 322, 323, and 324 on the Attorney General, the on-call judge, and any cabinet members involved tonight. If you agree, please nod.'

O'Sullivan gave a subtle nod. Quickly, he phoned **General Collins** at the Pentagon:

"Execute the instructions I'm texting now. I need to ensure no infiltration."

"Understood, sir," Collins responded. **"We'll check if anyone's compromised. We'll also get a court reporter lined up. And a backup judge, as requested."**

The Conversation with Thomas

Leaving the others, O'Sullivan headed down the hall to a small guest room where **Layton Thomas** was waiting. He found the former President half-dozing in the dark.

"Layton, get ready," he said quietly. **"We leave in fifteen minutes."**

Thomas stirred, blinking. **"It's three A.M. Where are we going?"**

"An emergency federal court hearing," O'Sullivan replied. **"We'll charge your co-conspirators—Secretary Gilbert, his nephew, and**

the others—with high treason. You won't be indicted, but there *will* be consequences. We'll discuss that once this is done."

Thomas sat up, realizing the gravity of what was about to unfold.

Chapter 42

Washington, D.C. – Emergency Federal Court Hearing (2016, Day 3, 8:52 A.M. ET)

By **3:30 A.M.**, all twenty-two indicted conspirators—**including** the Secretary of Defense, his nephew, and various judges, lawyers, and businessmen—were seated in the courtroom, hands cuffed and ankles shackled. Fear, anger, and disbelief etched their faces. President **Kelly O'Sullivan** arrived at **3:45**, accompanied by **Nicolás Tosh**, the Secretary of State, the Chief of Staff, and **former President Layton Thomas**. The Attorney General, **Gene Cartwright**, and a cadre of defense lawyers followed.

At **4:00 A.M.**, **Judge Ryan Stevenson** took the bench:

"I've read the information brief. Mr. Attorney General, are you ready to proceed?"

The Bombshell Indictment

Cartwright rose and named each conspirator. Then he dropped a shock:

"We have conclusive evidence to charge you with high treason: you targeted a *strategic military asset* of the U.S. and the G-7— causing great harm and nearly securing his wrongful imprisonment. Penalties for high treason can include life in a maximum-security facility. If you plead guilty, we'll allow parole eligibility after *twenty-five years*."

Outrage rippled through the defendants, forcing Marshals and Secret Service agents to restrain them. Gasps, cursing, and near hysteria erupted.

Over the next two hours, prosecutors presented painstaking video proof—clips of bribes, undue influence, phone deliveries, and doctored lawsuits. Scenes flashed on-screen, **CDAs 323/324** capturing every conspirator from *their own viewpoint* as they plotted against Tosh. Most stared at their live footage, uncomprehending how every incriminating moment had been recorded. **Kenneth Livingstone** and **Jonathan Stanza** glared at Thomas, silently furious that **he** wasn't on their side of the aisle.

A Recess & A Revelation

Mid-trial, President O'Sullivan received a private mental nudge from **Tosh**:

'Mr. President, General Collins says Livingstone and Stanza plan to denounce Thomas as the mastermind. Should we halt the proceedings for a recess?'

O'Sullivan nodded discreetly. Moments later, a Secret Service note reached Cartwright. He asked the judge for a fifteen-minute pause. The judge agreed to thirty minutes. O'Sullivan stepped into the hallway, enabling direct "identifier" communication with Livingstone and Stanza:

"Gentlemen, this is the President. We're hearing your every thought. You meddled with the man who built one of our most powerful weapons. Now, ironically, *that same weapon* monitors you. If you dare stand and accuse Thomas, we will pursue maximum sentences. Your choice."

Stanza and Livingstone exchanged stunned looks, realizing there was no escape.

Guilty Pleas & Sentencing

By **7:00 A.M.**, evidence resumed for fifteen more minutes. Judge Stevenson demanded to know the legal basis for the recordings:

"Under a G-7 resolution, Your Honor," Cartwright explained, handing over documents.

The judge, reassured by the G-7 stamp, asked for extended clips. At one point, a beep masked a certain name:

"Who's missing?" the judge asked. **"Classified. National security,"** Cartwright replied.

Thomas felt every eye on him. Finally, the judge invited the defense attorneys to consult with the accused. Cartwright quietly offered a stark deal: **plead guilty**—life in prison, chance of parole after twenty-five years—or fight and face guaranteed no parole. Unable to contest the ironclad evidence, all conspirators pled guilty.

The judge pronounced their fate: **life imprisonment** at Englewood, a maximum-security facility—**twenty-five years** minimum before any parole hearing. The stunned conspirators were led out under heavy guard.

A Private Ultimatum for Thomas

As O'Sullivan left, he pulled **Layton Thomas** aside:

"Here's how you avoid prison: you'll withdraw from public life, close your foundation, and relocate abroad—*Argentina*, for now. Most important, you must consent to perpetual deployment of CDAs

322, 323, and 324 on yourself. Otherwise, I'll push a G-7 motion to scan your entire life, and we'll charge you for every crime you've ever committed. Understood?"

Thomas swallowed hard. **"I have no choice, do I?"** "None," the President confirmed. **"Sign the papers at the White House. Now, let's go."**

Tosh's Next Steps

Soon after, O'Sullivan summoned **Tosh**:

"Your identity remains secret, your *public persona* intact. What's next?"

Tosh shrugged. **"Back to teaching at UM Business School. I'll keep my philanthropic and business roles private, though I'll add a family security detail."**

"So, you'll stay the same?" the President asked with a wry smile. **"Yes, sir—though I'll watch more carefully. And I'll keep buying T-Bills whenever you ask,"** Tosh teased gently.

O'Sullivan nodded, then murmured:

"Any new algorithms coming?" **"Yes—CDA-325—but I'll explain at our next meeting."**

The President stood, offering a rare smile and an outstretched hand:

"Go home, Tosh. Your family's waiting."

And with that, **Nicolás Tosh** departed, returning to a life that looked unchanged—but was forever colored by the night's revelations in a secret federal courtroom.

Chapter 43

Washington, D.C. – The White House (2016, Day 3, 8:25 A.M. ET)

By **9:00 A.M.**, **Layton Thomas** had signed his final agreement with President **Kelly O'Sullivan**: relinquishing public life, closing his foundation, and consenting to permanent **CDA** monitoring. By **11:00 A.M.**, Thomas and his wife were bound for Argentina aboard a government plane. President O'Sullivan took a short break, then returned to his regular Oval Office duties around noon—an astonishing sense of normalcy after the frantic overnight proceedings.

Headline Aftermath

That same day, **Miami** headlines exploded with news of an "emergency federal court hearing." The public learned that a top circle of **twenty high-profile figures**—judges, lawyers, business moguls, FBI agents, even the Secretary of Defense—had been convicted of **high treason** for conspiring to destroy a "strategic U.S. military asset." No mention was made of **former President Thomas** or **Nicolás Tosh**.

Officially, **Tosh's** conviction was reversed by **Judge Beltran** right before her own arrest. Several prominent Miami entities were implicated—**City Business Daily**'s editor-in-chief, two of its journalists, plus the entire lead team of **Livingstone, White & Stawskoski** (notably Kenneth Livingstone). In D.C., the big splash was the **Secretary of Defense** and his nephew going down for treason, unlinked by the media to the Miami fiasco.

Ocando in the Clear

One person who dodged the net was **Jimmy "The Handler" Ocando**. Under **CDA-323** scrutiny, it became clear he was clueless about the plot's real target; he'd just delivered phones, unaware of their true purpose. Freed of suspicion, he dropped out of sight.

Tosh's Lingering Silence

For **Nicolás Tosh**, the final revelations felt surreal. The arrests proved his innocence, but he hadn't spoken to his family in months. His terrifying conviction had shattered them, and since his sentencing was cloaked in secrecy, even his defense attorneys were kept in the dark about his whereabouts and eventual exoneration.

Now, having finished last-minute briefings in Washington, Tosh boarded the same **Falcon jet** that had brought him here. At **9:30 A.M.**, he flew out of **Andrews Air Force Base**, bound for Miami—but in practical terms, he was *off the grid*. Officially, his travel never happened, leaving his wife **Alejandra** and their two children, Emilia and Sebastián, unaware he was safe. They only knew the rumored "terrorism" charges had been dismissed and that he might return home soon.

Tosh gazed out the window, unable to dial his family just yet. He wanted to wait until he landed, to avoid explaining his presence in D.C. or how he'd sat in a top-secret court hearing with the President. He closed his eyes, remembering Alejandra's steadfast support during those harrowing months, and picturing his children's faces. A weary smile tugged at his lips.

Despite all that had happened—the humiliating arrest, the venomous media campaign, and the clandestine legal meltdown—Tosh felt a surge of relief. *He was going home.* And for now, that was all that mattered.

Chapter 44

San Carlos de Bariloche, Argentina – Cerro Catedral (1983)

While **Rainer** stayed behind to finalize the new joint research contracts with **Professors Borjes** and **Schneiderman**, **Nicolás Tosh** drove out of the university campus, following **Lago Nahuel Huapi**'s winding shore. He eventually turned up the steep route toward the base of **Cerro Catedral**'s ski resort. Despite the heavy snow, he parked near the pine trees.

A few minutes' walk brought him to a tiny **wooden cabin**—his mother **Isabela Tosh**'s old ski-instructor hideaway—where he'd spent countless childhood hours. Tucked behind tall pines, the place always soothed him, though he hadn't visited in years.

At the door, he found it locked and no spare key under the mat. Circling back, he forced open a stubborn rear window and climbed inside.

A Mother's Sanctuary

Dust motes swirled as he stepped in, noticing the familiar blend of old wood and a faint trace of his mother's perfume. Isabela's belongings remained as though she'd only been gone a day—ski gear, photo albums, and clothes neatly stacked. **Camila**, his aunt, must still be maintaining it. He felt a surge of gratitude, scanning the living room until curiosity drew him to a **closet** door left ajar in the bedroom. Two unfamiliar **duffel bags** lay inside.

"We've never stored anything like that here…" Nicolás murmured.

He knelt to unzip one, but a gruff voice startled him from behind:

"Who are you?"

He spun around to face a **shotgun barrel** pressed against his chest—and immediately recognized the man holding it.

"Bruno?" Tosh gasped. **"Yes. Who—"** The stranger paused, searching his face. **"I'm Nicolás Tosh."**

Bruno's eyes went wide, the gun slipping from his grip. A stunned moment later, he embraced Nicolás.

"Son…my son! I've looked for you everywhere these last six years."

Father & Son

Nicolás let himself be pulled in, then gently separated. He stared at his father: **Bruno Buonarroti**, tall and solid, white-haired yet strikingly fit for his fifty-some years. They moved to the **living room**—Bruno sank onto the sofa, Tosh settled into his mother's old rocking chair. The memory of her nightly lullabies washed over him.

"What are you doing here?" Tosh asked, voice subdued. **"You vanished. Your friends are worried. But more important—why did you only start searching for me six years ago? What about my first twenty years?"**

Bruno looked stricken. **"You never heard? Your aunt and mother kept it from me. I didn't even know you existed until you were twenty."**

"Why?"

"It's a long story. You want the truth?" Bruno exhaled. "Also, I guess you heard I stirred up trouble in Buenos Aires. A bunch of furious people want my head."

Nicolás nodded, shoulders taut. "We have time. Start at the beginning. I've waited my whole life for this conversation."

A sad smile ghosted across Bruno's face. "Alright. It all began thirty years ago, on a sun-drenched Italian island…"

Chapter 45

Emerald Coast, Sardinia, Italy (1954)

Bruno had been chasing the grouper for nearly half an hour, spear gun in one hand, fishing knife in the other. He dove repeatedly to **thirty-five feet**, carefully weaving through rows of coral, checking each nook for that massive tail he'd glimpsed. He could stay down about *three minutes* at a time—an impressive feat, even for a recent spear-gun world champion like him.

At last, he spotted the telltale flick of the grouper's tail. Bruno circled around the coral reef, slid in behind it, and fired. The **spear** punched clean through the fish's head. Trapped between coral walls, the mortally wounded grouper thrashed, tail snapping violently. Bruno yanked on the rope, but the huge fish—*easily five feet, over 150 pounds*—wedged deeper. He had to surface for air again.

An Enthralled Audience

Nearby, **Isabela and Camila Tosh**—two Swiss sisters on vacation—were snorkeling. They'd been quietly watching Bruno's repeated dives. Intrigued by how long he could hold his breath, they moved closer to see him make the kill. Now, from the water's surface, they watched him wrestle the wounded grouper free with a final thrust of his knife, then haul it upward.

Dripping and triumphant, Bruno hoisted the giant fish onto the sandy shore to clean it. Only then did he notice the two onlookers—fair-haired, wide-eyed with admiration.

"Looks like you'll be dining well tonight," said one sister, introducing herself as **Isabela**. Her pale blond curls framed bright blue eyes that caught Bruno's attention.

"Several dinners," he quipped, flashing a grin. **"I'm Bruno Buonarroti, from Lignano on Italy's northeastern coast."**

Isabela explained that she and her sister **Camila** hailed from **Zermatt**, Switzerland. Bruno's ears perked up:

"Zermatt? I climbed the Matterhorn twice last summer. Tough going—*and* you need a proper guide."

They all laughed, warmed by the Mediterranean sun and the shared excitement of the moment. Eventually, Isabela glanced at the time.

"We should go—need a shower and a change. But maybe we can meet up later?"

Bruno's smile widened. **"Absolutely. How about that Irish pub in town around seven?"**

The sisters giggled and agreed, promising to see him that evening. As they strolled away, Bruno admired their cheerful camaraderie, heart still pounding from the dive—and from the chance encounter that felt like more than just a coincidence.

Chapter 46

San Carlos de Bariloche, Argentina – Cerro Catedral (1983)

Rainer stayed behind, finalizing the data-center arrangements with Professors **Borjes** and **Schneiderman**, while **Nicolás Tosh** left the university brimming with excitement. He drove along the **Lago Nahuel Huapi** shore, then turned up the slope toward **Cerro Catedral**. Near the ski resort's base, he parked and trudged through pine-shaded snow until he reached a small **wooden cabin**—his late mother **Isabela**'s old hideaway.

He entered by forcing a stuck rear window (the usual spare key was missing). Inside, time seemed frozen: her books, ski gear, even a faint whiff of perfume. **Camila**, his aunt, clearly still maintained it monthly. Moving through the modest living room, he noticed something off in the master bedroom: two duffel bags that didn't belong.

Crouching to unzip one, he heard a voice behind him, rough and alarmed.

"Who are you?"

Nicolás spun, meeting the muzzle of a **shotgun** pressed to his chest. Then he recognized the man holding it.

"Bruno?" **"Yes. Who—"** The man's eyes narrowed—until shock registered. **"Nicolás Tosh?"**

He dropped the gun and gasped, pulling Nicolás into a trembling hug.

"Son...my son! I've been searching everywhere these past six years."

Breaking Decades of Silence

They drew apart. Bruno Buonarroti, tall and powerfully built with white hair, looked younger than his mid-fifties. Nicolás sank into a small rocking chair—where his mother once sang him lullabies—while Bruno sat on the worn sofa facing him.

"We all feared you vanished," Nicolás said quietly. **"People in town are worried. But more pressing—why only search for me six years ago? Why not from my birth?"**

Bruno sighed. **"Your aunt and mother never told me you existed. I learned after your mother had already died—when you were twenty, gone from Bariloche."**

Nicolás's brow furrowed. **"I was told you left because you had an affair with Aunt Camila."**

"That was a lie," Bruno said bitterly. **"Your mother and I never even argued—she left me days before our wedding, leaving a note: 'Bruno, I'm sorry. I can't burden you. Forgive me.'"**

Nicolás's anger softened into confusion. **"She was pregnant then."**

"Yes. She'd discovered she had ALS. She chose to raise you alone, convinced her illness would kill her soon. She died when you were six. I learned the truth much later and tried to find you, but you'd already left."

Mother's Memory

A hush settled. They recounted the past, clarifying lies. Bruno described Isabela as an *angelic athlete* who loved the outdoors and had a gentle heart. She decided not to chain Bruno with her terminal diagnosis.

Emotions overwhelmed Nicolás. **"All this time, I believed you abandoned us."**

"Son, I never stopped loving your mother—or you."

They embraced, tears releasing the hurt and confusion of decades. For hours, father and son traded life stories in breathless wonder: Bruno's global pursuits—*climbing, diving, surfing*—and Nicolás's hidden career forging **mathematical marvels** that reshaped the world. The distance between them dissolved with each new anecdote.

A New Mystery

Eventually, Nicolás recalled the trouble in Buenos Aires:

"Bruno, you said you're lying low—some group in the capital wants your head. What happened?"

Bruno's jaw tightened. **"It all started at the end of the Falklands War..."**

Chapter 47

Buenos Aires, Argentina (1983 – Two Months Earlier)

Bruno Buonarroti unlocked the door to his fifth-floor office on **Avenida 9 de Julio**—one of the world's widest avenues—lugging a pilot's briefcase packed with pesos. Inside, every drawer, closet, and file cabinet overflowed with the highest-denomination Argentine bills. *His currency jackpot* was now virtually worthless.

When the **Falklands War** began, Argentineans stopped trusting banks. Businesses hoarded money in back rooms and closets. For Bruno, a world-class diver from Italy who'd emigrated here years ago, the war initially seemed a godsend: his **neoprene wetsuit factory** scored a colossal order from the Argentine Air Force, delivering months' worth of products in just weeks. He was paid in full—vast piles of pesos.

Then disaster struck: Argentina lost the war, toppled into bankruptcy, and the currency **nosedived** in value. Bruno had no place to spend the pesos profitably because raw material costs shot up over 500%. His windfall was turning to dust.

The "Three Magnificent Italians"

Bruno was one of three childhood buddies from **Lignano** on Italy's northeastern coast—**Américo** in Brazil, **Claudio** in Venezuela, and him in Argentina. All had become champion spear-fishermen and built **marine-related businesses** in South America. Desperate for advice, Bruno phoned **Américo Ceccoto**—no help—and then **Claudio Di Buccio**, who proposed a bold idea:

"Use those pesos fast—buy any finished goods you can. Then ship them here to Venezuela. We'll sell them and convert to stable currency."

Bruno discovered Argentine shops brimming with unsold inventory—**anything but** food or medicines, which flew off shelves. Those businesses hadn't sold to the government (like Bruno had), so their merchandise lay idle.

Armed with his **pilot's briefcase** full of pesos—returning to his office for refills each time—Bruno scoured the city, purchasing every leftover product: clothing, tools, furniture, electronics. Within days, he amassed enough to fill *eighty shipping containers*, dispatched postwar on the first cargo vessel out of Argentina.

Turmoil & Hideout

The plan worked—until local demand **skyrocketed** right after the war ended. Inflation soared, and suddenly, manufacturers who'd sold everything to Bruno had nothing left to meet frantic consumer orders. Furious, they blamed him for taking their stock at "fire-sale" prices and shipping it abroad. Threats poured in, culminating in a break-in that trashed his office. *Now* Bruno was on the run.

"I figured I'd lay low in your mother's cabin," he explained to **Nicolás Tosh**, seated in the cozy living area. **"I never expected *you* to find me."**

Nicolás observed his father's anxious gaze.

"Any luck so far, dealing with these angry suppliers?" he asked wryly.

Bruno sighed. **"I've always relied on good fortune."**

Nicolás's eyes crinkled with a half-smile.

"Luck's a fickle friend. Yours held a long time, Bruno."

He paused, meeting his father's eyes with calm assurance. *If Bruno needed a rescue plan, perhaps Nicolás could help—and after decades apart, the idea of helping his father felt strangely right.*

Chapter 48

San Carlos de Bariloche, Argentina – Cerro Catedral (1983)

"All right, Bruno—let's fix your Buenos Aires problem," said **Nicolás Tosh** calmly. He pulled out his *beeper-like* device and registered Bruno on his **neural network**, then explained the "CDA" algorithms.

"Some of these math tools I've created are dangerous. We're pushing for them to be designated as WMDs by the major world powers," Nicolás said. Bruno, a life-long sportsman, listened in awe as his son described how the data center worked, how they could **download** someone's memories and communicate mind-to-mind.

Enlisting "Black Leather Jackets" Help

They tested it immediately. Tosh used **CDA-319** to send his thoughts directly into Bruno's mind. Shocked but fascinated, Bruno responded out loud. Soon, Nicolás let him know they'd "loaded" **CDA-323** on him, enabling silent thought-exchange like seasoned "carriers" in the system.

"Now, let's call a policeman in Buenos Aires—Ruben Borjes," Nicolás said, handing Bruno a spare "identifier." Within seconds, they reached Ruben telepathically.

Borjes, a recent recruit to Tosh's organization, recognized Bruno's name:

"We've received about twenty complaints against you, Mr. Buonarroti," he admitted. **"Nothing illegal in your mass buying and exporting, but you made powerful enemies."**

Bruno explained every detail. Borjes paused, then offered a solution:

"Many of those angry businessmen have ties to our Walkyria business or the Experta Foundation. We'll smooth things over— small contract discounts, additional pledges. That should keep them off your back."

Nicolás ended the call before Bruno could thank Borjes, explaining:

"He's helping me, not you," he said gently. **"He doesn't condone your hustle, but he's doing this for our organization."**

Healing Old Wounds

Afterward, Bruno suggested they **visit Camila**. Nicolás recalled his aunt's guilt and how he'd cut contact. But first, Nicolás connected telepathically with **Rainer**, his friend and collaborator, waiting at the mountain base with rented skis.

"Bruno, let's get our gear and join Rainer," Nicolás said. They locked the cabin and trekked to Cerro Catedral's lifts.

In the fading daylight, the three men rode up three chairlifts, then squeezed in one last ski run across a frozen lake. Bruno beamed—*this* was his natural element. At the far summit, Nicolás told him:

"I met Rainer up here, with a 360-degree view of the Andes. That's where the idea for my CDA algorithms took root."

"Truly magnificent," Bruno murmured, breath pluming in the cold. The trio skied back in near-dusk, weaving through pine shadows and finishing just as darkness fell.

That evening, **father and son** paid a visit to **Aunt Camila** and cleared up the final deceptions lingering since Isabela's death. She apologized for her role in perpetuating the fiction of Bruno's "affair," and they forgave each other.

A New Path

Over the next **twenty-five years**, Bruno Buonarroti worked in Tosh's **new security division**, bolstering its protection protocols. He eventually sold his dive-equipment business and built a small computer reseller firm. Though maintaining a level of independence, he stayed close to Nicolás—regularly meeting in **Bariloche** each year to ski, spend time at Isabela's cabin, and visit Camila.

Bruno retired a few years ago, moving to Miami to be near **Nicolás's wife, Alejandra**, and the grandchildren. Truthfully, he also craved the sea again—a chance to fish and dive under a warm sun. For Bruno, it was a richly **deserved peace** after decades of wandering, trouble—and a final reunion with the son he never truly lost.

Chapter 49

Buenos Aires, Argentina – Bruno Buonarroti's Computer Store (Spring 1989)

Alejandra Martínez-López, at twenty-three, seemed to do it all: she owned a small software company, taught AI at the city's top university, danced flamenco, cooked gourmet meals, rode horses, played piano, and even led aerobics classes. Raised in a tight-knit Catholic family, she radiated warmth and success. Countless "wannabe" suitors lined up, but none ever measured up to her standards. She'd even been accepted to **MIT** and **Stanford**—though she couldn't decide about leaving Buenos Aires, a place she adored.

Today, *running late* as usual, Alejandra was racing to her first appointment: a potential **sublet** in a new black-glass shopping center. Having just secured fresh contracts with the Argentine Army and a major brewery, she planned to double her development team from twenty-eight to nearly sixty and needed more office space fast.

Her parking job nearly ended in disaster, but she shrugged off her shaky nerves, sprinting inside, already fifteen minutes behind schedule. There, a tall, distinguished man with white hair greeted her:

"Good morning—Miss Martínez-López?" "Yes. I'm so sorry I'm late—traffic," she explained breathlessly.

The owner, **Bruno Buonarroti**, guided her through the sleek storefront and into a partitioned office area. Alejandra's eyes lit up at the open layout—perfect for her team's future growth. A quick call to her business partner confirmed they both loved it.

They sat in a small conference room, hashing out rental terms with surprising ease. Finally, Bruno hesitated before speaking:

"I hope you won't take this wrong, but... you're quite young to be handling all this."

Alejandra smiled, unoffended.

"I get that a lot. My father's backing me—he's a prominent attorney—and he'll come by tomorrow. If necessary, he'll co-sign."

Bruno nodded, impressed by her self-assurance. They shook hands, sealing an informal agreement. As Alejandra hurried off, phone pressed to her ear, Bruno couldn't help admiring her drive and energy—there was something special about this bright, fast-talking young woman who tackled software deals and salsa dancing with equal gusto.

Chapter 50

San Carlos de Bariloche, Argentina – University Lab (Spring 1989, Twenty-Four Hours Earlier)

Nicolás Tosh hadn't set foot in Argentina for six years, not since reconnecting with his father. But a week earlier, **Bruno** had called from Bariloche, urging him to come immediately: there was a *major security breach* in the local lab. So Tosh flew from Zurich to Buenos Aires, transferred to a domestic flight, and by mid-morning, he was seated with **Professor Benjamín Borjes** at the university.

"What happened, Professor?" Tosh asked. **"We suspect sabotage,"** Borjes replied gravely. **"Or maybe theft. Some of our CDA constructs look…tampered with."**

An Unusual "Sabotage"

They discussed how **twenty students**, split into five groups, each coded isolated portions of new **CDA-323** modules. One group's segment had malfunctioned, and entire formulas seemed missing. Others had odd changes that didn't fit the system.

"Why would anyone do that?" Tosh asked. **"No idea,"** Borjes shrugged. **"I planned to cancel today's class, but if you want—" "No, hold it. Let's go on as usual. Introduce me as your *former student* so I can see who knows enough to sabotage or deviate our code."**

Tosh quickly scanned the suspect formulas. His eyes flicked across the lines, mind racing with permutations.

"Professor, look here. It's not truly 'stolen' or 'sabotaged'—this chunk is a random substitution. Some lines are amateurish but show

promise. And for the *missing* bit: it seems the students hit a wall and just left it blank."

Borjes relaxed slightly. **"So the code's fixable?"** "Yes. Let's see which student might have tried tinkering."

Spotting the Prodigy

In class half an hour later, Professor Borjes let Tosh deliver a mini-lecture on "discrete algorithms for future software." Tosh deliberately demonstrated the same formula strings that had been altered. One student, **Dieter Jürgen**, perked up, following each step with rapt attention. After class, Borjes and Tosh asked him to stay behind.

"We noticed a certain *creative twist* in your group's code," Borjes began. **"I…just experimented,"** Dieter admitted. **"But the logic was too advanced for me."**

Tosh introduced himself as the algorithm's original developer.

"I admire your curiosity, Dieter. Would you like to join my organization? We can nurture talent like yours." "Yes, sir. I'd be honored," Dieter said, eyes shining.

Over the coming years, **Dieter Jürgen** became part of Tosh's data center team, initially under Professor Borjes in Bariloche, later moving to **Zermatt** as head of the supercomputer network. Conveniently, Dieter had Swiss nationality—his parents had immigrated to Argentina two decades prior—making the transfer seamless.

A Quick Buenos Aires Stop

With the local lab crisis resolved, Tosh dropped by **Aunt Camila**'s place for a short visit, then caught an afternoon flight back to Buenos

Aires. That evening, he met **Bruno** for dinner—father and son shared a plate of **chivito** at a little eatery on La Valle Pedestrian Street, capping it off with *Martin Fierro* (cheese-and-dulce-de-leche). Over coffee, they caught up on Bruno's ongoing business ventures. Although he worked part-time for Nicolás's organization, Bruno insisted on maintaining his own independent reseller company.

"No problem," Tosh said, amused. **"As long as you've left the diving industry behind."**

They turned in early, since Tosh's flight to Zurich left at noon the next day. **Bruno** planned to show him his computer store in the morning—just enough time for a quick father-son check-in before Tosh jetted off to resume his quiet, extraordinary double life.

Chapter 51

Buenos Aires, Argentina – Bruno Buonarroti's Computer Store (Spring, 1989)

"Deal it is, then," said **Alejandra Martínez-López**, shaking hands with **Bruno Buonarroti**. She'd found her perfect sublet for her expanding software team. Bruno escorted her back to the showroom, pausing as they approached a small group testing an **IBM PC** with two floppy drives, a 250 MB hard disk, and 2 MB of RAM—state-of-the-art at the moment.

"Let me introduce you to my son," Bruno said quietly.

First Look

Seated behind the gleaming PC was **Nicolás Tosh**, glancing up just in time to notice Alejandra's pastel-green business dress and confident posture. For an instant, their eyes met, and each felt an unexpected rush of warmth. In Alejandra's view, Nicolás exuded easy charisma—his strong hands, a subtle intensity in his gaze. Nicolás, in turn, found himself captivated by her sparkling aura and razor-sharp energy.

Sensing the sparks, **Bruno** tactfully stepped away.

"I'm Alejandra Martínez-López," she said, offering a friendly smile. **"Nicolás Tosh,"** he replied, his voice steady despite his pounding heart. **"Care for a cup of coffee?"**

They slipped into the **mall café** next door. In minutes, it felt as though they'd known each other for years. She teased about the near-crash in the parking lot; he confessed he traveled constantly between Argentina and

Europe. Warm laughter turned into deeper conversation, each fascinated by the other's drive and outlook.

A Swift, All-Consuming Romance

After that day, whenever Nicolás was abroad, they spoke by phone for hours—Alejandra ignoring her usual wariness, Nicolás postponing lab deadlines just to hear her voice. He flew to Buenos Aires more often, extending each stay; she visited Switzerland, relishing the quiet grandeur of the Alps with him. Their friends and families watched in awe as this high-octane pair—a rising software entrepreneur and a globe-trotting mathematician—grew inseparable.

Within **three months**, they saw no reason to wait on formalities. Under a moonless night sky in **Las Vegas**, they slipped away to a tiny chapel, far from prying eyes, forging their union in a swift, private wedding. In that moment—driven by love, unencumbered by expectations—**Alejandra Martínez-López** and **Nicolás Tosh** sealed the start of the next exhilarating chapter of their entwined lives.

Chapter 52

*Las Vegas, Nevada – Caesars Palace Honeymoon Suite
(Autumn, 1989)*

Nicolás Tosh lay deep asleep in a plush honeymoon suite at **Caesars Palace** when his "identifier" started buzzing. Instantly, **Rainer Sábato**'s thoughts poured into his mind:

"Okay, *lovebird*, how do you plan to juggle marriage *and* your three organizations?"

Rainer was half-teasing, half-serious. Since **Nicolás** met **Alejandra**, he'd seemingly put everything else second. Yet no major crises had arisen, so it hadn't caused real issues—*so far.*

"I know what you're thinking," Nicolás replied silently. **"But I've never missed a key call or deadline, right?"** **"True. But answer me—what's your plan?"**

Nicolás sighed, turning on his side so he wouldn't wake Alejandra, still dozing next to him:

"I need time to settle my personal life. I haven't told her anything about the CDAs or the data center. I want her to live *normally*—no secrets, no hidden burdens." **"That's a big choice,"** Rainer said. **"So what's next?"** **"I'll try being a regular businessman—*or* a professor if that doesn't work—without leveraging my math tools or capital. My plan is for Walkyria to sponsor an R&D center at a university wherever we settle, so I can teach discreetly. If we move to Düsseldorf, I'll be only two hours from Switzerland."**

Rainer relaxed somewhat:

"You're serious... Good luck. You deserve happiness. When do I meet *her*?" **"Give me a few months. We still have a *traditional* wedding in Buenos Aires for her family."**

They ended the call, leaving **Rainer** both relieved and a bit skeptical. *Nicolás in "normal life" mode?* It was hard to picture.

Back to Buenos Aires

Not long after their Vegas elopement, **Alejandra** and **Nicolás** returned to **Buenos Aires** and began planning a more formal ceremony with her parents. Alejandra persuaded her father to swap the family's usual Christmas trip to Lake Placid for **Zermatt, Switzerland**—**Nicolás's** annual ski destination and the old hometown of his late mother.

A few weeks later, the entire family crossed the Atlantic to that **magical Alpine village** beneath the Matterhorn. For Tosh, it was a homecoming that beckoned his dual identity—data center founder, newlywed husband, and the man who yearned to keep it all in perfect balance.

Chapter 53

Buenos Aires, Argentina – Alejandra Martínez-López's Home (Autumn 1989)

Alejandra's father, **Nelson Martínez-López**, was a self-made Cuban-born attorney who emigrated to Argentina at eight years old. He built a strong reputation working nights through law school, representing an influential local German community. Through one German client, he'd met **Lane Woodward**, the FBI's station chief in Buenos Aires.

Concerned Father, Mysterious Fiancé

Over coffee in Nelson's study, Woodward tried reassuring him:

"Your future son-in-law is a math genius—graduated with honors from the *Universidad de los Andes* in Bariloche. He has dual nationality from his Swiss mother, who died of ALS when he was six. His father's an Italian living in Argentina for three decades."

"So how does he earn a living?" Nelson pressed. **"No public record after graduation,"** Woodward replied. **"Given his skill set, we suspect *government-related* classified work—probably for Switzerland."**

That only half-satisfied Nelson. He'd noticed **Nicolás Tosh** constantly carrying a small buzzing device, tapping it silently every few minutes. No word or gesture—just a flicker in his eyes. Nelson was determined to dig deeper, especially since his daughter's wedding drew near.

A Firm Yet Loving Mother

Nelson's wife, **María,** was the family's anchor—a devout Catholic who'd guided him through night school. She adored Nicolás:

"Nelson, enough," she told him gently. **"Alejandra is marrying someone she loves; he's clearly no criminal. Let her start her own family in peace."**

Nelson promised to drop it—but privately, he kept testing **Nicolás**. He sent his two burly sons to challenge him at various sports: soccer (the near-semi-pro brothers launched lethal shots), racquetball (the star brother ended up crawling off the court). Both returned impressed, admitting Nicolás played at a *remarkably* high level.

"Dad, he's no pushover," they conceded, chuckling at how Nelson nicknamed the slimmer man "Bones."

Off to Switzerland

By the time they were all set to travel for the winter holiday—swapping their usual Lake Placid trip for Zermatt at Alejandra's request—Nelson remained determined to find out everything about his elusive new in-law. Yet beneath the protectiveness, a grudging respect for **Nicolás Tosh** had already begun to take root in his heart.

Chapter 54

Zermatt, Switzerland – Christmas, 1989

It was almost noon when **Nelson Martínez-Lopez** parked the rental van beside the Alpine hotel in Zermatt. He'd driven up with his wife and two sons, while **Nicolás** and **Alejandra** took a helicopter over from Geneva. As soon as the young couple reappeared—flushed and grinning—Nelson recognized precisely *why* they were running late.

"Nicolás, help me with these bags, please." Without complaint, Tosh hefted the heaviest suitcase into the lobby.

A Father's Quirky Rules

Once they reached the assigned room, Nelson calmly declared:

"You two aren't *officially* married yet. So, Nicolás, you'll bunk here with my sons—see the third bed in the middle? That's for *you*."

Alejandra bit back a laugh, exchanging a quick wink with Nicolás. She knew exactly how to circumvent her father's strict "no sleeping together" rule.

For the next few days, **Nicolás** wore out Alejandra's brothers on the slopes, choosing steep trails, cross-country paths, and challenging routes only a high-level skier could love. By early afternoon, the brothers collapsed, allowing Alejandra and Nicolás to slip away to their hidden bed-and-breakfast, free to enjoy each other's company *in private*.

A Surprising Revelation

On the fifth evening, **Nelson** cornered Nicolás in the hotel's **Turkish bath**. Grinning, he teased:

"My sons can barely move. You beat them every day on those runs, eh?" Then his voice softened. "I think you'll do fine looking after my daughter. I see that now."

Nicolás exhaled in relief. He'd gained the father's acceptance.

"Sir," he said quietly, "I'd like to show you something—just the two of us."

The Secret Data Center

A half-hour later, they slipped into a back elevator leading to the hotel's rooftop. To Nelson's amazement, the walls opened to reveal a hidden corridor. Inside was a **state-of-the-art data center** connected to an even larger facility beneath the mountain. **Rainer Sábato** and **Peter Friedli** greeted them, explaining that this was **Nicolás's** private domain—an advanced lab for his classified *CDA* work.

"**No nuclear bombs**," Nicolás clarified, amused at Nelson's rumor-based assumptions. "**But I'd appreciate your silence. If you consent, you'll become a 'carrier,' gaining lifetime protection from our organization—but with the condition that you *never* reveal this to Alejandra or anyone else.**"

Nelson, impressed by what he saw, ultimately nodded in agreement:

"**I understand, son. My daughter's job is also *top secret* in Argentina's military. So, ironically, you two hide your work from each other. But I see now you both share a sense of duty. You have my trust.**"

One More "Runaway" Moment

That evening, Nelson let his wife in on the simpler truth—**Nicolás** had explained enough to earn the father's blessing. Relieved, Alejandra and Nicolás spontaneously sneaked away again, weaving through Zermatt's snowy streets under a bright moon. Within minutes, they reached their **gasthoff** love nest. She dropped her overcoat, revealing nothing beneath but winter boots. Laughing, Nicolás scooped her into his arms...

They returned before dawn with rosy cheeks, just in time for the day's final surprise: *a proper Argentine wedding.*

A Formal Celebration

Less than two months later, **Alejandra Martínez-López** and **Nicolás Tosh** hosted a grand ceremony in Buenos Aires—complete with extended family, friends, and all the traditions. Amid lively music and toasts, they stood hand in hand, ready to begin a new chapter of life. Unbeknownst to everyone else, each carried a secret that only deepened their bond—a clandestine passion for two separate callings, woven together in the most unpredictable and perfect of ways.

Chapter 55

Miami, Florida – Day 3 (12:00 Noon)

The **FBI Falcon Jet** touched down at **Opa-locka Airport** right at noon. Dressed in borrowed Secret Service clothes, **Nicolás Tosh** walked out a free man, newly exonerated. He requested a ride to the **Federal Detention Center** gate—a grim place he'd left behind only hours earlier—so he could meet his family without the hush of secrecy.

Alejandra picked up on the first ring:

"Where are you?" **"Standing outside the FDC,"** he said. **"I'm free. Where are you?"** **"At your attorney's office, just a few blocks away."**

Moments later, **Alejandra** and their two children, Emilia and Sebastián, spotted him, sprinted across the street, and threw themselves into a tearful embrace. They wrapped him in fierce hugs, kisses, and laughter, half-sobbing with relief. Several Secret Service agents watched from a polite distance.

Home to Bayside

Soon, they piled into the family car and drove to **Bayside**, their gated community along Biscayne Bay, not far from downtown Miami and the airport. The 5,000-square-foot ranch house—updated several times since they'd moved from Germany—felt both comforting and surreal after six months of turmoil.

Gathered in the living room, **Nicolás** addressed them all:

"I'm proud of how you handled this nightmare. We had no plan for what happened—but we survived. I hope now we can be more

grateful for what we have and for each other. Life changes in an instant. Let's never forget that."

Then he asked for a few moments alone with **Alejandra**. She clung to his arm, as though afraid to let go again.

"Baby," he began softly, **"I have a confession. Something I should've told you years ago. If you'd known, maybe the last six months wouldn't have been so terrifying."**

Alejandra's eyes narrowed, still raw from the ordeal.

"You mean the trial's accusations? Were any of them…true?"

Nicolás shook his head. **"No, none of that. But there *is* a reason they called me a 'military asset.' And it's not illegal, or for personal gain—it's a…mission. Something I started decades ago in Bariloche, but I kept it secret from you, even though you're my partner, my rock. I regret that deeply."**

Alejandra stayed silent, trying to absorb his words.

"Look at these news reports," Nicolás said, showing her coverage of the conspirators' conviction for attempting to destroy a "U.S. military asset." **"Those twenty people? They *targeted me*. They framed me, got me convicted. But the President separated it from my exoneration so the public wouldn't realize a single human could be a strategic asset."**

She stared, stunned. **"So you…are some kind of government operative?"**

Nicolás let out a slow breath, took her hand:

"Not a spy. Nothing illegal. Everything we've done is for the greater good—call it a 'grand plan' from thirty-five years ago on a ski mountain in San Carlos de Bariloche."

He paused, eyes full of resolve. It was time to share everything.

Chapter 56

Washington, D.C. – The White House (2016, Day 3, 3:00 P.M. ET)

Waiting to greet Japan's Prime Minister, **President Kelly O'Sullivan** took a call from **General Collins**:

"Mr. President, we've finished downloading data from former President Thomas." "So soon?" O'Sullivan asked, checking the clock. **"We had to obtain written consent from all G-7 members first,"** Collins explained. **"Thomas isn't on the standard list of U.S. government posts authorized for CDA-323."**

O'Sullivan frowned. **"Meaning Tosh's system only generates 'unlocking codes' if it verifies all approvals?"**

"Yes, sir. The AI runs it—no human intervention on Tosh's side. Both we and their system must sign off. Now all codes have expired again."

Renewed Frustration

The President realized that once codes expired, they could only deploy the CDAs on Americans *explicitly designated* by G-7 rules.

"So, we're back to the old list," O'Sullivan said wearily. **"But now it includes *former* presidents."** **"Precisely. That's the new G-7 agreement. The Office of the President is subject to CDAs 322–324 for national security reasons, *including* ex-presidents."**

The President asked if the White House could **seize** or replicate Tosh's data center. Collins reminded him:

"They keep multiple duplicates—some in Fort Knox, others in the Pentagon, updated every second. Even if Tosh's main data center shut down, the backups would activate automatically, but we'd still need their code to interpret certain discrete-algorithm segments."

Collins added that mathematicians in the government had tried reverse-engineering Tosh's algorithms, to no avail:

"Sir, we're decades from fully grasping how they're formulated. It's revolutionary."

G-7 Debates & President's Decision

Further complicating matters, some G-7 leaders wanted the data center supervised by an international board. But the existing protocols—classifying **CDAs** as WMDs—ensured no unilateral expansions or exploitations. If any single nation tried overriding the rules, **Tosh's organization** would pull the plug entirely.

"They truly cornered us," O'Sullivan murmured. "No wonder we can't just 'increase usage.'"

Collins confirmed:

"Yes, sir. They rely on each of the seven powers to keep the others in check. And if all else fails, they'd yank the CDAs forever."

Shortly after, the Undersecretary of Defense, **William T. Brown**, was sworn in as the new Secretary of Defense, automatically subject to the CDAs. All went smoothly— "spotless," in Collins's words.

"One less thing to worry about," O'Sullivan muttered.

But the President still seethed over the fiasco in Miami. Determined to curb corruption and potential sabotage, he decided to expand the list of government officials under mandatory disclosure, possibly including

federal judges, prosecutors, law enforcement, intelligence officers, and any staff overseeing nuclear programs. That afternoon, he convened a small team in the Oval Office:

"We need a commission to recommend which posts require *absolute* **transparency,"** O'Sullivan said, handing them a rough outline. **"Take all the time you need. I want a serious, deep dive."**

The team understood: they'd be shaping how far the country's leaders would come under the secret watch of **CDAs 322–324**—even if it meant treading carefully around Tosh's intangible fortress of power.

Chapter 57

Miami, Florida – The Tosh Home (2016, Day 3, 3:00 P.M. ET)

Nicolás Tosh sensed the tension as soon as he and **Alejandra** stepped into the living room. With the entire family finally reunited, he had something urgent to confess—especially to his wife.

"Alejandra," he began, **"everything we share is real. You and the kids matter more than anything. But yes, I've kept a separate life, for good reasons—so I thought."**

She folded her arms, uneasy. **"So, that other life just…collided with ours?"**

He nodded:

"I believed I could keep my secret work hidden. I was wrong. Had you known, maybe the frame-up wouldn't have succeeded. I regret it more than anything."

In a soft, almost resigned voice, Alejandra murmured:

"All those times you stared off, absent-minded… you were *communicating* with your data center, right?"

Nicolás pulled out his small "identifier" device:

"Yes. Let me show you."

He handed her the device. Closing his eyes, he mentally contacted the data center:

'Rainer, please register Alejandra on the network.' 'Are you sure?' came **Rainer Sábato**'s silent reply. **'I am.'**

Alejandra noticed Nicolás's faraway look. She'd asked him a question, but he was clearly *elsewhere*.

"Hello? I'm talking to you, Nic—"

Suddenly, **Rainer**'s voice filled her mind:

'**Hi, Alejandra. Don't be scared; the device bridges your brain waves to our neural network. Your husband is a mathematician who invented 'CDA' discrete algorithms…we run three entities: the for-profit Walkyria, the Experta Foundation, and the Zermatt Data Center. This device is *not* licensed; it's too powerful and must stay secret.**'

Alejandra sat, stunned. She managed a breath:

"**So, you're reading my brain?**" '**Not exactly, only bridging signals. Think of it like Wi-Fi for thoughts.**'

She ended the call, demanding a "normal" talk with Nicolás. He explained how *some* conspirators had discovered he was a **U.S. military asset** and framed him; eventually, the President and the G-7 approved deploying the more powerful CDAs to expose them. The notion rattled Alejandra:

"**So, *this* is why they convicted you of terrorism? They had no idea you were that 'asset.' You could've used your technology earlier to avoid jail!**"

He spread his hands. "**I tried protecting my identity—but yes, I messed up.**"

The Real Bombshell: Natalia

Alejandra's voice dropped to a whisper:

"**So, what about the rumor of an affair? Did you know a 'Natalia Barrios'—the same woman married to ex-President Thomas?**"

Nicolás winced, **"Yes…once, long ago. It was a single night, and I regret it."**

She felt her stomach knot. **"She called me months ago. I hung up, thinking it was nonsense. I can't believe—"**

"Ale, I slipped. I was young, naive. She and I…" He trailed off, guilt flooding his face.

Her eyes filled with tears. **"Get out,"** she said. **"I can't look at you right now."**

Nicolás left quietly, heart pounded with remorse.

Alejandra's Call

Desperate for clarity, Alejandra remembered Natalia's old phone number. She dialed; after foreign rings, a woman picked up:

"This is Emanuella Thomas. Who's speaking?" **"Natalia?"** Alejandra said, voice tight.

A pause. **"You want to talk now?"**

"Yes. I dismissed you before, but…please, I need the truth."

Natalia sighed:

"It was one night. I lied about more, out of spite. I wanted to hurt Nicolás—and you—since *my* husband found out and blamed us both. I envied you. Let's be honest: he loves you. I manipulated him for an old promise, but his heart wasn't in it. That's all."

Alejandra's hand shook. **"I see. If my trust is broken, I suppose…there's no second chance, right?"**

"If you ever cast him aside, let me know," Natalia said, somewhat snidely. **"But truly—he belongs to you. He's *yours*."**

The call ended. Alejandra stared at her phone, mind swirling. Emotion warred with hurt, and anger at herself for not believing Natalia's earlier call. She pressed another number:

"Nicolás?" she said firmly. **"We have to talk. Can you come back?" "I'll be there in fifteen,"** he murmured.

She inhaled, bracing to face her husband again, uncertain but determined to find the path forward in the aftermath of so many lies.

Chapter 58

Miami, Florida – The Tosh Home (2016, Day 3, 6:00 P.M. ET)

Nicolás Tosh had just wrapped up a meeting at **Zaptec**, where **General Pinkus** described how easily public opinion can be manipulated—first by the media demonizing a target, then by prosecutors bolstered by that hostile narrative. Now, driving home through Miami's evening traffic, Nicolás's thoughts spun: **Alejandra** had called, wanting to talk *immediately*. He had no idea how she felt or what she would say.

Arriving at their gated house, he saw **Alejandra** standing outside. She gestured for him to join her on a walk along the quiet sidewalk. For a minute or two, they strolled in silence, the weight of unspoken words pressing in.

"Nicolás, I talked to Natalia today." Her voice was level, but he sensed her anger. He tensed. **"I…figured she might reach out again." "You don't want to know what she said?" "Not really,"** he admitted, voice low.

Alejandra stopped, folding her arms. **"What did you *promise* her?"**

Nicolás closed his eyes at the painful memory. The affair with *Natalia* was an old scar he'd hoped never to revisit. Yet Alejandra's calm gaze demanded an explanation.

"I'm sorry for betraying you," he whispered. **"I never loved her. I never wanted to hurt you. But yes, it happened, and I've no excuse. I told no one—especially not you, because…"**

"**Because you were following orders—from the President?**" she cut in, shock on her face. "**He asked me not to embarrass the** *former* **president publicly,**" Nicolás said, frustration etched in his voice. "**I was supposed to consult him first, but I didn't.**"

Alejandra's eyes flared. "**So you conceal the** *affair* **for a politician's sake? Or to hide your double life from me?**"

Nicolás exhaled, tears gathering. "**Both. Natalia used my mother's memory to manipulate me. I still can't talk about it without breaking down.**"

Alejandra saw the anguish in his face. "**Fine. Let's drop it. For now.**" She inhaled deeply. "**But how did that single encounter with Natalia lead to us nearly losing everything?**"

Nicolás admitted that **ex-President Thomas** discovered the betrayal and orchestrated the false terrorism charges to destroy him, unaware of Nicolás's status as a U.S. "military asset." Alejandra stood stunned.

"**He hates you that much?**" "**Yes—and once it all came out, he realized I never knew he'd married Natalia. But by then, the damage was done.**"

They resumed walking, heading back toward the house's front steps. Alejandra perched on the porch edge, and Nicolás sat beside her.

"**So,**" she said softly, "**the hush-hush operation you run—these** *CDAs*—**caught the conspirators, but also put us under a bigger spotlight than ever?**" "**Exactly,**" he said. "**The entire G-7 is more aware now; we always feared they'd try controlling or exploiting us if they realized how powerful our algorithms are.**"

Alejandra nodded, grasping the burden he carried alone:

"I understand better why you separated these worlds—ours and your hidden math-lab universe. But I'm not the same. My own work is top-secret. We've both kept each other in the dark."

Nicolás turned, eyes wide. "I suspected you had certain duties. I never pushed."

She reached for his hand:

"Let's keep it simple. If you want me or the kids involved, you'll decide how and when. We won't pry. We'll give you space to work out the details—just don't shut us out anymore."

Nicolás exhaled, relief and guilt mingling. "Thank you."

They went inside. Alejandra soon fell into a troubled sleep, her face lined with exhaustion. Nicolás watched her, realizing even now she did not feel safe. Gently, he tucked a blanket over her. He vowed then that if he ever faced another crisis, he would involve her—his partner, confidante, and wife—from the start.

Chapter 59

Miami, Florida & Washington, D.C. – Day 3 (10:00 P.M. ET)

After ensuring **Alejandra** was resting, **Nicolás Tosh** slipped quietly into his study. He turned on an older "identifier" device and contacted **President O'Sullivan**:

'**Mr. President, good evening.**' The President answered in a half-joking tone, **"I hope you're not in *another* crisis already?"** '**Not yet, sir. Just tying up loose ends.**'

Nicolás first thanked the President for his swift intervention, noting how crucial it was in securing his release.

"You deserved it," O'Sullivan replied. **"Someday we'll honor your contributions openly."** '**Respectfully, sir, I hope that day never comes. Remaining discreet is why we can continue doing what we do.**'

Revisiting the Conspirators' Data

Nicolás brought up his concern that some conspirators might still be at large:

'**I believe your team only ran CDA-324 on those in *authorized government posts*. Others from the conspiracy could've influenced or been influenced by them. We still have seventy-two hours before the current codes expire—enough time to search deeper.**'

The President hesitated:

"General Collins told me the codes had expired." '**They haven't *yet*. We can still apply CDA-324 to *all* conspirators—then find**

whomever they've interacted with, possibly run it on those new individuals as well.'

O'Sullivan, weary of more potential scandal, conceded:

"Understood. Let's bring General Collins on this call."

Nicolás scrolled through his outdated device to locate Collins in the directory. After a few keystrokes, Collins's voice chimed in:

"Good evening, Mr. Tosh, Mr. President."

Nicolás explained the oversight with CDA-324. Collins confirmed:

"Yes, sir. We can do it quickly with your approval. Also, about Senator Molina…"

Senator Molina's Mystery

Christopher Musial, who was standing by at Tosh's request, joined the call. He explained that:

"Senator Gilbert Molina is *not* on the indicted list, but we suspect he has *some* link. His father, Leroy Sinclair, was *the* conspirators' mastermind, arrested in Telluride. We only discovered it through Pinkus's security firm."

The President recalled:

"When Sinclair was apprehended, Molina had just left. I warned him on the phone to stay out of it."

Collins added:

"We never thoroughly cleared Molina, because he didn't show up on the phone ring. Could be a coincidence—or he could be part of something deeper."

The President told Collins:

"All right. I'm authorizing a CDA-324 run on Senator Molina. If it flags anything suspicious, we expand."

Collins noted that *ex*-Secretary of Defense Gilbert and his nephew were also in question, but with Gilbert deceased, the President said:

"Check posthumous data and linkages—whatever's left. We must be sure no conspirator's gone unnoticed."

The President's Reluctance

Nicolás sensed O'Sullivan's unease: more revelations could spawn yet another fiasco. But the President pressed on, asking **Nicolás** to contact *ex*-President Thomas if needed.

'Yes, sir. I'll locate him in Buenos Aires. The data center can figure out the closest "carrier."'

O'Sullivan's executive assistant quickly provided Thomas's Argentine address. Nicolás ended the call, old beeper-like device in hand, already planning how best to approach the former president—someone who had unwittingly caused *so much* chaos.

Chapter 60

Buenos Aires, Argentina (Day 3, 12:00 A.M. ET/ART)

Late Work for Borjes

Ruben Borjes no longer wore the black leather jacket of his old police days. For twenty years he'd worked for **Nicolás Tosh**, helping set up Walkyria's operations in South America and managing the **Experta Foundation** programs in Argentina, Brazil, and Chile. Since his uncle, **Professor Benjamín Borjes**, had passed away the previous year, the lab in Bariloche had finally closed, consolidating everything in Zermatt.

Tonight, Ruben had stayed late, finalizing the foundation's annual budget. Driving home around midnight, he was lost in memory— thinking of his uncle's integral role in designing Tosh's most recent CDA algorithms—when his *identifier* buzzed.

'Ruben, buenas noches,' came **Nicolás Tosh**'s familiar mental voice. **'I have an address in Buenos Aires. Need to know if you're nearby.'** **'Sure, Nic. Go on.'** **'Barrio del Inglés, number 322.'** **'But I live there! I'm five minutes away. Whom are we visiting?'** **'Layton Thomas.'** **'The** *former* **U.S. President?'**

Ruben's heart skipped a beat. He'd read about Thomas's abrupt exile. Tosh explained:

'Yes, I need to connect him to President O'Sullivan. Ready?'

Calling Ex-President Thomas

Nicolás tapped on his directory, selecting the name:

'Mr. Thomas, this is Nicolás Tosh. I'm here with President O'Sullivan.'

A startled voice responded:

"I have no *identifier*, how are you—?" 'There's one in your vicinity, sir. We're bridging the call through it.'

O'Sullivan spoke up:

"Layton, we have questions. First: was *ex*-Secretary Gilbert involved in the conspiracy at any point?" "No," Thomas said curtly. **"I disliked him, never worked with him. He had no part in *my* fiasco."**

"What about Senator Molina of Florida?" O'Sullivan pressed. **"No relationship there, either,"** Thomas insisted. **"Look, the CDA records from *my* brain will confirm it. Now, if you'll excuse me..."**

"Thank you, Layton," O'Sullivan said, ending the call. **"We'll be in touch."**

Thomas let out a tense sigh, silently fearing what new twist might come next—knowing that any CDA search could unearth more secrets he hoped to bury.

Chapter 61

Washington, D.C. – The White House (2016, Day 4, 1:00 A.M. ET)

"Where is Senator Molina now?" President O'Sullivan demanded as soon as the call connected.

Nicolás Tosh responded, mental voice crisp:

'If he's still in D.C., we need an 'identifier' near him, sir. Let me check…'

Moments later, Nicolás asked the President:

'Can you turn your device on, Mr. President?' "Sure," O'Sullivan said, powering it up. **"Am I the only 'identifier' in D.C.?"**

Nicolás sighed:

'At this moment, yes. Until now, your unit was *read-only*, but I'll push a software update so you can actively search the directory. Give me a minute…'

A quick download ensued, prompting the President to reset his "identifier." He scanned the new features:

"I see a 'DIRECTORY' option. I'm searching Molina… Huh, no signal."

Nicolás then initiated a broader worldwide trace using 730 active "identifiers" carried by "carriers" plus 10,000 installed at major transportation hubs. After a brief pause:

'Mr. President, you'll find this surprising. Molina left the country two hours after Christopher last saw him. We picked up traces at Dulles Airport, then Narita in Tokyo twelve hours later, then Shanghai a few hours ago. That's the last signal we have.'

The President let out a low whistle:

"So you have 'identifiers' at nearly every major airport worldwide—like a giant fishing net." 'Yes, sir. We have a two-mile range, so we monitor whenever a *registered* brain is in proximity.'

O'Sullivan exhaled wearily:

"Could be desertion or something bigger. I'll call the CIA—no telling what Gilbert and Molina *really* wanted. CDA-324 should give more answers. Let's hope it clarifies their link to the conspirators."

Nicolás and Christopher both signed off, leaving the President to address his final concerns:

"By the looks of it," he muttered, **"you two might end up working here. Good night, gentlemen."**

He placed the "identifier" on his desk, already envisioning another long night—one where the lines between open government, intelligence, and a private data network blurred further than ever.

Chapter 62

Miami, Florida & Washington, D.C. – Day 4 (2:00 A.M. ET)

Nicolás Tosh stayed on the line with **Christopher Musial**, then looped in **Rainer Sábato** waking in Zermatt. They relayed the night's events, focusing on **Senator Molina**'s abrupt disappearance.

"Gilbert must have warned Molina in time," Christopher speculated. **"But if Molina wasn't part of the conspiracy,"** Nicolás said, **"why meet the ringleader and three key conspirators in Telluride?" "And what's his tie to Secretary Gilbert?"** Rainer added. **"It leads back to China, apparently."**

Just then, **Nicolás's** *identifier* buzzed: the **President** again. With a touch, Nicolás connected him—and **General Collins**—into the conversation.

Presidential Update

O'Sullivan spoke first:

"We reviewed Secretary Gilbert's CDA data. After your arrest, Gilbert recognized your voice from a *YouTube* UM lecture—and realized you were the same 'Nic Tosh' advising the White House. He'd been funneling billions in contracts to the conspirators' mastermind, Leroy Sinclair, for decades, so he tried warning them without revealing state secrets."

Nicolás grimaced. **"So that's Gilbert's motive for helping them: self-preservation."**

Collins continued:

"He assumed *Senator Molina* was also part of it, but he wasn't. Molina's father is Sinclair, and he'd only dropped by Telluride under pressure—he left just before the arrests. Learning of a potential tip-off, Gilbert tried contacting Molina, but it was a botched attempt. In truth, Molina knew about the conspiracy but never participated."

Nicolás frowned. **"Then why bolt to China?"**

"That's CIA territory," the President said. **"Unrelated to your organization or the conspiracy."**

Loose Ends & a Change Ahead

A brief silence fell. Finally, **O'Sullivan** admitted:

"Nicolás, Gilbert's accidental discovery of your identity worries me. Tomorrow night, I'd like a private talk—about how your system is set up. Forty years ago, your approach made sense, but the world and your organization have both changed."

Unease crept into Nicolás's voice:

"I understand, sir."

With that, they ended the call—each aware that the simplest solutions were gone, and a more complicated era for **Tosh's** secret enterprise loomed.

Chapter 63

Miami, Florida – Day 4 (3:00 A.M. ET)

Closing the call with **President O'Sullivan** at past three in the morning, **Nicolás Tosh** leaned back, exhausted. **Rainer Sábato**, on the line from Zermatt, spoke first:

"Nicolás, we've always lacked a robust personal-security system. You've relied on G-7 governments to protect Zermatt but look at *Secretary Gilbert*. Personal agendas can override any official stance."

Nicolás nodded reluctantly:

"You're right. Tomorrow, I'll hear what the President wants. But I suspect his pitch will revolve around more *oversight* of our technology."

Rainer's voice had an edge:

"And you'll reject it? Look, you can't ignore that we live in a hyper-connected world, dealing with the mightiest powers on earth."

Nicolás exhaled slowly:

"I'll keep an open mind—so long as our autonomy remains. But, yes, we do need better security. This fiasco proved we're vulnerable to even *one* official's greed."

They ended the conversation with the faint sense that life for the **Zermatt Data Center** was about to shift dramatically—and **Nicolás** readied himself for a delicate balancing act between *safeguarding* his organization's independence and *placating* the world's most powerful government.

Chapter 64

Miami, Florida (The Tosh Home) / Washington, D.C. (The White House) – Day 5 (10:30 P.M. ET)

Nicolás Tosh spent most of the day in remote meetings with **Rainer** and his Zurich legal team, strategizing how to preserve the **Zermatt Data Center**'s anonymity. By **10:30 P.M.**, his *identifier* buzzed: **President O'Sullivan** again.

'Good evening, Mr. President.' "**Nicolás, we need your help. We've designated Senator Molina a co-conspirator. Track him via his 'identifier number' and run CDAs 323 and 324 under the G-7's resolution.**"

Nicolás's mind raced. The **CIA** must have lost Molina in Shanghai, and now the White House wanted a direct approach:

'Understood, sir. Should I reconnect with the Pentagon?' "**No—do it yourself. We'll send the written authorization in minutes.**"

President's "Housekeeping"

O'Sullivan added:

"**We'll keep protecting you, but you must share your data center's personnel and location with General Collins once we sign an agreement.**"

Nicolás bristled:

'Sir, we don't require external protection. Our independence is vital.'

The President soldiered on:

"General Collins also wants to know who in Walkyria, Experta, or your back office are aware of your team's facilities. How many 'identifiers' you have, etc."

Nicolás gave a clipped reply:

'That's classified, Mr. President.'

Though the tension rose, **O'Sullivan** pressed for clarity:

"We assume you detect when a registered subject arrives at or departs from a city, but not exact in-city locations—correct?"

Nicolás half-shrugged:

'We can deploy fixed 'identifiers' throughout a city if needed, hooking them wirelessly to cover wide areas. But I'd rather focus on the G-7 resolution, sir. Where do you want CDAs next?'

O'Sullivan replied firmly:

"Find Molina, run CDAs 322–324 on him, and *do not* alert him."

Nicolás acknowledged:

'Yes, sir. It'll take under twelve hours.'

They ended the call with *both* sides on edge—**Washington** seeking control, **Zermatt** defending secrecy—and Molina's pursuit caught in the middle.

Chapter 65

Shanghai, China / Zermatt, Switzerland (Data Center) – Day 5 (12:00 P.M. CST / 12:00 Noon CET)

At Zermatt's Data Center, the quantum supercomputer launched the search for **Gilbert Molina** with a single swift command. Within a second, **fifty "identifiers"** around Shanghai—positioned at major airports, transit stations, and central hubs—activated in sync. Thin, invisible laser beams crisscrossed the city in a web, each *identifier* linking to every other. In under a minute, Shanghai was blanketed by a seamless **neural network** signal.

Once coverage was confirmed, the data center sent a second command to **ping Molina's brain ID**. Now, the moment Molina crossed any of the **5,000** invisible signal vectors, he would be connected without realizing it. Immediately, **CDAs 322, 323, and 324** would deploy, silently uploading his entire life data to Zermatt in under two hours. **Gilbert Molina** would remain completely unaware of his mind's infiltration— and by day's end, the **Data Center** in Zermatt would know everything there was to learn.

Chapter 66

Shanghai, China – Day 6 (12:00 Noon CST / 12:00 Midnight ET / 6:00 A.M. CET)

Gilbert Molina woke late in his 57th-floor suite at the Pudong Hyatt, overlooking the teeming Huangpu River. He had stayed up until dawn calling his U.S. contact, **Mr. Chen**, who confirmed that **Molina** faced *no* conspiracy indictment and his father, Leroy Sinclair, had been sentenced to life with a shot at parole in twenty-five years. The entire case was sealed in the American courts.

Chen assured him it was safe to return home—once they wrapped up a final "delivery." Hungry and restless, **Molina** headed out to stroll a few blocks to the Glass Cube Apple Store. Unaware that **Zermatt**'s invisible "vector" lines now veined the city, Molina crossed one in a quiet pedestrian plaza—and at that moment, his brain's **identifier** pinged the neural network.

He was connected. And he had no idea.

Chapter 67

Zermatt, Switzerland (Zermatt Data Center) – Day 6 (7:00 A.M. CET / 1:00 P.M. ET / 1:00 P.M. CST Next Day)

In under an hour, the **quantum supercomputer** at Zermatt downloaded **Molina's** entire brain data, then shut down the **Shanghai neural network**. During that brief window, coded signals notified **Tosh** and **Rainer** of the operation's success. By deactivating the network so swiftly—only sixty minutes from start to finish—the team minimized any risk of detection by Chinese authorities. Better yet, they completed the mission over eleven hours before **President O'Sullivan**'s deadline.

Now, with the extra time, they could parse Molina's data and see precisely why the President had insisted on total secrecy. **Nicolás Tosh** approved of the outcome: swift, discreet, and entirely under the radar— just the way he preferred it.

Chapter 68

Washington, D.C. – The White House, 2016, Day 6 (2:00 P.M. ET)

Nicolás Tosh spent the flight from Miami to D.C. conferring with **Rainer** on the final data gleaned from **Molina**'s neural imprint. When the plane landed, a White House car collected him, depositing him at the West Wing by mid-afternoon. Soon he was ushered into **President O'Sullivan**'s office, where **General Collins** also waited.

"Mr. President," Tosh said immediately, **"I want to reiterate that our organization will remain autonomous, and that you will never ask us to circumvent the G-7 rules on the CDA WMDs."**

O'Sullivan nodded:

"You have my word. Now, let's show you what we've been working on."

They led Tosh downstairs to an underground bunker area, where a small crew bustled around a newly installed **supercomputer**.

"We moved our CDA server here from the Pentagon," General Collins explained. **"We'll keep minimal staff at the old site."**

Tosh studied the equipment:

"So, you're centralizing your CDA operations here?" **"Yes,"** Collins said. **"And we're not posting any official 'protection' for Zermatt, Walkyria, or Experta, if that remains your preference."**

Tosh gave a curt nod. **O'Sullivan** continued:

"Tell me more about these 'carriers.' How exactly do they work?"

Tosh clarified that *carriers* are individuals who opt in to **CDA-321**, enabling mental thought-communication. The President regarded Tosh intently:

"So, you can embed data in someone's brain?" **"Only with their consent,"** Tosh said. **"Otherwise, the algorithm remains dormant and harmless."**

O'Sullivan then turned to the immediate matter:

"Do you have Molina's data?"

Tosh confirmed:

"Yes, sir—ready to transfer once this supercomputer's active. For now, we can patch in direct. We also learned that Andy Chen is secretly funding certain U.S. politicians, including rising stars like Senator Molina. It's a vast infiltration ring."

Stunned, the President stepped away, placed a call, then returned:

"The CIA is joining us via conference. No mention of the CDAs or your data center, understood?"

Tosh nodded. **General Collins** quickly explained that Chen's network included four categories of recruits—**students, Chinese-born U.S. citizens, business executives, and politicians**. The President then got **CIA Director Mark Thiel** on speaker, summarizing the infiltration. After a tense exchange, they agreed on an immediate briefing at **CIA headquarters**.

Before leaving, **O'Sullivan** made one request:

"Nicolás, I need your data center to register my top six CIA officials for future *carriership*, in case we need them on the neural

network. They won't know about you or CDAs yet. But it's crucial we're ready."

Tosh agreed:

"Understood, Mr. President. Just send their details, and we'll have them in the system—*inactive*, for now."

The moment they emerged from the bunker, the President's motorcade was already mobilizing to head for **Langley**—and **Nicolás Tosh** braced for the next wave of hush-hush intelligence briefings. He had no illusions about the volatile line he walked between full *cooperation* and preserving the **Zermatt Data Center**'s *sovereignty*—but for now, at least, the White House was keeping its word.

Chapter 69

Langley, Virginia—CIA Headquarters, 2016, Day 6 (4:00 P.M. ET)

The **presidential motorcade** swept into **Langley** by mid-afternoon, carrying **President O'Sullivan**, **General Collins**, and **Nicolás Tosh**. Within minutes, they were seated in a private conference room across from **CIA Director Mark Thiel** and his top six officers. Before stepping inside, Tosh discreetly **activated his "identifier"**—the tiny device that automatically registered the brain signals of anyone nearby.

As they exchanged greetings, the *identifier* finished scanning the group. **Tosh quickly sent a mental thought** to the President:

Sir, we have the six CIA officers' IDs.

O'Sullivan silently replied:

Run CDA-322 through 324. We need to confirm none has ties to Chen.

Though Tosh bristled at this borderline use of the WMD-level algorithms, he complied. **General Collins** noticed the tension between Tosh and the President. O'Sullivan gave Tosh a reassuring look—**the two would talk afterward**.

Meanwhile, the President steered the discussion toward **Andy Chen**. Over the last day, Tosh's data center had traced Chen's infiltration network. The CIA had partial intelligence on him, but not the scope of Chen's U.S.-based recruits.

Half an hour in, the "identifier" concluded its quick search of the CIA officers. **Tosh signaled** O'Sullivan: one of them, a young officer named **Whitmore**, appeared to be compromised by Chen.

The President kept his composure and said, "Mr. Whitmore, step outside with me and Director Thiel, please." In **Thiel's** office, O'Sullivan confronted the officer: they found a phone recording app running in his pocket. The shaken officer was arrested on the spot.

Returning to the room, **O'Sullivan** briskly told the others they would soon coordinate a joint operation with the **FBI** to dismantle Chen's ring. Additional details, including a final timeline, would remain classified until the President gave the go-ahead. Sobered by Whitmore's betrayal, everyone silently grasped the network's scale.

When the meeting ended, the President led Tosh and Collins back to the motorcade. During the quiet ride to the White House, **O'Sullivan** turned to Tosh:

"We need to talk about your philosophical concerns. This incident proves we must ensure total secrecy and alignment with G-7 protocols. But I won't deny there may be times we ask for your help—pushing right up to the edges of those protocols."

Tosh nodded, both uneasy and resolved. He had **crossed a red line** in scanning Whitmore without explicit G-7 authorization, and that uneasy feeling only deepened. Whatever trust he still had in the President, he realized, must be guarded carefully going forward.

Chapter 70

Zermatt, Switzerland – Zermatt Data Center 2016– *Day 7, 7:00 A.M. (CET)*

Rainer rubbed his temples, fighting fatigue as he sat in the glass-walled office overlooking the Quantum supercomputer. He had been working straight through the night, reviewing every byte of data extracted from Andy Chen's CDA-323 file. After all the earlier drama—Chen's infiltration network, Senator Molina's flight—this new trove promised leads on dozens of U.S. operatives and Silicon Valley insiders whom Chen had recruited. Yet the raw lists offered little certainty. They named former and current employees of big tech firms but left question marks everywhere: addresses missing, job statuses unknown, no guarantee these contacts were still active.

It frustrated Rainer how even a technological marvel like the Zermatt Data Center couldn't simply conjure up all the missing details. With Chen's memories downloaded, they had glimpses—faces, phone numbers, scraps of e-mails—but verifying each lead would require the old-fashioned "gumshoe" approach the CIA and FBI were preparing to launch. According to General Collins, massive raids would unfold soon, hopefully catching every suspect by surprise. But Rainer knew better: even the best agencies struggled to coordinate simultaneous arrests in multiple states without tipping someone off. There was always a risk of leaks or timing failures.

He scanned the control terminal—no keyboard, just voice or thought commands feeding into the neural network. At times, it felt almost primitive compared to the data center's power. Pacing in the hush of his office, he wondered if they were missing a more direct way to confirm each suspect's current location.

Suddenly, an idea struck him: *Wait—these were Chen's memories, not just a random data dump. Chen always kept his U.S. contact info somewhere. Maybe he had a more precise record stored...*

Rainer pulled up Andy Chen's CDA-323 archive, the full "life playback" that recorded Chen's experiences. He typed the mental command: **Search: "ADDRESS BOOK USA."**

A list of video clips appeared instantly. Rainer selected them, watching from Chen's viewpoint as Chen accessed contacts on his iPad. Chen always used an app called **mSecure**, apparently containing every operative's detailed info—addresses, phone numbers, even e-mails. From Chen's own eyes, Rainer saw the password each time Chen typed it, saw the user ID on a piece of paper, saw the iPad's passcode. It was all there, hidden in plain sight within the neural recording.

A surge of excitement replaced Rainer's earlier fatigue. *This is more than a vague list—this is direct evidence.* He found the specific scene where Chen opened mSecure. There it was: lines of text with each operative's data. Rainer froze the playback on the moment Chen typed the master password. Perfect. They could log into Chen's personal iPad or a backup and retrieve the entire network's contact files.

With a thought command, Rainer minimized Chen's archived memory feed and switched to a live CDA-322 channel. The screen displayed a grid of active "icons"—tiny silhouettes representing everyone currently under live observation. Most were locked—G-7 leaders, top government officials—unavailable without fresh authorization. He scrolled to the two icons that were part of the new White House Special Operations push: **Gilbert Molina** and **Andy Chen**.

He selected **Chen**, immediately seeing a real-time feed of the man's own vision. It was jarring, as always, to slip into someone else's viewpoint. Chen appeared to be in a nondescript hotel lobby—perhaps Hong Kong, maybe Singapore, it was hard to tell. He wore a crisp suit and carried a leather briefcase. Before Rainer could glean much more, Chen ended a phone call and turned toward the exit. The feed flickered as he walked outside into bright daylight, and Rainer glimpsed tall buildings stretching overhead.

Rainer suppressed a shiver. No matter how many times he used these algorithms, the ethical weight never vanished. Simply spying through Chen's eyes felt invasive, even if Chen was a confirmed threat. But this was the tool—one Rainer and Tosh had built decades ago and deemed a last-resort measure for moments exactly like this. They couldn't let an industrial-espionage mastermind continue unchecked.

All around him, the hum of servers reminded Rainer of the data center's vast reach. He forced himself to focus, memorizing everything in Chen's immediate field of view. Soon, the CIA and FBI would move in, guided by the addresses gleaned from mSecure. If all went to plan, they would roll up Chen's network in one coordinated strike across the country. The key was to remain unseen, preserving the shock factor.

Taking one last look at Chen's vantage, Rainer whispered under his breath: "Got you—and every one of your associates."

Then he ended the live feed, heart pounding, and prepared to forward the password-laden images to General Collins. The old FBI method might still be needed to confirm each suspect's status, but now at least they had precise targets. For the first time that night, Rainer felt they stood a real chance at shutting Chen down before he vanished again.

Chapter 71

Shanghai, China – 2016, Day 7, 7:30 A.M. (CST)

Andy Chen's Shanghai base was a sleek condo in a sprawling twenty-story complex, deep in the heart of the Pudong District. From his balcony, he could glimpse the silver spire of the Pudong Hyatt—a mere fifteen-minute walk away—where Senator Molina and several of Chen's visiting contacts were currently holed up. Chen had been awake for hours, juggling phone calls to the United States and piecing together grim news: Leroy Sinclair and the rest of Molina's co-conspirators had disappeared into a maximum-security prison. Family members reported no contact, no visiting privileges for at least thirty days. No one in Chen's government or legal network could offer details.

Despite the ominous silence, Chen was under pressure to send Molina back stateside. An absent senator would raise suspicions in Washington; at best, they had a two- or three-day grace period before someone sounded the alarm. Even Chen, typically unflappable, felt his confidence slip. Did the meltdown in the U.S. risk exposing his entire network?

He slumped onto a minimalist black sofa, iPad perched on the low glass coffee table in front of him. Tapping to unlock **mSecure**, his private digital vault, he retrieved a number he rarely dialed—one of the highest contacts in his chain. He reached for his satellite phone, keyed in the digits, and waited for a response.

While the call rang, Chen's eyes flicked to the corner of the iPad's screen, where a small icon indicated it was auto-synchronizing. He allowed himself a faint smile—he loved how technology saved him from tedious backup tasks. Routine sync or not, the device held the lifeblood of his operation: addresses, phone numbers, personal notes on each American recruit. It never crossed his mind that this very moment, the data was being siphoned off remotely—used against him by unseen hands at a secret data center half a world away.

Finally, the call clicked through with a muffled voice. Chen steadied himself.

"Are we compromised?" he asked without preamble. The person on the other line said something curt in Mandarin, the tone jittery.

Chen frowned. The news was worse than he'd expected—confirmation that multiple arrests in the U.S. had toppled key players. If he held Molina here any longer, the senator's prolonged absence would draw dangerous scrutiny. But sending him back to Washington too soon risked walking straight into a trap.

"Understood," Chen said tersely, cutting the call. He set the satellite phone aside and glanced again at the iPad's screen. The progress bar was nearly complete, innocuously finishing its backup. Chen gave it no more thought; soon he'd pack his bag, meet Molina at the Hyatt, and decide their next move.

For Andy Chen, the swirling sense of crisis was real enough—yet he still had no idea just how critical the breach of his digital fortress had become.

Chapter 72

Zermatt, Switzerland – Zermatt Data Center 2016 – Day 7, 7:30 A.M. (CET)

From his office high above the Quantum supercomputer, Rainer leaned back and marveled at how **simple** it could be to breach a formidable spy master's defense. Using Chen's own Apple credentials—gleaned straight from Chen's CDA-323 life archive—Rainer had just logged into **iTunes** via the web. Next, he piggybacked onto Chen's home network in Shanghai, thanks to "carrier" Perry Zuh quietly stationed in a nearby hotel. Perry's **identifier** had detected Chen's Wi-Fi signal, giving Rainer a window to trigger the iPad's **iCloud** backup remotely.

Within minutes, Rainer had a perfect copy of Chen's iPad right on his own terminal. Every contact, password, and note for the massive U.S. espionage network lay exposed. The Zermatt Data Center's system then parsed the data in seconds, mapping out precise addresses for nearly all of Chen's operatives—spanning Silicon Valley, the broader Bay Area, and cities across the country.

Standing at the console, Rainer scanned the results:

- Twelve **fixed identifiers** in Silicon Valley were already close enough to cover most suspects.

- Another **ten** would suffice to catch 90% of Chen's recruits with minimal movement.

- The last 10%—dozens of people scattered across seventeen smaller cities—posed a trickier challenge.

"Okay," he muttered to himself. "Let's start with the easier 90%." He fired off an update to the **carriers** in San Francisco, instructing them to install ten temporary identifiers before midnight local time—less than two hours away on the West Coast. They confirmed immediately, dispatching a three-person team for the job.

Next, Rainer examined major metro areas. New York, Miami, Chicago, and Boston already had enough **fixed identifiers** to sweep up the remaining targets there. Dallas and Los Angeles were more spread out; he messaged local carriers to place five additional units in Dallas and eight in L.A. They promised completion within a few hours.

The system also combed social-media profiles, e-mails, and group chats linked to Chen's operatives. Although it revealed an elaborate scheme of coded "green light" or "stop" signals, there was no sign of **alarm**—they didn't yet know their network was compromised.

By 8:30 A.M. Swiss time, Rainer felt exhaustion pressing in—he'd been awake all night. Still, the wheels were in motion: squads of carriers were on the move across the U.S., prepping to intercept Chen's operatives before they caught wind of any crackdown. Satisfied for the moment, he shut off his console and headed home to sleep, knowing he'd need to be back by afternoon—when America's East Coast burst into life, and the next phase of this covert operation began in earnest.

Chapter 73

Palo Alto, California – 2016, Day 8, 3:00 A.M. (PT)

Sang-Chang Lin lay awake, staring at the ceiling of his cramped apartment. He'd convinced himself that once he repaid his "scholarship loan," the demands would end. Yet just hours ago, Andy Chen had delivered crushing news: the future scholarship for Lin's younger brother depended on Sang-Chang continuing his espionage. He was trapped—facing a stark choice between betraying his conscience and risking his entire family's future.

He rolled over, clutching the corner of his pillow. By now, he'd stolen far too many corporate secrets to walk away clean. If the FBI or his employer discovered what he had done, he'd likely face decades behind bars. And still, the pressure to keep funneling data didn't let up. Even if he wanted to stop, "they" wouldn't allow it. His nightmares were no longer about failing a test or disappointing his parents—they revolved around a knock at the door, federal agents seizing him in a dawn raid.

His journey to this point had started innocently enough. The day he arrived in the U.S. to attend Stanford, he also began an internship at a prominent Palo Alto firm specializing in router and switch technology. After graduation, the company fast-tracked him into its R&D department, giving him near-total access to every prototype or cutting-edge product. Through the 3G era into 4G, and now the leaps toward 5G/LTE, Lin had been at the center of each breakthrough. Unbeknownst to his American employers, a rival tech giant in southern China enjoyed front-row seats to every one of Lin's stolen developments.

Now, at three in the morning, he wondered whether he'd crossed a final line. Each new theft carried greater risk. The moral weight, once so easy to brush aside, felt intolerable. And still, he saw no exit. Tired yet unable to sleep, Lin rose and stared out the window at the quiet neighborhood—a blur of streetlamps and dark silhouettes. In a few hours, he'd be back at the lab, logging in, making updates, sifting through project code. How much longer could he conceal the siphoning of data for Andy Chen?

He pressed a hand over his eyes. He couldn't imagine a future free of these demands, but continuing on meant damning himself further. Either way, it felt inevitable that eventually he'd lose it all.

Chapter 74

Boston, Massachusetts – 2016, Day 8, 6:45 P.M. (ET)

Joe Lee stared at his reflection in the bedroom mirror, struggling to knot his tie with trembling fingers. This should have been another routine evening—heading to his office for a late shift of coding. But a knot of dread coiled in his stomach, telling him everything was about to unravel.

He was American-born, the child of Chinese immigrants who arrived with nothing three decades ago. His parents had toiled ceaselessly to give him a shot at Harvard, and Joe paid them back by graduating **magna cum laude**. Life looked bright—until, three years ago, their family's good fortune in China caught up with him. His parents had found a "friend" to remit money to relatives in a remote western province; soon, those same relatives received government stipends and lavish gifts they didn't have to repay. It all seemed like a stroke of luck—until **Andy Chen** called Joe in Boston with a threat:

"Work for us, or we'll take everything away."

That was the beginning. Whenever Joe tried to break free, Chen repeated the same ultimatum, reminding him that half his extended family's livelihood depended on China's "beneficence." And each time Joe asked when he could stop, Chen's answer never changed:

"When I say so."

Joe worked for a data intelligence firm that specialized in market analysis and visualization apps. He had top-level access to the core **object-oriented** code behind each project—much of it so sensitive that the company's legal counsel worried about misuse if it ever fell into the wrong hands. Yet over time, he'd siphoned everything to Chen.

Now, as he stepped into his shoes and straightened his collar, a chill washed over him. Deep down, he sensed the end was near—either the FBI would catch him, or his company would unmask him, or Chen would push him to steal an even bigger prize that would tip the scales. He paused at the door, trying to steady his breathing. But nothing eased that gnawing certainty that his life, and the lives of those he cared about, were balanced on the sharpest of knives.

Chapter 75

Miami, Florida – The Tosh Home 2016, Day 8, 7:00 A.M. (ET)

By the time Rainer's message arrived at **2:30 A.M.**, *Nicolás Tosh* was too exhausted to process all the details. He slept just four hours before waking with a sharp new insight—one that could change everything. As he grappled with how to pitch it, his **identifier** buzzed.

"Nicolás, good morning."

"Mr. President, good morning. We're already linked to you."

"I know. How goes the investigation?"

"Right now," Tosh said, "we're transferring all CDA data on Chen's operatives to the White House bunker's supercomputer. It'll be done in a couple of hours."

The President sounded astonished.

"How did you—?"

"Rainer figured it out," Tosh explained. "We duplicated Chen's iPad through his home network, recognized every address, and deployed 'identifiers' in multiple cities. I green-lit it over an hour ago."

"Fantastic! The CIA and FBI were still two or three days away from the same conclusion. Once I let General Collins share your data, they can move in within hours."

Tosh inhaled.

"Sir, about that—I actually think we should let the *Chinese* operatives go free. Only arrest the U.S. citizens on the list."

A startled pause crackled through the connection.

"I beg your pardon?" asked the President.

"With CDAs on them," Tosh continued, "they're perfect unwitting spies. Keeping them in prison wastes the opportunity. Let them go back to China as heroes—and likely gain high-level positions. Meanwhile, they're feeding us intel every day, no payoffs or drop-offs needed. We'll make it look like we only caught the U.S. traitors. Their social networks will carry that warning, which we've already rigged with a couple of test messages."

Silence. Then the President spoke in a different tone—calculating, impressed.

"You're suggesting we avoid the embarrassment of having over a thousand foreign spies operating here undetected. Instead, we bust a few dozen American conspirators, salvage the intel, and gain a major win. Brilliant, Nicolás. I'm calling off the order now."

The line clicked over. Tosh overheard the President loop in the Attorney General, the FBI Director, and CIA Director Mark Thiel:

"Gentlemen, new plan," the President announced. "Arrest only the U.S. businessmen and politicians. Stand down on everyone else. The 'evidence' was inconclusive, so I don't want them touched or even surveilled. Understood?"

They all answered yes, though Thiel voiced surprise:

"What changed, sir?"

"Classified," the President replied flatly. "But this is in our national interest, it keeps you employed with honors, and we'll use these individuals as future assets. Also, stop any evacuation of our own people in China immediately."

He ended the call. Returning to Tosh's line, the President chuckled softly:

"We've exceeded my wildest expectations. Now we both have tasks. Bring General Collins up to speed."

"Yes, sir," Tosh said.

Moments later, Tosh connected General Collins and Rainer. The President rejoined them briefly:

"Gentlemen, let me summarize." He did so, then fired off orders: "Rainer, once the data finishes transferring, insert those 'warning' messages in their social feeds to confirm they'll run. Then we let the chips fall where they may."

General Collins exhaled, a rare note of emotion coloring his voice:

"Nicolás, this is the smartest political move we could make—turning these infiltrators into *our* spies. It transforms a fiasco into a gold mine."

"Agreed," Tosh said, feeling relief and a sense of awe.

They closed the connection. Rainer, alone at the data center in Zermatt, stared at the empty screen and allowed himself a grin.

"Wow," he murmured.

Chapter 76

*Zermatt, Switzerland | Washington, D.C. | Miami, Florida
2016 – Day 8, 7:30 A.M. (CET) / 1:30 P.M. (ET)*

In the hush of Zermatt's data center, *Rainer* watched the final data-transfer status inch toward completion. From his office, he maintained a live connection with both *General Collins* and *Nicolás Tosh*—the three men stationed in different corners of the globe yet unified by a single objective.

At last, the status bar blinked **COMPLETE**.

"Done," Rainer announced. "We've got it all, gentlemen."

There was no time for congratulations. Tosh's voice, coming through the neural link, cut in:

"Rainer, we need that social-network chatter online immediately. Every second counts."

Rainer glanced at his console, where the pre-scripted "warning" messages awaited deployment across the targeted accounts. They had been meticulously designed to alert Chen's operatives that a U.S. crackdown was imminent—thus pushing them to flee, while unwittingly carrying their *identifiers* (and feeding intelligence back to Zermatt).

"Right away, Nicolás," Rainer replied. "We're starting now."

He tapped a simple command. Across the quantum supercomputer's interface, message after coded message cascaded into the digital channels of Chen's network—tiny ripples that would soon create a wave of panic, fueling an exodus the White House eagerly anticipated.

Chapter 77

Shanghai, China – 2016, Day 8, 7:45 P.M. (CST)

Andy Chen scowled as his iPad lit up with yet another automatic sync. *Really need to fix that,* he thought. He'd just returned from Pudong International Airport after watching Senator Molina board a flight back to D.C. Taking the Maglev train at over 400 kph might have been exhilarating under better circumstances, but all Chen could feel was unease. Unbeknownst to him, every moment—Molina's departure, Chen's own ride—was already logged in Zermatt's data center and mirrored in the White House bunker.

Now, in his Shanghai condo, Chen positioned himself at his desktop, ready to post cryptic messages on Twitter and Facebook—his preferred channel for issuing instructions to the **operatives** he oversaw. Ostensibly, these were spiritual or philosophical quotes—Confucius proverbs weaving gentle lessons on life. But each phrase signaled a specific command: confirming pickups, scheduling deliveries, authorizing payments. Chen was the only one allowed to craft these messages, a self-appointed "spiritual guide." Replies like "Thank you for your guidance" meant the instructions were received; "Your wisdom enlightens us" confirmed a mission's success.

He was about to post the first set of cues when he noticed a bizarre new message on Facebook:

"The enemies of the enemy are at the gates."

Frowning, he snatched his satellite phone and punched in a trusted contact's number.

"I just found a message on our group feed I didn't write," he barked. "Can you see who posted it?"

Before the line could respond, another alert pinged—this time on Twitter:

"Today, before sundown your army will fall to the swords of the avenger."

Chen's grip tightened on the phone.

"There's another one," he muttered grimly. "What the hell is going on?"

He was too preoccupied to notice that yet another auto-backup window blinked onto his iPad screen, an invisible sign of just how compromised his entire operation had become.

Chapter 78

Zermatt, Switzerland | Washington, D.C. | Miami, Florida
2016 – Day 8, 8:00 A.M. (ET) / 2:00 P.M. (CET)

A world map glowed on the **Zermatt Data Center** monitors, outlining the surging lines of social-media traffic. *Rainer* poised at the console, while *General Collins* and *Nicolás Tosh* observed from their respective locations, neural connections uniting them.

"We're ready," Rainer said. "The system will intercept unusual spikes headed to Facebook and Twitter, redirecting them to Eastern Europe. The data hidden on those servers details today's raids on the U.S. businessmen and politicians. Soon enough, the rumor-mill will leak it."

Green vectors flashed across the screen—thousands of posts from Chen's network, all funneling into the social platforms before bouncing to Russian Federation and Eastern Bloc servers.

"Looks solid," Tosh murmured. "We've got them locked."

Then something else caught Tosh's eye: a small linguistic tag in the corner of Chen's feed.

"Wait—did you notice the language?" Tosh asked quietly. "Yes," General Collins said. "Cantonese."

Tosh's mind churned.

"Rainer, query Chen's archived data for any meetings or contacts with official **Chinese** government representatives."

A few seconds later, the result was stark: **none**.

"Gentlemen," Tosh said, "Chen isn't working for the People's Republic of China. He's working for **Taiwan**."

Rainer's eyebrows rose. "But we've seen intel flowing into mainland China."

"Likely via Taiwan-based companies," Tosh replied. "It's a neat cover to keep them competitive with China's rapid growth. So, in effect, a thousand-plus operatives are about to stampede into China believing they're Chinese agents—when they're actually working for Taiwan…and, inadvertently, for **us**."

They ran a quick AI check: Did Chen's recruits *know* they were working for Taiwan?

Answer: *No.* They believed it was the Chinese government.

"They've never been explicitly told," Collins observed. "All they see are lavish gifts, bribes, or nepotistic job placements," Tosh added. "A *real* Chinese state operation rarely works this way. Taiwan, though, can slip around Mainland corruption to support Chen's network."

He paused, letting the new discovery settle in.

"We'll keep them in play, let them run straight home. In the end, it benefits us. For now…we watch."

The connections ended, each man quietly absorbing the scope of Chen's ruse—and the advantage the Zermatt Data Center had just gained in the global spy game.

Chapter 79

Shanghai, China – 2016, Day 8, 8:30 P.M. (CST)

"Mr. Chen, we traced the mystery posts. They originated from Eastern European servers aligned with the Russian Federation," reported the network manager. "They're hinting at massive raids and arrests coming soon. The Russians seem to have caught wind of it, too."

Chen felt a cold knot in his stomach. He regretted letting Senator Molina fly home. Now, ten ominous messages had appeared in his group channels, sparking a frenzy among his **operatives**, who bombarded him with pleas— "Guide us, master." He had spent over a decade building this network. Its very existence was now at stake, and there was no contingency plan for the U.S. businessmen or politicians he'd recruited. They couldn't just vanish into China.

A new post flared across his feeds:

"The master can now move his army and face the real enemy inside their castle."

Who was behind this? Possibly an insider. Yet Chen could do little but trigger his last-resort fail-safe. He typed a single command:

"Wisdom awaits you. Follow the path to righteousness."

That cryptic phrase, posted on both Facebook and Twitter, meant every Chinese national and American-born Chinese operative was to **drop everything**—grab travel papers, head to the airport, and flee immediately. No questions, no delays. Chen hated sacrificing the American collaborators, but he had no plan to shelter them in China. They'd become liabilities, likely arrested, possibly exposing him. But the larger network might survive without them.

Within seconds, the Zermatt Data Center's quantum system registered Chen's evacuation signal. *General Collins*, *Rainer*, and *Nicolás Tosh* received an automatic alert.

"Gentlemen, Phase One is complete," Collins said. "They're on the run, just as we intended. I'll inform the President."

Tosh lingered, an uneasy twinge gnawing at him. *We've crossed a line,* he thought. *There's no going back now.*

Chapter 80

*Zermatt, Switzerland | Washington, D.C. | Miami, Florida
2016 – Day 8, 9:00 A.M. (ET) / 3:00 P.M. (CET)*

After **General Collins** briefed the President on Andy Chen's frantic orders for his U.S. operatives to flee, the general added a political note:

"Mr. President, we'd like you to offer plea deals to each of the American businessmen and politicians—including Senator Molina—in return for confidentiality. Their testimonies should be sealed to protect Chen's identity."

He knew *Nicolás Tosh* had proposed letting the Chinese operatives slip away, so this would prevent the U.S. conspirators from blowing the entire ruse.

The President nodded thoughtfully:

"Agreed. I'll issue those instructions immediately."

"We'll figure out how to pass that along to Chen, sir," Collins said. "A gesture to show we aren't after him directly."

"Keep me posted," the President replied, ending the call.

In short order, White House aides began drafting the confidential plea offers—a quiet move that would keep both domestic fallout and further escalations with foreign powers to a minimum. Meanwhile, at the Zermatt Data Center, Tosh and Collins coordinated how best to discreetly convey the news to Chen, preserving the delicate balance that kept Chen's network—and the U.S. advantage—intact.

Chapter 81

Boston, Massachusetts – 2016, Day 8, 9:00 A.M. (ET)

Joe Lee's hands shook as he scrolled through the alarming messages on Facebook and Twitter. The final instruction—*leave the country immediately*—sealed his fate. His life in the United States was over, and the only question left was whether he'd make it out as a free man.

He'd just arrived at his office when the directive flashed onto his screen. His resignation letter, prepared months ago in a pang of paranoia, was still tucked in his desk drawer. He printed it, scribbled a signature, and left it on his manager's desk—citing "family reasons" and waiving any final salary or benefits. He packed a few personal items, eyes darting nervously at coworkers who had no clue he'd vanish within minutes.

Five minutes later, he was in the elevator, heart pounding. He barely glanced back as he exited the building. A quick cab ride to **Logan International** put him on a last-minute flight to **New York's JFK**, departing within the hour. By noon, he'd be bound for **Beijing**. The entire pivot—from receiving Andy Chen's message to fleeing U.S. soil—took barely three hours.

Joe sank into his airplane seat, forcing back the panic clenching his chest. He pictured the team he'd left behind, the half-finished projects he'd abruptly abandoned. Guilt flared, but fear won out. For better or worse, he was following the only directive that might keep him out of prison—or worse.

Chapter 82

Palo Alto, California – 2016, Day 8, 6:00 A.M. (PT)

The moment the cryptic command appeared on *San-Chang Lin's* Facebook wall, he knew his American dream was finished. Within minutes, he had stuffed a rolling suitcase with only his most essential belongings. A moving company would eventually deal with whatever remained. He printed out his resignation letter—nearly identical to Joe Lee's—slipped it into an envelope, and drove to his office.

In the hushed lobby, he collected a handful of personal items, leaving the rest behind without a second glance. He placed the sealed letter on his admin's desk, feeling the finality of it hit him. As he returned to the car, he tapped a quick tweet to Joe:

"I'm going to see the master, today."

Joe's reply was instant:

"Me, as well. Everyone I know is going."

A few more messages to mutual contacts confirmed the exodus was widespread. They were all heading "home," or so Chen had decreed. By *7:00 A.M.* Pacific Time, a hired sedan deposited San-Chang at **San Francisco International Airport**. Three hours later, he was in the air on a flight to Tokyo, connecting onward to Shanghai. The life he had built in California—job, friendships, quiet ambitions—now lay behind him, sacrificed to the silent pull of a distant master he had never even met in person.

Chapter 83

Zermatt, Switzerland | Washington, D.C. | Miami, Florida
2016 – Day 8, 11:00 A.M. (ET) / 5:00 P.M. (CET)

In the last three hours, *General Collins*, *Rainer*, and *Nicolás Tosh* observed a staggering exodus of **Andy Chen's** operatives. One by one, they boarded planes—most bound for Asia, a few hopping domestic flights to bigger hubs for international connections. By mid-afternoon on the East Coast, nearly all had left U.S. soil.

"Rainer," Tosh remarked, "we owe you big time." "What—am I more important than the Quantum supercomputer?" Rainer teased. "Let's just say without you, we'd still be relying on grainy visuals and guesswork."

Earlier, the President had briefly joined their feed to confirm that the **CIA** and **FBI** were set to arrest the American conspirators, keeping the entire operation sealed off from most government channels. Only a tight circle of officials knew the plan. The President also finalized a structure shielding Chen's identity—on condition that Chen remain *far* from U.S. territory indefinitely. Sometime in the future, the U.S. might lean on Chen's China-based network if needed; in return, if he crossed any lines, Washington would tip off the Chinese government about his true activities.

By late morning, as soon as the data center confirmed that every operative was airborne or en route, General Collins placed a call to the President:

"Sir, they're out—or nearly so."

That was all the President needed. He gave the Joint CIA-FBI Task Force the final green light to launch the arrests, sealing the fate of the

U.S. co-conspirators—and leaving Chen's unknowing "army" safely under watch half a world away.

Chapter 84

San Antonio, Texas – 2016, Day 8, 12:00 P.M. (CT)

Antonio Barrios was a natural bridge between worlds: the son of a Nicaraguan immigrant mechanic and an All-American Olympic swimmer. Born and raised in San Antonio, he'd grown up bilingual and street-smart, mastering the art of fitting in with both Hispanic and Anglo communities. At **six-foot-two** with a compact, muscular frame, a military-style haircut, and a permanent five-o'clock shadow, he looked more like a Navy SEAL than a rising politician. Yet here he was, serving in the **Texas State Legislature** with eyes on a future seat in the U.S. Congress.

Years earlier, he'd solved his campaign-funding woes through a swift maneuver that cost him nothing, courtesy of a donor connection with **Andy Chen**—though Barrios never felt beholden to him. Chen might have believed he had Barrios in his pocket, but the lawmaker had no intention of bending to any unlawful demands.

That afternoon, Barrios drove his massive double-cab pickup into a modest church parking lot, preparing to meet local leaders about deportation concerns—pregnant women, legal residents married to U.S. citizens, and children torn from families. He had to walk a political tightrope: show empathy for the Hispanic community while maintaining a tough stance on illegal immigration to satisfy much of his voter base.

He was just stepping out of his truck when a convoy of black SUVs roared into the lot, blocking his path. A knot of **FBI agents** jumped out, weapons holstered but hands near the grips, their stances bristling with authority. One stepped forward, badge flashing.

"Antonio Barrios?" "Yes," Barrios said warily.

"You're under arrest."

Before he could respond, they spun him around, cuffing his wrists, then hustled him into a vehicle. Inside, they read him his rights, calmly stating charges of **espionage** and **high treason**. The SUVs sped off as quickly as they'd arrived, leaving the church group and stunned constituents staring at each other in disbelief—car keys in hand, no idea what to do with the idling pickup.

In under a minute, everything Barrios had worked for—his position, his reputation, his dreams for higher office—shattered like glass.

Chapter 85

Chicago, Illinois – 2016, Day 8, 12:00 P.M. (CT)

Roland Keough stood at the pinnacle of success. His company had developed a cutting-edge **hand dryer**—a sleek device that dried hands in fifteen seconds by sucking in and dehumidifying air before blasting it back out. Recently, Keough's engineering team had gone further, rolling out an innovative sink with a motion-sensitive soap dispenser on the left, a water faucet in the middle, and the dryer to the right, all integrated into one seamless unit. It was poised to debut nationally, and Keough's sales staff from around the country had converged in Chicago for the launch.

Not long ago, things had been far from rosy. Keough lacked the capital to push his advanced "dry-air" technology beyond prototypes, and sales of older dryer models were plummeting. Then he met **Andy Chen** at a trade show. Suddenly, funding flowed, though Keough never fully grasped what Chen might expect in return.

That morning, he entered the large conference room where his entire sales team waited, brimming with optimism. But before he could speak, a clamor erupted behind him—shouts, the crash of overturned chairs. Spinning around, Keough found himself face-to-face with armed **FBI agents** storming toward him. Within minutes, he was under arrest, accused of espionage and high treason. As he was led away, his stunned employees looked on, the company's grand launch and bright future dissolving in an instant.

Chapter 86

Zermatt, Switzerland | Washington, D.C. | Miami, Florida
2016 – Day 8, 8:00 P.M. (CET) / 2:00 P.M. (ET)

For the past three hours, *General Collins*, *Rainer*, and *Nicolás Tosh* had monitored the exodus of Andy Chen's operatives. Nearly all had departed U.S. soil, while the FBI prepared arrests for the remaining **American businessmen** and **politicians**. Yet one issue nagged Rainer:

"General, many of these people never actually delivered anything illegal. Some were never even asked. Are we labeling them traitors simply by association with Chen?"

Collins shrugged:

"That's for the Attorney General to decide. Some folks may be guilty only of receiving Chen's funds, not espionage."

Tosh chimed in:

"And we already have everything we need in the CDA data. Why burn resources on interrogations?"

Collins grinned:

"Let's bring in the President. He's been on the line all day."

A calm voice sounded:

"Gentlemen, I'm here. One moment—I'm signing documents with my aide unaware I'm talking to you."

A minute later, the President returned:

"All right, fill me in."

Collins explained that many suspects—some perhaps naive—never provided *anything* to Chen, though they were part of the same network. The President then looped in Attorney General **Gene Cartwright**, who reaffirmed they could impose varying charges: from **conspiracy** to outright **industrial espionage**, or lesser penalties like **money-laundering fines**.

Meanwhile, Rainer ran a quick search on who had actually stolen or delivered data. The results showed:

1.   **Seven** had explicitly been told to collect or provide illegal material in exchange for Chen's funds.

2.   **Only three** of those seven actually delivered something—one leaked classified Army docs, two shared proprietary corporate data.

3.   The rest either did nothing or didn't realize they were part of a conspiracy.

"Clean as a whistle," Cartwright noted, reviewing Rainer's confirmation that the money originally came from the *Taiwan Central Bank*—i.e., not from an overtly criminal source.

"So, Mr. President," Cartwright concluded, "we can charge one with espionage, two with industrial espionage, and four with conspiracy. Everyone else can face milder sanctions—perhaps refunds of Chen's 'loans'—so long as they sign confidentiality agreements."

The President concurred:

"Yes. Have them sign NDAs and repay the money. Keep the rest out of jail. Of the seven, none are elected officials, correct?"

Collins scanned the data:

"Correct. Senator Molina isn't involved at that level."

"In that case, let him go too," the President said. "He's part of the mass release, provided he signs the usual confidentiality terms. I'll handle him personally."

Finally, the President dialed **CIA Director Mark Thiel**:

"Mark, new directives: release everyone except those seven. Before release, each must sign an NDA and vow no further contact with Andy Chen on penalty of treason charges. They also must repay Chen's loans. Gene Cartwright will draft the documents."

"Understood, Mr. President," Thiel answered. "We'll halt their transfers and get the paperwork done locally."

With that, the President signed off, leaving the group scrambling to execute his orders. Within hours, a wave of suspects found themselves freed—under ironclad gag orders—while a select few now faced the highest charges, caught by the evidence gleaned from the Zermatt Data Center's unstoppable algorithms.

Chapter 87

San Antonio, Texas – FBI Interrogation Room 2016 – Day 8, 5:00 P.M. (CT)

Antonio Barrios felt his world crumble in a matter of hours. Shortly after his arrest, FBI agents grilled him relentlessly. Yes, he admitted, he had accepted legally documented "loans" from Andy Chen—but he had never done anything in return, nor had he been asked. He insisted he would never betray his country.

The agents threatened him with life in prison, treason charges, the end of his political career. Yet they had scant evidence linking him to espionage; their head office offered no new leads for three hours straight. Nonetheless, they planned to transfer him to Washington, D.C. by evening.

Just as they marched Barrios away to change into a jumpsuit, an official notice flashed on every agent's phone: new orders from Washington. One agent stepped forward:

"Barrios, looks like you caught a break. Call your attorney—*now*."

Barrios had no criminal lawyer, but within minutes, his staff arranged for the best defense attorney in town: **Luis Felipe Rodríguez**. Furious at Barrios's treatment, Rodríguez sped to the FBI office, fuming about constitutional violations—until his phone rang:

"Mr. Rodríguez? One moment, please, for the U.S. Attorney General."

Rodríguez froze. **Gene Cartwright** came on the line:

"Luis Felipe, it's been a while. Listen, your client took $5.5 million in loans from Andy Chen—a foreign spy—fueling Barrios's campaigns.

Initially, we planned to charge him with conspiracy. But with the President's approval, we won't charge him *if* he accepts the following terms:

1. Pay a $250,000 fine.

2. Repay Chen's loans as they come due.

3. Sign a strict confidentiality agreement (and you, too).

4. No further contact with Chen or his people—under surveillance at all times. Any breach, and we prosecute."

Cartwright ended the call abruptly. Stunned, Rodríguez drove on to the FBI office, where an anxious Barrios paced an interrogation room.

"Luis Felipe, this is outrageous—" Barrios began.

"Shut up and sit," the lawyer snapped. "You're in deep trouble."

An FBI agent appeared with a stack of documents. Rodríguez studied them, then explained each point to Barrios:

"Violate this deal, and they *will* charge you. Understood?"

Barrios nodded. With a notary present, he signed everything. Rodríguez likewise added his signature to the confidentiality clause. Minutes later, they walked out of the FBI office under the fading Texas sunlight.

"Thank you," Barrios began.

Rodríguez cut him off:

"Antonio, I'm *disappointed.* You'll pay my legal bill in full. Our friendship is done, and you've lost my vote—forever."

Barrios said nothing, realizing how close he'd come to watching his entire life truly implode.

Chapter 88

Chicago, Illinois – FBI Office 2016 – Day 8, 6:00 P.M. (CT)

Ronald Keough exhaled with relief, stepping out of the FBI building beside his attorney. Just hours ago, he'd faced the threat of espionage charges; now, his signature on a strict confidentiality agreement spared him that fate.

"Ronald, you used terrible judgment," his lawyer admonished. "Look," Keough replied, "without Chen's money, I'd have gone under. I couldn't even cover rent or payroll—he never asked for a thing in return."

"Good thing, or you'd be in prison. Make sure you never contact him again."

Across the country, dozens of Chen's other associates experienced similar scenes—walking free under gag orders and repayment terms. Only **seven** faced formal charges, each pleading guilty under sealed agreements. Six received sentences of two to five years; one, caught with top-secret military documents, was sentenced to life with the possibility of parole. Per the President's directive, the entire operation wrapped up before midnight, leaving Chen's U.S. network gutted and its would-be conspirators either jailed or bound by the tightest legal constraints imaginable.

Chapter 89

Washington, D.C. – Dulles Airport/FBI Office 2016 – Day 8, 6:00 A.M. (ET)

Gilbert Molina stepped off the plane feeling raw and on the verge of collapse. The moment he cleared the jetway, two men approached:

"Senator, please come with us."

"FBI?" Molina's voice wavered. "Yes, sir. It'll go smoother if you cooperate."

He nodded numbly. They ushered him through Immigration, collected his passport, then led him into a cramped FBI office located inside **Dulles International Airport**. There, one agent spoke firmly:

"You'll need to call your attorney. Make sure it's a **criminal** defense lawyer."

A sick swirl of dread tightened in Molina's gut. Still, he clung to the hope that he wasn't actually charged. He dialed **Phil Duncan**, the seasoned defense attorney he'd used for minor dustups in the past:

"Phil? It's Gilbert— "Gilbert, what happened?" "I just landed from Shanghai. FBI picked me up at the gate; they won't say much, only that I need counsel present." "Have they charged you?" "No." "Then likely it's some sort of deal. Let me guess—something to do with your father?" "I don't know. Can you come right now?" "I'm on my way."

Molina hung up, informing the agents that his lawyer was en route. Meanwhile, Duncan inwardly cursed the timing. He had never liked **Leroy Sinclair**, Gilbert's father, and now this fiasco smelled far worse than standard political trouble. Still, Duncan would defend Gilbert regardless—he was in too deep to back out now.

Chapter 90

Zermatt, Switzerland – Zermatt Data Center 2016 – Day 8, 12:30 P.M. (CET)

Sitting at his console in the glass-walled nerve center, *Rainer* multitasked at an almost superhuman level. With one mental thread, he tracked **Andy Chen**—keeping an eye on Chen's frantic coordination of operatives, financial transactions, and potential new "drops" or clandestine payments. Yet another channel zeroed in on **Senator Gilbert Molina**, listening to every flicker of his thoughts.

Molina was pivotal: the only U.S. Congressman linked directly to Chen's funding. *Were these two conspiracies—Molina's circle and Chen's network—truly separate events, or different faces of the same operation?* Rainer didn't have a final answer, but he intended to find one.

He silently approved of **General Collins's** plan to intercept Molina the moment he landed at Dulles, pressuring him to sign a strict confidentiality agreement before leaving the airport. One more scandal among U.S. lawmakers was the last thing anyone needed—especially on the heels of headlines about one businessman charged with espionage and six more indicted for conspiracy.

Alongside this hush-hush approach, Rainer also prepared "identifiers" at Dulles so **Molina's attorney, Phil Duncan** could be scanned and registered in the network. With the President's authorization, they'd deploy **CDAs 322–324** on Duncan to probe any hidden ties to Chen. Two identifiers aimed at the FBI's Dulles office soon picked up Molina's brain signals—already in the system courtesy of Christopher Musial's earlier registration. By passively scanning for any new signals within that office, Rainer ensured Duncan's arrival would be captured instantly.

When Duncan walks in, Rainer thought, *we'll snare him too.* Once again, Zermatt's invisible architecture would slip another unsuspecting mind into the web, gleaning answers they had no other way to obtain.

Chapter 91

Washington, D.C. – Dulles Airport/FBI Office 2016 – Day 8, 7:00 A.M. (ET)

Attorney **Phil Duncan** entered the cramped FBI office determined to make quick work of whatever crisis had drawn him here. An agent handed him a single-page agreement, summarizing **Senator Gilbert Molina's** predicament in clipped, matter-of-fact terms. Duncan spent several minutes in silence, scrutinizing each clause. Finally, he turned to Molina:

"Gilbert, it's straightforward:

1.   You avoid all future contact with **Andy Chen**.

2.   You pay back Chen's so-called 'loans' on schedule.

3.   You sign this confidentiality agreement. Understood?"

Molina nodded wearily.

"Yes."

"Because you involved me," Duncan added, "I also have to sign the NDA."

Both men jotted their signatures. No one spoke further as they left the FBI office together, returning to the bustling airport corridors.

"Got luggage?" Duncan asked.   "Just this carry-on," Molina murmured.

They reached Duncan's car. Once inside, the lawyer's exasperation boiled over:

"Of all the attorneys in D.C., you had to drag *me* into this?"

Molina's only response was a half-sullen shrug. In truth, this was exactly the "break glass in case of emergency" scenario he'd foreseen. But it felt more like a moral free-fall than a rescue.

Unseen by them, **Zermatt Data Center** had already latched onto Duncan's brain signals. As he drove toward downtown Washington, his entire life—secrets, contacts, ambitions—began streaming into Rainer's neural network. Duncan's ominous feeling of discomfort turned out to be more justified than he could possibly imagine.

Chapter 92

Zermatt, Switzerland – Zermatt Data Center 2016 – Day 8, 2:30 P.M. (CET)

Rainer and *General Collins* spent half an hour poring over the neural data on **Phil Duncan**. They confirmed he'd never been involved with **ex-President Thomas** nor had direct dealings with **Andy Chen**—those were the *only* clear points. Beyond that, the situation turned far more complicated.

Duncan, it turned out, was a longstanding **recruiter** for the **Taiwanese government**. His role: identify up-and-coming politicians lacking funds (like Molina), entrepreneurs with ties to China, and promising Chinese-American university students in STEM fields. Duncan funneled these names to Taiwan's embassy, which typically responded within two weeks, telling him which prospects to cultivate. Over the past decade, he'd contributed thousands of leads.

To maintain cover, Duncan acquired a struggling **weekly business journal** in D.C. five years earlier—keeping just enough staff and freelance printing services to publish four hours' worth of content each week. In reality, his small team posed as journalists while scouring commercial registries, local media, and universities across the country in search of new prospects. None of them realized how or why this intel was being compiled.

In exchange, Taipei paid Duncan millions over the years—most notably a **$250,000 monthly retainer**. Now, thanks to Rainer's neural network sweeps, the full picture of Duncan's clandestine role lay exposed on the Zermatt Data Center's screens. Rainer and Collins exchanged a tense glance: *This infiltration ran deeper than they'd ever suspected.*

Chapter 93

Washington, D.C. – The White House Bunker 2016 – Day 8, 2:45 P.M. (ET)

General Collins's war-room bunker thrummed with activity. His team pored over the lives of **1,270** identified **Chen** operatives—an effort that could stretch for months. The next step loomed even bigger: analyzing everyone those operatives had ever interacted with. *Rainer* had already volunteered the **Zermatt Data Center** for that broader sweep.

"What do you think?" Rainer asked over the secure line. "I see multiple networks," Collins replied. "Chen never met **Phil Duncan**, yet Duncan's intel to Taiwan eventually funnels to Chen."

They recapped how **Duncan** would first spot likely recruits—politicians in need of campaign cash, entrepreneurs with China links, promising Chinese-American STEM students. Duncan would pose as a wealthy attorney, feeling them out over months. Once he approved, Taipei took over, feeding the data to Chen, who handled the final recruitment. Meanwhile, **Chinese nationals** were scouted directly by Chen's team in mainland China and sent abroad.

"I'll request time with the President," Collins said, "to discuss these new revelations. I'll get back to you with a slot."

"Fine," Rainer answered. "And about *Chen*—we should contact him soon." "Agreed. I'll handle it," Collins said.

With that, they ended the call, each aware that the U.S. government's newfound knowledge might permanently shift the balance in this silent, high-stakes power struggle.

Chapter 94

Zermatt, Switzerland – Zermatt Data Center 2016 – Day 8, 10:00 P.M. (CET)

After General Collins gave *Rainer* the green light, the Zermatt Data Center began processing **CDA-324** data on everyone Chen's 1,270 operatives had interacted with—an exponentially larger dataset than Chen's own CDA-323 file. For now, Rainer honed in on one key question: *Which individuals outside Chen's known roster also showed up consistently in the same social networks?*

He ran a query, letting the system sift through extended social-media links. After fifteen minutes, the result appeared: **seven** such individuals. Another half-hour of cross-referencing revealed something startling:

1.   Chen hosted **20** private network groups.

2.   The system found over **500** additional social-media groups linked to those same networks.

3.   Those **same 7** "outsiders" appeared in *all* 500 groups, though they rarely posted.

4.   In the last two days, they'd been conspicuously probing for info about Chen's vanished U.S. network.

Rainer asked the AI:

"What do these 7 'observers' actually do?" **System**: *They appear as silent members across hundreds of groups. Historically, minimal activity. Recently, they've been active—inquiring about Chen's operation.*

He pressed further:

"Any link to Chen or **Phil Duncan**?" **System**: *An indirect link. Some of the 500 groups also contain individuals Duncan once scouted. However, the 7 observers aren't direct recruits of Duncan or Chen. They simply inhabit every corner of these overlapping networks.*

An uneasy realization dawned: **Taiwan** was potentially scooping an entire knowledge base of American vulnerabilities, right under everyone's nose. Rainer flagged this as an emergency. Within an hour, he was on a secure conference call with General Collins and *Nicolás Tosh*, sounding the alarm that the infiltration might run deeper than any of them had imagined.

Chapter 95

Zermatt, Switzerland | Washington, D.C. | Miami, Florida 2016 – Day 8, 11:00 P.M. (CET) / 5:00 P.M. (ET)

Over a secure video link, *Rainer* presented every finding about the seven mysterious "observers" infiltrating hundreds of social-media groups, outlining their possible ties to Chen's network and **Phil Duncan**'s scouting. *The President* spoke first:

"We need to bring Chen on board as we planned. **Tosh, Rainer**, repeat what you did with Chen's previous operatives—register these seven observers via CDA and find out if anyone in Duncan's 'scout list' has already been recruited. Take no chances and waste no time. We won't 'spook' these newcomers until we know exactly what they're doing, who they contact, and what they've accomplished.

General Collins and I will maintain *radio silence* with our own agencies—CIA, FBI—to give you the freedom to operate without tipping anyone off. Let us know how long you'll need."

Rainer nodded on-screen, the neural net's glow visible in the background.

"Yes, Mr. President. First step: locate these seven physically so we can deploy the necessary 'identifiers' and 'carriers.' We'll also re-check every scouted individual to see if any slipped past our net. That'll take a few days."

The President leaned forward:

"Good. As for contacting Chen—let's do it now."

Chapter 96

*Shanghai, China | Washington, D.C. – White House Bunker
2016 – Day 9, 6:00 A.M. (CST) / 6:00 P.M. (ET)*

Andy Chen was running on fumes. For two days, he had juggled frantic phone calls and accommodations for operatives fleeing the U.S. Now, with a flight to Hong Kong leaving in two hours, he was ready to meet his superiors—**Lin Chang** first, then the true boss behind everything.

Luggage in hand, Chen headed for the door when a voice—silent yet unmistakable—spoke inside his head:

"Mr. Chen, good morning. Relax. Have a seat. We need to talk. I'm transmitting my thoughts into your mind directly. You can speak aloud, and I'll hear you. No devices are in your home or on your body. We could do this anywhere. Also, we've already downloaded your entire life story—recorded in high-definition. We see and hear every thought you have, live."

Stunned, Chen set his bag down and obeyed.

"We suggest you call your Hong Kong boss right now. Cancel your trip. You won't be going."

Chen complied, hands trembling, canceling the flight he had been sure was critical.

"Mr. Chen," the voice continued, **"we know everything about you, your network, and your employer. Two choices: we can turn you over to the Chinese government or you can work for us, maintaining your operation as usual—on condition that you never again set foot in the U.S."**

Chen swallowed. **"So I'm serving two masters?"**

"Your current employer will never know. If you even think of telling them, we'll see it in real time."

"What do you want me to do?" Chen asked.

"Carry on, just as you planned: reorganize in China, use your operatives as you see fit. We won't intervene unless you jeopardize U.S. interests. We'll also place them where *we* need them. Now watch..."

A flurry of vivid images—Chen's entire life—flashed through his mind, followed by a text log of his *most private thoughts*. He saw lines like: *I'll find a way to warn my superiors. Be patient. Imperialist pigs— I'm smarter than you. I'll be your docile servant until I defeat you.*

Silence fell, leaving him chilled.

"Mr. Chen," the voice resumed, **"you truly have no choice. And if you try evading us or disclaiming what's happening, we'll release proof of your corruption and treachery to your government. You'd be finished."**

Realizing he was cornered, Chen exhaled in defeat. **"Who...are you?"**

"Call me Freedom-Hawk. Continue your normal routines. When we need you, you'll know."

Chen could only sit there, heart pounding, as the driver honked outside—unaware his boss had just become a double agent under the tightest surveillance imaginable.

Chapter 97

*Washington, D.C. – The White House 2016 – Day 9, 7:00
P.M. (ET)*

General Collins ended his direct neural exchange with **Andy Chen** and allowed himself a slow exhale. Mentally, he observed *Nicolás Tosh* and the President, whose faces were visible via secure link.

"This man hates America with a passion," the President said gravely. "He's like a feral animal, and I'm not sure we can tame him. But you covered every angle I can think of, General."

"Team effort, sir," Collins replied, nodding toward Tosh. "I couldn't have done it alone."

The President stood, checking his watch with a wry smile:

"We still have pressing issues, gentlemen, but there's a state dinner tonight—ironically, with the **Chinese president**. He's here lobbying for G-7 acceptance. I need to go play host. Let's reconvene after the event or tomorrow morning."

With that, the President left, his mind already juggling the delicate diplomatic role ahead—even as, behind the scenes, he and his team had just coerced one of China's fiercest covert agents into unthinkable compliance.

Chapter 98

Washington, D.C. – The White House 2016 – Day 9, 11:00 P.M. (ET)

The President entered the Oval Office still in his formal attire from the state dinner—ironic, given the Chinese President was the evening's guest of honor. Loosening his bow tie, he addressed General Collins (linked via the White House bunker) and *Rainer* and *Nicolás Tosh* (connected remotely):

"Gentlemen, thank you for waiting. Let's hear the latest."

General Collins began:

"Sir, after analyzing Chen's social-media groups, Rainer found **seven individuals** who appear in every group but don't appear in Chen's known network. They also join **500** other media groups, each hosting at least one recruit scouted by **Phil Duncan**. At first glance, these seven are mostly silent, only recently asking about Chen's fiasco."

Nodding, the President turned to Tosh:

"And Duncan?"

"He scouts potential recruits—politicians who need campaign funds, businessmen who need capital, and Chinese American students—then hands names to Taiwan's embassy. But we still lack clarity on who's *actually* compromised."

Rainer explained:

"We're gathering ID info on all of Duncan's scouted individuals. Parallel to that, we'll watch for signs of recruitment—like travel plans to China. Also, we can cross-reference his **CDA-324** data to see who's actively become part of Chen's network."

The President let out a grim sigh:

"And if Taiwan can plant 1,270 operatives here through Chen, I wonder who else has done the same. If word got out, it'd devastate our credibility—domestically and globally. Let's keep this strictly between us."

They all agreed. The President straightened his posture:

"Carry on with your plan. I'm available twenty-four/seven. Let's end this quietly."

With that, the meeting ended. The President lingered for a moment, pondering how close a brush this was with national humiliation. At least, he told himself, the synergy between Collins's team and Tosh's mathematical breakthroughs had already brought major results—and might yet shield the country from an even deeper crisis.

Chapter 99

Zermatt, Switzerland | The White House, Washington, D.C. | Miami, Florida 2016 – Day 10, 6:00 A.M. (CET) / 12:00 P.M. (ET)

"Mr. Sábato, how do you plan to get started?" Rainer heard General Collins's question echo through the secure neural link.

"We'll access Phil Duncan's CDA-323 file, extracting every name he proposed to Taiwan's government—people they actually cleared."

Nicolás Tosh stayed silent, worried about pressing the limits of the G-7 resolution. He made a mental note to have his Zurich legal team review how far the President's directives could stretch the protocol on "Weapons of Mass Destruction–level" CDAs.

Once Tosh and Collins ended their call, Rainer turned to the data center systems. He searched Duncan's archived *memory feed* for instances where the Taiwanese Embassy "cleared" a name. Then, to avoid missing anything, he also looked for any follow-up meetings Duncan held with each candidate.

On a giant screen dominating the rock-hewn lobby, glimpses of Duncan's life played at high speed. Rainer braced himself—he knew the final list of "cleared" recruits would be massive. Once identified, they would need to be **registered** on the neural network and have their lives downloaded, exactly like Chen's people. With only so many *carriers* and *identifier* devices, Rainer worried they might have to stage the operation in smaller waves or scale up quickly.

As each thousand names poured in, he forwarded them to **General Collins**. After four hours, the final tally emerged:

• Duncan had recommended *roughly ten individuals per day* for **ten years**, totaling **36,500**.

• **Cross-referencing** them against Chen's 1,270 known operatives found an 87% overlap, leaving **34,770** who might be "scouted but not recruited."

• None appeared to be **U.S. government employees**—this was more a pool of **business** and **political** figures, plus private citizens.

• The system flagged **43** businessmen and **17** politicians among them.

It was a vast new frontier. Rainer repeated the location-based method they used on Chen's network: mapping addresses against fixed **identifier** sites. For about 10,500 addresses—roughly 30%—they could aim an existing device immediately that same night. The command went out, and over a hundred identifiers rotated in **17 U.S. cities**, scanning for brain signals and then silently applying **CDAs 319–324**. It was, by far, the **largest** single CDA deployment to date.

While overseeing the operation, Rainer noticed a **small red icon** flashing in his neural interface—an alert from the AI system, not triggered by any known infiltration. Selecting it, he saw it concerned **Gilbert Molina's** old memories from a helicopter flight **years earlier**. Possibly unremarkable, but the AI had flagged it as significant given recent queries about *spy networks*.

Rainer frowned and opened the video. *Something*, he realized, lay hidden there—and it might reshape everything they assumed about the infiltration they were trying to contain.

Chapter 100

Shanghai, China – 2009 (Six Years Earlier)

At **seventy-three**, *Andy Chen* was well past retirement. Yet there he stood at **Pudong International Airport**, anxious about a delayed flight and glancing repeatedly at the digital display showing the **Maglev** train's top speed of *423 km/h*. Less than fifteen minutes earlier, he had traveled the 42 kilometers from downtown Shanghai to the airport—a reminder of the city's futuristic edge. Dozens of skyscrapers soared above fifty stories high, while Western-style malls, global fashion brands, and luxury car dealerships dotted the skyline. Coupled with state-of-the-art museums and performing arts centers, Shanghai's breakneck modernization left even lifelong residents in awe. Its historic Bund and vibrant pedestrian boulevards contrasted sharply with the modern, high-tech Pudong district.

Just as Chen was contemplating the city's growth, a voice interrupted:

"Mr. Chen?" "Yes." "I'm Gilbert Molina."

Chen blinked. He hadn't expected the newcomer so abruptly.

"Welcome to China," Chen said smoothly. **"How was your flight?"** **"Smooth, thanks,"** Molina replied.

Outside, an American town car waited with open doors. As they climbed in, Chen leaned forward:

"Heliport."

Molina frowned.

"Where exactly are we going?" "An island up the coast—about a forty-minute ride." "What about our first meeting?" "Already set. We're meeting the president in an hour."

Ten minutes later, they lifted off in a waiting helicopter, banking out over dark, moonlit waters. Molina was puzzled and mildly uneasy. He'd come to China for campaign funding—long-term loans Chen had promised. He hadn't expected a clandestine nighttime flight over the ocean. Yet, following Andy Chen's lead, he sat in silence as the chopper throbbed toward a mysterious island and the promise of high-level introductions he never imagined.

Chapter 101

Island off the Coast of China – Aboard an Agusta Helicopter (2009)

Gilbert Molina felt both excitement and annoyance as the **Agusta helicopter** skimmed low over calm seas under a bright full moon. He'd traveled all this way only because *Andy Chen* had offered to fund his political campaigns through long-term loans. Why China's highest echelons wanted an *unofficial* meeting, he couldn't guess—and Chen had stayed silent the entire flight.

After nearly an hour, Molina saw the silhouette of a **small island** rising like a jagged mountain. Through the helicopter's window, he watched as massive doors opened on the cliffside, revealing a perfectly round opening. The Agusta descended into a hidden hangar, a full **hundred feet** underground. The place teemed with hundreds of people, bustling about like a massive subterranean hub.

Chen led him down a corridor into a small conference room—only one man inside. The man rose with a gleaming smile.

"Gilbert, my friend! It's been ages."

Molina's eyes widened:

"Artemis? What on earth…?"

His old **childhood friend**, *Artemis Wang*, was the last person he expected. Molina had braced for a high-powered Chinese political delegation; instead, here stood the founder of the world's largest social networking and e-commerce empire, **Lingtao**—a behemoth with *2.5 billion* users. Artemis, born in the U.S. but of Taiwanese descent, had merged his upstart social site with China's biggest online marketplace, forging a global giant. Now, apparently, he also operated from this **underground complex** miles off the coast.

"Gilbert, we haven't seen each other since college," Artemis said warmly, ushering him outside to an **electric cart**. **"Come—let me show you our facility."**

They drove through towering rows of servers: this was **Lingtao's** beating heart, the data center fueling their integrated social, shopping, dating, and streaming platform. Artemis explained it was **100 square miles** of subterranean space, housing **25,000** engineers, support staff, and families in a hidden city—complete with transparent ceilings that displayed the night sky overhead. All of it, Artemis boasted, sat beyond typical government oversight.

"Gilbert, we're like our own nation. We have minimal regulations—just taxes and basic user data rules. Yet we have immense power over billions of users, shaping what they see, buy, and believe. Now, I want you to be part of this future. That's why you're here."

Molina nodded, mind spinning. Artemis spelled it out: *Andy Chen* would provide loans for Molina's political rise, expecting **no immediate favors**—only future influence, should Molina someday climb to national office.

"We might not contact you for years," Artemis said. **"If politics fizzles out, come work for me. Either way, your debts will be forgiven in time. I brought you here, so you'd understand exactly who you're dealing with."**

Molina stayed **24 hours**, touring the site. He gained enough insight into Lingtao's global dominion to realize how easily Artemis could reshape political discourse if he wished. By the time he took the helicopter back, his arrangement with Chen was formalized, and over the next seven years he saw Artemis only casually—drinks at their favorite bar, no mention of secret deals. Not until recently, when the entire network crumbled in the face of a massive U.S. crackdown.

Chapter 102

Hong Kong Island, China – 2016, Day 10, 3:00 P.M. (HKT)

"Mr. Chen, your error was inexcusable," Master Chang said. **"You acted on emotion, without evidence—and now your entire U.S. network is gone."**

Andy Chen bowed his head. **"I know I reacted impulsively,"** he admitted, **"but look at the outcome: every businessman and politician in my group was arrested that same day. Seven were never released."**

Chang, an elderly figure with measured composure, paused briefly. When he finally spoke, his tone remained calm:

"It's difficult to judge without standing in your place. So, what do you plan next?"

Chen lifted his gaze:

"I'll move the operation into Mainland China."

A spark lit in Chang's eyes, signaling approval of the idea. **"You intend to propose this to the organization?"**

"Yes," Chen replied.

Chapter 103

Zermatt, Switzerland – Zermatt Data Center 2016 – Day 10, 9:00 A.M. (CET)

While much of the United States slept, *Rainer* sat alone in the data center, grappling with a new possibility. **Andy Chen** might not actually work for Taiwan's government—or he could be playing multiple sides, or perhaps he served only **Artemis Wang**. The truth was unclear.

Determined to find answers, Rainer delved into Chen's archived **video data**. Simultaneously, he checked **CDA-322's** live feed, which showed Chen's current location in **Hong Kong**. As usual, the neural system allowed Rainer to see through Chen's eyes and hear his conversations and thoughts in real time. He caught sight of an elderly man seated across from Chen in a bustling restaurant, both speaking rapid **Cantonese**. Animated hand gestures suggested a tense exchange.

With a mental command, Rainer activated Zermatt's **automatic translation** software, selecting English for the transcript. He listened intently as he tried to piece together whether Andy Chen had been honest about his employer—or whether he was deeply enmeshed in a double or triple game far beyond what any of them had imagined.

Chapter 104

Zermatt, Switzerland – Zermatt Data Center 2016 – Day 10, 9:15 A.M. (CET)

Seated at his console, *Rainer* zoomed in on **Andy Chen's** live geolocation feed: Hong Kong's **Canal Road**, pinpointing the restaurant where Chen was meeting the unknown man. Because the other individual wasn't yet in the system, Rainer couldn't simply blanket-scan the entire space. He needed a direct ID.

At last, Chen and his companion finished lunch and headed for the exit. Rainer seized the moment: he nudged the **identifier** stationed near Canal Road, guiding its angle to pick up both **brain signals**. The system instantly discarded Chen's, already recognized, focusing on the second:

"Got you," Rainer muttered.

CDA-319 deployed in seconds, registering the subject. Rainer immediately ran **CDAs 319–324**, firing a quick note to *General Collins* explaining he was "asking forgiveness, not permission." His priority was to see who this man was.

The initial data trickled in—just a **name**—**Lin Chang**. A few minutes later, more details:

• Chang was a high-ranking official in **Taiwan's National Intelligence Office**, operating under the façade of a retired professor who'd lived in America for thirty years.

    • **He also led Taiwan's entire spy network in China.**

    • The bombshell: **Lin Chang** was **Artemis Wang's father**.

Stunned, Rainer realized he needed to grasp the full scope of **Artemis Wang**'s ties to Taiwan's government. Switching to **CDA-322** live feed on Lin Chang, he watched the older man's perspective—hoping to unravel how Wang's mega-corporation and Taiwan's intelligence apparatus converged.

Chapter 105

Hong Kong Island, China – 2016, Day 10, 3:30 P.M. (HKT)

Seated in the back of a **town car**, *Lin Chang* watched as the driver dropped **Andy Chen** at the Peninsula Hotel. Once Chen stepped out, Chang instructed the driver to continue. Moments later, he placed a call to Taiwan, speaking in **Cantonese**:

"I met with Chen—no evidence he'll expose our government."

A clipped voice on the other end replied:

"We agree. But if another incident occurs, we're severing cooperation. We can't risk a crisis with our second-largest trade partner over favors owed to Artemis. Effective immediately, our Central Bank will pay any outstanding invoices directly to Artemis's organization, *not* to scattered individuals in the U.S. The Embassy in D.C. also won't accept or courier documents for attorney Duncan anymore. Make sure your son gets formal notice."

At **Zermatt**, *Rainer* observed every moment through **Chang's eyes**, thanks to the neural network's live feed. He both saw Chang's surroundings in high-definition and overheard each word of the phone conversation—along with Chang's unspoken thoughts.

Meanwhile, *Andy Chen* boarded a plane back to Shanghai, convinced that high-altitude flight would block the watchers. He resented them— *they* were the enemy. He intended to see his boss on a remote island, hoping to escape scrutiny there, too.

Yet Chen was wrong. The neural net tracked him uninterrupted. Within seconds, Rainer received fresh signals from **Chen's** vantage, waiting for any next move—and any next slip.

Chapter 106

Zermatt, Switzerland – Zermatt Data Center 2016 – Day 10, 9:45 A.M. (CET)

Rainer leaned back in his chair, letting the truth settle: **Artemis Wang**—one of America's wealthiest entrepreneurs—had orchestrated everything. The Taiwanese government had mostly acted as couriers, not the real masterminds. Wang's goal, Rainer realized, wasn't serving any national cause; it was to siphon technology from rival companies, propping up his global e-commerce and social media empire.

A data cross-check confirmed it: every employer tied to **Chen's 1,270 operatives** either competed with Wang's **Lingtao** group or possessed crucial tech that could threaten Wang's platform. **No** other scouted individuals had been formally recruited—*only* Chen's network was active. And the seven "observers"? Not people at all, but Wang's **server bots**, silently monitoring social-media chatter.

That sealed it. Rainer descended the stairs to find **Peter Friedli**, hunched over a neural-network console:

"Peter, I need to widen our coverage for an island a hundred miles off Shanghai," Rainer said. "Do you have coordinates?" Peter asked. "Yes."

Rainer extracted them from **Gilbert Molina**'s helicopter memory feed—pulling exact GPS points from the moment the chopper landed years ago. Peter fed the location into the data-center grid. On the big screen, an **oval** extended over the coastal waters, turning yellow, then red, as one of the twelve satellites they controlled recalibrated. Now they could track *any* registered user at that secret island.

With that, Rainer quietly set a final process in motion: finishing the **CDA** registration for the thousands of new recruits. Then, compiling a detailed briefing for the **President**, **General Collins**, and **Nicolás Tosh**—who were still asleep half a world away. They would wake to discover that the entire puzzle had been solved in the night.

Satisfied, Rainer decided it was time for a reward. **Powder-snow skiing** beckoned on the Klein Matterhorn slopes just outside Zermatt—his chance to clear his head after a marathon of revelations that threatened to reshape the balance of power across three continents.

Chapter 107

Shanghai, China – 2016, Day 10, 8:30 P.M. (CST)

General Collins had digested Rainer's latest findings and prepared accordingly. Meanwhile, *Andy Chen* arrived back in **Shanghai** under driving rain and high winds. As he traversed **Pudong International Airport**, he mulled over his discussion with **Artemis Wang** in Hong Kong, who eagerly endorsed Chen's idea of relocating his network to **Mainland China**—a move that would hugely benefit Wang's operation. But *Taiwan's* abrupt pullback from U.S. infiltration efforts dampened Chen's spirits.

Awaiting him on the tarmac was a helicopter. Just as he boarded, a detested message arrived:

"Mr. Chen, we've extended our neural coverage to the island you're visiting. We'll have you online even if you go underground."

Chen clenched his jaw, refusing to reply.

"Shall we notify Mr. Wang of your location?" the voice pressed. **"That won't be necessary."**

"Excellent. We'll contact you again to confirm our reach."

Feeling cornered, Chen endured a rough flight through stormy skies. Finally, the chopper touched down on the island's hidden helipad. The moment the skids hit concrete, *General Collins* spoke again in Chen's mind:

"Mr. Chen, we see you've landed. Remember, we're watching."

Chen responded with icy disdain:

"Fine by me, sir."

Then the connection clicked off, leaving Chen alone in the swirling downpour—caught between the unstoppable watchers and the powerful boss he still needed to face.

Chapter 108

Washington, D.C. – The White House Bunker 2016 – Day 10, 8:00 A.M. (ET)

General Collins arrived before dawn, spending hours digesting the extensive digital file *Rainer* had sent from Zermatt. He knew both *Nicolás Tosh* and the President were reviewing the same intel; they had agreed to convene whenever the President's schedule permitted. Meanwhile, Collins had already contacted **Andy Chen** per Rainer's request—an attempt to keep a tight grip on Chen's unpredictable nature. **Artemis Wang** was a different dilemma altogether, one Collins suspected only the President could address. A persistent question nagged him: *Why was Chen's spy network the only one fully activated?* Perhaps they'd only learn the answer once **Artemis Wang** himself was registered in the neural network.

A call lit up Collins's phone: one of the President's secretaries.

"General, President O'Sullivan will be available after 11:00 A.M. He's finished reviewing the material."

Collins thanked her and returned to one last puzzle. He checked **Andy Chen's** neural-video archive. Curiously, Rainer hadn't included the footage of **Chen's helicopter ride with Senator Molina** years ago—likely because Chen **never** met Wang during that journey. Only Molina did. That explained why earlier analyses missed any direct Chen–Wang connection. Now, however, Chen's current off-shore trip was even more intriguing—especially with **Artemis Wang** waiting somewhere in the shadows.

Chapter 109

Island off the Coast, China – 2016 – Day 10, 9:30 P.M. (CST)

Andy Chen had never met **Artemis Wang** face-to-face. Their interactions happened via a secure video link on this hidden island, preceded by an obligatory stop in Hong Kong to confer with Wang's father, **Master Chang**. Tonight, as usual, Chen flew in under cover of darkness, traveled through the island's private corridors, and settled into the stark, white-walled conference room. A single camera lens blinked at him, reflecting his own uneasy expression.

He'd already been waiting twenty minutes before Wang finally appeared on screen. The instant Chen saw Wang's grim face, he knew this would not be an easy conversation. Without pause, Chen launched into a blunt, step-by-step report of the U.S. fiasco: how the FBI had cornered his American conspirators—businessmen, politicians—and how every one of them had cut ties rather than risk prison.

When Chen finished, laying out his plan to redeploy all remaining operatives in China, Wang said nothing, silent in obvious frustration. After a tense beat, he spoke:

Wang: "All those businessmen and politicians in the U.S. cut off contact?" **Chen:** "Yes. They've either fled or cut deals with the Department of Justice."

Wang's eyes flickered. "Which means they gave the government everything they had on you, Andy."

Chen pressed his lips together, trying not to betray the churn of anger and fear. "Nobody in that group knows each other," he said, "and none knows the engineers who were feeding us technology."

Wang: "Maybe that kept the larger network safe. But those politicians and executives are out, and you're still exposed in America. Let's be realistic—you're finished there."

Chen swallowed. "That's exactly what I want to discuss. If I take the same team—"

Wang cut in sharply. "You put them in China, you mean?"

Chen nodded. "Yes. Shift the entire operation here. Let them refocus under your umbrella."

Wang drummed his fingers against the desk, considering. "Fine. But I want you to wait for my instructions over the next few days before deploying anyone. No rash moves, Andy."

Chen inclined his head in agreement, then detailed his recent talk with Master Chang and the abrupt notification from Taiwan's government. Wang waved it off with casual assurance:

Wang: "No problem. I've already lined up another embassy to handle any 'support' we need. You won't rely on Taiwan alone."

With that, Wang severed the connection. The screen went dark, leaving Chen gazing at his own reflection—a man who had lost everything he'd built in the United States but still grasped at a new path in China. The hush of the conference room felt stifling.

He rose slowly, raking a hand through his hair. Despite Wang's outward calm, Chen knew the stakes were higher than ever—and that if he misstepped again, his next call with Artemis Wang might be his last.

Chapter 110

Washington, D.C. – The White House Bunker 2016 – Day 10 – 9:30 A.M. (ET)

General Collins ended the video feed from Andy Chen's latest conversation with Artemis Wang, feeling both relief and renewed urgency. Chen's deference to Wang was clear—though little else in the exchange was truly new. The real challenge lay in confirming Wang's role, especially if he intended to rebuild Chen's network in China.

He glanced at the countdown on a wall monitor: **3 hours, 30 minutes** until the President's scheduled conference. Collins wanted hard answers before then. He tapped a small device on his desk—the "identifier"—and selected **Nicolás Tosh**.

Collins (thought-speak): *Nicolás, good morning. Any updates from Rainer's data?*

Tosh (thought-speak): *Yes, General. I reviewed everything first thing this morning.*

Collins spoke aloud, trusting the neural link to carry each word:

"Good. We have to register Artemis Wang on the network immediately."

Tosh's mental voice came back, calm as always: *I know.*

"When can we do this?"

I'm en route to San Francisco right now—to do it myself.

Collins blinked at that. "Personally? Why?"

Wang's among my biggest customers worldwide. He only knows me as a math consultant and software vendor—once his professor at the University of Miami.

Collins frowned. "Does Rainer know about your connection?"

No. Rainer has zero visibility on our for-profit ventures.

"So, Nicolás—can you still make the President's 11:00 A.M. call?"

Yes, sir. Absolutely. My meeting with Wang happens in about an hour, assuming no delays.

Collins drummed his fingers on the table. "How much does Wang actually know about you?"

Only that I'm an advanced-math business owner, one of his key partners. Nothing else.

"Fine. Will we have him registered on the neural network before the President's conference?"

That's my plan, General. If time permits, I'll deploy CDAs 323 and 324 on him as well.

Collins allowed himself a small nod. "Excellent. Confirm the moment it's done."

Will do, sir.

The connection went silent, leaving Collins alone with the bunker's steady hum. **Artemis Wang**—the unseen force behind Chen's infiltration—was now in Nicolás Tosh's crosshairs. If Tosh succeeded, they might finally glean Wang's true intentions in time for the President's briefing. And for the first time since Chen's meltdown, Collins felt the momentum tipping back to their side.

Chapter 111

San Francisco, California – San Francisco International Airport 2016 – Day 11 – 6:30 A.M. (PT)

A **Bombardier Global Express** touched down with barely a jolt on the tarmac at San Francisco International Airport. **Nicolás Tosh** had left Miami's Opa-locka Airport at three-thirty that morning (ET), determined to reach the West Coast before dawn. The moment he discovered that **Artemis Wang** headed a vast, clandestine network of industrial espionage operatives—led by **Andy Chen**—Tosh summoned his company jet. Rarely did he use it for domestic flights, but this was an exception.

Tosh's history with Wang went back years to their days at the University of Miami—where Tosh was the brilliant professor and Wang an ambitious undergraduate. Yet only now, as fresh intelligence traced Chen's infiltration directly to Wang's empire, did Tosh realize how deeply their worlds had interwoven. As a precaution, he ran a quick check of his own database to ensure none of **Walkyria's** employees appeared on Wang's spy roster. Satisfied, he stepped off the plane and into a waiting town car bound for **Lingtao** headquarters, just minutes from the airport.

Lingtao Headquarters

Lingtao's campus sprawled across dozens of acres—a ring of twelve glass-and-steel cylinders, each about twelve stories high, plus a towering central building of twenty-five floors. The driver let Tosh out at the main lobby, where **Eric Lenard**, Wang's COO, and **Monica Miller**, his executive assistant, waited.

Eric: "Welcome, Nicolás." **Tosh:** "Good morning, Eric. Monica. Thanks for meeting me so early." **Monica:** "Artemis arrived a short while ago. He's expecting you."

They led him into a sleek, glass-enclosed elevator that whisked them upward to the top floor. Floor-to-ceiling windows revealed a breathtaking sweep of San Francisco Bay and the distant runways of SFO. Inside a grand office, **Artemis Wang** approached with a bright but uneasy smile.

Wang: "Nicolás Tosh—my teacher and mentor. It's been ages!" **Tosh:** "Artemis, this isn't a social visit. I'm here on a serious matter. First, let me disclose something: I own and run the math-software vendor **Walkyria**—your largest strategic supplier. We've been with you since your startup days."

Wang's eyes went wide. Tosh saw shock flare across his ex-student's face, as if decades of speculation had finally snapped into focus. Wang always prided himself on not relying on outsiders, yet ironically, his entire platform hinged on Tosh's advanced math. His attempts to probe Walkyria had failed; his engineers never managed to crack Tosh's proprietary algorithms or neural network.

Wang: "Nicolás…this is…wow. I had no idea you were behind Walkyria." **Tosh (activating his "identifier" in his pocket):** "How are you, Artemis?"

Unbeknownst to Wang, **CDA-319** was already homing in on his brain's unique signature, registering him on Tosh's neural network. A flicker of data streamed behind Tosh's calm gaze.

Wang: "I'm okay, I suppose, but your sudden call was a surprise. It's six-thirty in the morning. What's so urgent?" **Tosh:** "Are you aware of what happened to me recently—my six-month ordeal?"

Wang nodded.

Wang: "I heard rumors. Some frame-up, but then you were cleared." **Tosh:** "Yes, and the conspirators who set me up are serving long prison terms now." **Wang:** "So…who was the mastermind?" **Tosh:** "Ever heard of **Leroy Sinclair**?" **Wang:** "Sinclair…? Wait, that name's connected to a college buddy's father. My friend uses his mother's last name… **Gilbert Molina**, right?" **Tosh (quietly deploying CDA-320 through 324):** "Exactly. Molina traveled with his father on multiple occasions as the conspiracy developed. The FBI picked him up at Dulles after a flight from Shanghai. Now he's under a Justice Department confidentiality agreement, forbidding contact with a Chinese-American suspected of working for a foreign spy ring—a man named Andy Chen."

Wang blinked, fear tightening in his features.

Wang: "Andy Chen financed Molina's career. But what's that got to do with me?" **Tosh:** "Molina says **Chen works for you**."

A stunned hush fell. Wang sank back in his chair, pressing his palms over his face for a long moment. Finally, he looked up.

Wang: "All right, Nicolás. What does…whoever is investigating me want?" **Tosh:** "I can't reveal specifics, but they'll likely call you soon— today. My advice? Stay here. Don't make any calls or send instructions that might look suspicious. They're watching every move, and they'll know instantly if you try to run."

Wang swallowed hard.

Wang: "Why warn me?" **Tosh:** "Because if you panic and vanish, it triggers a bigger crisis for all of us. Get your top criminal attorney here now, and lie low until you're officially contacted."

Wang realized the U.S. government treated national security threats mercilessly. His earlier bravado vanished.

Wang: "Should I call my lawyer immediately?" **Tosh:** "Yes. And get the best you can afford. I'll stay here until they reach out—I might help, in a small way."

Wang picked up his phone and dialed **Lewton Sanders**, the trusted attorney who'd guided him from the start. Within minutes, Sanders was on the way. Meanwhile, Wang tried to bury himself in routine tasks, but the tension was palpable. Tosh sat in the office's lounge, eyes distant, quietly conferring with **Rainer** and **General Collins** via the neural network in his mind.

Neural Network Check-In

Tosh (thought-speak): *Gentlemen, I've informed Wang he's under investigation. He's paralyzed—fearful to act except calling his lawyer.*

Collins (thought-speak): *Why divulge that? We wanted to watch him, see if he ran…*

Tosh: *My instincts said leaving him free for two hours—until the President decides—was too risky. He might flee or destroy evidence. Now he's too shaken to do anything but wait. And we can see everything he's thinking via CDA-322.*

Collins: *You're right. Good call. We're capturing his entire life archive, too. Rainer says it'll be complete before the President's meeting.*

Tosh: *Yes, I'm watching the progress. We'll reconvene once it's done.*

They ended the mental link. Moments later, Artemis Wang approached Tosh, who sat staring off into space, lost in silent conversation. Wang hovered uncomfortably before finally speaking out loud:

Wang: "Nicolás? Hello?"

Tosh blinked back, returning to the moment.

Tosh: "Artemis—sorry, was thinking about my schedule. Everything okay?" **Wang:** "Lewton's on his way. But…where were you just now? I stood here calling your name, but you looked like you were gone." **Tosh (half-smiling):** "I zone out sometimes—my wife complains about it, too. Just lost in thought."

Wang studied him, troubled.

Wang: "You can't tell me anything else?" **Tosh:** "I'm not part of the investigation. I'm only letting you know…something's coming. You'll need counsel. As for your company—I doubt the government wants to cripple Lingtao. It's too big, too strategic to fail."

Even as Tosh said it, he regretted the implication. Wang's face fell. He paced away, wrestling with how much the Feds already knew. If they had Chen's entire network, how much deeper might it go? With Chen effectively sidelined, were Wang's other secrets still hidden?

By eight o'clock local time, the neural network finished extracting **Artemis Wang's** entire life record. Whatever came next would be revealed in the upcoming White House briefing—where Tosh and the others could decide Wang's fate in a matter of hours.

Chapter 112

Zermatt, Switzerland | Washington, D.C., USA | San Francisco, California, USA Lingtao World Headquarters – Day 11 (2016) 5:00 P.M. CET / 11:00 A.M. ET / 8:00 A.M. PT

General Collins, **Rainer**, and **Nicolás Tosh** sat before a wall of screens in their respective locations—Zermatt's data center for Rainer, the White House bunker for Collins, and an office lobby at Lingtao's Bay Area campus for Tosh. From three time zones, they joined forces to watch **Artemis Wang's** life unfold in a high-speed panorama, gleaned from the full CDA-324 download completed just moments ago.

It was both a dazzling and disquieting reel—Wang's meteoric rise from college prodigy to CEO, culminating in his landmark merger that formed **Lingtao**, then the gradual turn toward obsessive ambition, industrial espionage, and illusions of global influence.

They paused the playback just minutes before the scheduled 11:00 A.M. (ET) conference with President O'Sullivan.

Presidential Conference – 11:00 A.M. ET

President (speakerphone / neural link): "Gentlemen, how are you holding up?"

They answered one by one. The President singled out Rainer for high praise, commending him on his breakthrough the previous night.

Collins: "Sir, we can confirm Artemis Wang is the real mastermind—**not** any foreign government. Chen's infiltration network was the only one fully active, aimed at fueling Wang's corporate empire. Wang sees his massive social-media platform as a borderless cybernation—he's obsessed with technology that grants him influence, or even control, over 2.5 billion users. Over time, he believes Lingtao can overshadow most nation-states."

President: "If you can harness the loyalty or behavior of billions, you wield unimaginable power. I'm starting to see why he took such risky measures."

Collins: "Yes, sir. The question, then, is **what do we do about it**?"

Rainer: "It's more complex than simply taking him down. We can't afford to sink Lingtao. The blow to our own strategic and economic interests would be massive. Allow me to show a brief clip from a debate at Harvard Business School—our 'carrier,' Chris Musial, ran a session on the hazards of letting key 'digital pillars' collapse."

They shared a quick five-minute video. The President nodded.

President: "Understood: **too big and too strategic to fail**. All right, so if we forcibly dismantle or bankrupt Lingtao, we lose the platform's entire knowledge base, disrupt billions of user services, and spark severe global backlash."

Rainer: "Precisely, sir. So a public crackdown is unwise. We recommend we act behind the scenes—secure a smooth transition, quietly dismantle his spy ring, and minimize political fallout."

President: "Nicolás, what's your take?"

Tosh: "Mr. President, once I realized Wang was my former student— and that his company is one of my largest Walkyria clients—I flew to San Francisco first thing this morning. My priorities were:

1.   **Register** Wang on the neural network, which I did around six A.M. Pacific.

2.   **Prevent** him from taking any rash action that could harm the U.S. or sabotage Lingtao.

I succeeded on both. I used our conversation to keep him in his office and dissuade him from fleeing or giving damaging orders. Meanwhile, we've just finished downloading his entire life archive via CDAs 319 through 324."

Collins (to the President): "So that's where we stand, sir—**what** do we do next? We can't delay; the risk grows by the hour."

President: "Agreed. Let's loop in Cyberwarfare. I have limited time."

He picked up a secure phone, skillfully merging it with the neural link so all participants could hear.

Cyberwarfare Division – Conference Line

President: "General Statton, do you read me? I have General Collins, Rainer Sábato, and Nicolás Tosh on board as well."

Statton (over phone): "Yes, Mr. President."

President: "Lingtao—the largest web platform by traffic—may face 'abnormal operations' in the next few hours. I want a general alert, with the capacity to **shut it down** if needed."

Statton: "Sir, what exactly do you mean by 'abnormal operations'?"

Tosh (cutting in): "General, it could be sabotage from within. Wang might panic, or unknown players may attempt a cyberattack. We need you ready to intervene, but **only** on the President's direct order."

Statton: "Understood. We'll stand by, prepared to isolate or disable Lingtao's global servers on your command."

The President ended the call.

Back to the Presidential Briefing

Tosh: "What about Wang himself, Mr. President?"

President: "We do exactly what we did with Andy Chen. The Attorney General just sent me a draft plea agreement. Let's talk to Wang now."

Rainer: "Sir, if we're cutting a deal, we should demand **all** the data from the 'Duncan-scouted' and 'Chen-recruited' rosters. That would save us huge time verifying the rest of his infiltration networks."

President: "Excellent point. I'll have that added to the final terms. Let's begin."

Tosh: "One moment, sir—I'll enter Wang's office."

Lingtao Headquarters – Wang's Executive Floor

Tosh crossed the expanse of the top-floor suite, stopping near Wang's oversized desk with panoramic windows behind it. Wang and his attorney stood as Tosh approached.

Wang: "Nicolás, let me introduce you to—"

Without speaking aloud, Tosh transmitted a thought:

Tosh (thought-speak to Wang): *Artemis, ask your lawyer to step outside. This is crucial. Trust me.*

Wang's eyes bulged, but he gave no visible reaction. His attorney looked bewildered—the two men exchanged no words, yet their expressions suggested some silent conversation.

Wang (aloud): "Lee, please wait in the hallway. I'll call you if I need you."

Attorney: "Artemis, I strongly advise you not to say a thing without me present."

Wang: "I'm just talking to a friend, not a government official."

Attorney: "Everything you say could be used against you—"

Wang: "Please, Lee. Just five minutes."

Reluctantly, the lawyer left. Tosh then spoke silently:

Tosh (thought-speak): *Mr. President, we're ready.*

Across the neural link, the President's calm voice spoke directly into Wang's mind:

President: *Mr. Wang, good morning. With me are General Collins, Rainer Sábato, and Nicolás Tosh, who stands before you now. We're using a communicational technology allowing direct thought-to-brain contact. You may speak aloud in response; we'll hear you.*

Wang exhaled sharply. "Mister… President? May I ask why we're talking like this?"

President: *One: it's secure. Two: it concerns the technology itself. Since Mr. Tosh is intimately involved with it, he's here as well.*

Wang: "So this is an *unofficial* channel, correct?"

President: *Precisely. Tosh acts as our designated consultant for these algorithms. I'll be frank: we have serious matters to discuss, so I want you prepared.*

Wang: "I'm listening…"

President: *We have the means to see through your eyes, hear your words—and record your **every** thought in real time.*

A brief video feed flashed in Wang's mind, showing exactly what he saw moments ago, then a snippet of his internal monologue. His jaw tightened in alarm.

President: *We've also downloaded your life in HD—every memory, from your earliest years to now. Observe this clip...*

Footage of Wang's recent video conference with Andy Chen played in his mind's eye.

President: *Finally, we have data on those around you, including anyone else we've already registered. We're pulling footage from people you've interacted with—like Gilbert Molina. This is how deep our authority and capability run.*

Wang stood trembling, as though the air had been sucked from the room.

President: *Mr. Wang, you've committed grave crimes carrying potential life imprisonment. But I'm offering you a chance—cooperate fully, and we can discuss reduced sentences or parole. Are you ready to do that?*

Wang: "May I speak with my lawyer first...?"

President: *Of course. But show him these facts—that we have a complete record of your life. Under G-7 and Congressional approval, we can use this technology for national security threats. We know everything, Mr. Wang.*

At that final pronouncement, Wang realized how thoroughly cornered he was, mind spinning with panic. He opened his mouth to reply, but no words came. Outside the door, his attorney waited, oblivious to the silent war raging inside his client's thoughts—and to the momentous confrontation unfolding via the neural link that had just upended Artemis Wang's entire world.

Artemis Wang's mind reeled. He faced a silent room in his top-floor office, his lawyer waiting outside, the President of the United States and his team inside his head. The swirling mix of fear, shock, and resentment weighed on him like an iron mantle. He had built **Lingtao** from nothing into one of the most powerful digital platforms in the world—and now, in mere minutes, he risked losing it all.

Wang (speaking aloud): "Sir, how can I possibly explain all of this to my lawyer?"

President (thought-speak): *That's up to you, Mr. Wang. You may disclose as much or as little as you wish—subject to the confidentiality constraints we'll impose.*

Wang exhaled, shoulders slumped.

Wang: "What exactly do you want from me?"

President: *We'll send you a cooperation and confidentiality agreement for your attorney's review. Under it, you're forbidden to discuss our technology—or us—with anyone. In exchange, we'll grant leniency, channeling your case through the Department of Justice. We've left the specifics—like references to your crimes and to us—blank, so your attorney won't see certain details. Will you accept?*

Wang: "I agree."

President (to Tosh): *Nicolás, can you handle it?*

Tosh: *Yes, sir. I'll print the draft now.*

Tosh stepped to a nearby printer, issuing a silent command through the neural network to generate the document. In seconds, he handed it to **Lee Anderson**, Wang's criminal attorney, who had just been summoned back into the room.

Anderson skimmed the agreement, eyes flicking from one vague clause to the next.

Anderson: "Artemis, it says here you're *admitting guilt*. Don't do that. They have to prove wrongdoing first."

Wang: "Lee, I *am* guilty. We both know it."

Anderson: "Legally, that's for a jury to decide." He lowered his voice, agitated. "This is insane. Half the document's redacted or blank. I can't even see the full charges."

Wang (wearily): "Just finalize it. Let's get their counsel on the line."

Moments later, the White House legal team conferred with Anderson. Meanwhile, General Collins's firm but measured voice again filled Wang's mind:

Collins: *As you sign, remember: we see what you see. We know your thoughts. Our reach extends to your private island as well. Any sabotage or attempt to flee, we'll know—and we have a U.S. Cyberwarfare unit on standby to* **shut down** *Lingtao if needed.*

Wang: "I'd never harm our community—my entire career's built on it."

Back at the conference table, Anderson laid down his pen, shaking his head.

Anderson: "I've edited what I could, Artemis. Since half the content is classified, my hands are tied."

Wang: "Thank you, Lee."

A notary was summoned. The final pages printed again with Anderson's notes, and Wang scrawled his signature. Meanwhile,

President O'Sullivan glanced at his watch in Washington, clearing his schedule to finalize the arrangement.

The Terms

President: *Mr. Wang, first you'll provide a comprehensive database of every operative, plus all scouted or recruited candidates. Next, you'll resign as Chairman and CEO in about sixty days—time enough to dismantle the remaining spy network. You'll keep running the company as if you're in charge, but we'll assign a Co-Chairman/CEO who must approve every major move. Your official reason for departure will be 'health considerations.' Finally, you must donate all your shares to a nonprofit. Your future penalties and fines depend on your ongoing cooperation. Understood?*

Wang felt lightheaded, nodding wordlessly.

President (placing Wang on hold): *Gentlemen, one moment.*

Inside the White House bunker, O'Sullivan switched his neural feed to private mode with **Tosh.**

President (thought-speak): *Nicolás, I propose **you** become Co-Chairman/CEO—then permanent if you agree. We'll keep it confidential, so Wang remains the public face, but he'll answer to you in reality.*

Tosh: *I'm honored, sir, but—*

President: *Hear me out. Our nation owes you. You've done all this covertly—asked for nothing. Now we need you to ensure Lingtao remains stable. Wang's shares will transfer to your **Experta Foundation**. That's how we keep it philanthropic. Wang will remain visible but effectively subordinate. We'd only require your physical presence occasionally.*

The key is preventing a public meltdown with employees, media, and the market.

Tosh: *Yes, I see the logic. Let's finalize it then. Wang's waiting.*

Back to Wang

President (returning to main feed): *Mr. Wang, please sign all documents now.*

With an unsteady hand, Wang signed away operational control of his empire to **Nicolás Tosh**, transferring his shares to the **Experta Foundation**. The government's confidentiality and cooperation agreement required no formal confession—merely an acceptance of guilt. Wang found himself left with a fraction of his former wealth, perhaps a few hundred million dollars—still enormous by normal standards, but minuscule compared to his billions.

President: *Mr. Wang, we can't promise no prosecution. Your final fate hinges on your cooperation with Mr. Tosh and the U.S. However, refrain from touching your remaining assets beyond daily expenses. You'll face a large fine, and your behavior in the coming months decides whether you keep anything else.*

Wang stared off, ashen-faced. Then the President spoke once more:

President: *Is that clear, Mr. Wang?*

Wang (quietly): "Yes."

The line went dead. Tosh watched Wang sink into a chair, shoulders sagging, the tension crashing over him. After a moment, Tosh broke the silence:

Tosh: "Artemis, you've narrowly avoided a Supermax prison cell— no small mercy. Publicly, you remain CEO and keep your reputation intact. You'll still have a sizeable fortune, just not tens of billions. I suggest you make good use of it."

Wang (in a hollow voice): "What…do we do now?"

Tosh: "We have work, Artemis. A great deal of it."

In the hush of that grand, glass-walled office, it dawned on Wang that while he'd escaped the most brutal punishment, he'd lost the empire he'd shaped in his own image. And in the soft luminescence of a California morning, he prepared to step into a new reality—answering to the man who had once been his mentor…and who now commanded all that he had built.

EPILOGUE TO ALGORITHM–323

Zermatt, Switzerland – Several Weeks Later

A crisp alpine wind swept through the hidden canyon as Nicolás Tosh stepped out onto a newly built platform above the Zermatt Data Center. Far below, the quantum supercomputer pulsed with quiet power. Overhead, satellites silently updated, transmitting a constant pulse of data from every corner of the globe. The stone walls still smelled faintly of ozone after the last round of hardware upgrades—the system was bigger than ever.

He gazed out at the surrounding peaks, thinking how a single twist of fate had brought him from a teenage daydream in Bariloche to this.

- He had built Walkyria, then Experta.
- He had guided the G-7's usage of CDA-322 through 324, sparing entire governments from collapse.
- And recently, he had seized control—albeit quietly—of **Lingtao**, the largest social-media and e-commerce empire on Earth.

Artemis Wang remained the public face, but the world would have gasped to know that behind the scenes, it was Tosh—and his data center—deciding Lingtao's destiny. Any time Wang so much as typed a personal email, Tosh's neural network verified he wasn't hiding secrets. That had been part of Wang's plea deal, along with handing his fortune to the **Experta Foundation**. He got to stay free, but under a digital leash.

Tosh inhaled the thin mountain air. He told himself he had done good. The conspirators who framed him were gone. The infiltration ring run by Andy Chen had been flipped—its thousands of agents unwittingly feeding back intel to the U.S. Yet something felt unfinished. Power always invites a challenge, he thought, recalling a conversation with Rainer that very morning. **Rainer** had come across a set of unauthorized data pings: an unidentified group appeared to be testing the edges of the neural network. Perhaps it was the usual background noise, or perhaps a sign that someone else was on the verge of creating their own mind-tech.

A faint vibration in his pocket: his "identifier" device, on stand-by.

"Nicolás, do you read me?" came **Rainer's** *mental voice.*
"Yes. Any news?"
"A new wave of inbound signals. Not Chen, not Wang—someone else is sniffing around. Tied to an Eastern European domain. We can't confirm yet, but it's advanced."

Tosh closed his eyes. Every time he thought he could rest, a new threat materialized. The harsh truth: The deeper the Zermatt Data Center burrowed into global systems, the more they became a target. And with the White House now pushing for expansions in "transparency," someone—maybe an enemy government, maybe a rogue faction— would inevitably try to exploit these algorithms in ways Tosh never intended.

He made his way back inside, into the swirling hum of the data center's main atrium. Massive screens glowed with lines of code, real-time feeds, and the cosmic threads that connected billions of minds. "Algorithm–323," he reflected. "We labeled it a WMD. Yet we pushed it to the limit, all in the name of keeping the world safe." But new lines of code flickered. New illusions of control beckoned. And the next algorithm—CDA-325—loomed in the wings, holding even greater potential for rewriting human minds. Did he dare refine it further? Or lock it away, to spare humanity from unstoppable tyranny?

A fresh alarm pulsed on the master console. Rainer and a half-dozen operators rushed to respond, tension crackling through the air. Tosh's heart pounded.

One crisis had ended—but a new storm was gathering. Tomorrow, next week, next month, the race would continue. The question was no longer whether they could protect this technology from the unscrupulous; it was whether it could remain a shield rather than a sword. He exhaled and stepped up to the console, ready to face whatever came next.

In the hush of that subterranean fortress, the flicker of new code welcomed him into an uncertain future.

PROLOGUE TO ALGORITHM–325

One Year Later – Lingtao Campus, Bay Area

A massive crowd gathered beneath steel rafters in **Lingtao's** newly renovated auditorium. A glossy stage showcased two podiums bearing the company's swirling, modern logo. A flurry of camera flashes painted the air white. VIPs from Silicon Valley, heads of global NGOs, and even a discreet envoy from the White House sat in the front rows, eyes locked on the dais.

Artemis Wang—officially still Lingtao's Chairman & CEO—stepped forward to applause.

"Welcome, everyone," he began, voice echoing in the hush. "Today marks a new era of transparent data solutions. Lingtao is proud to partner with the **Experta Foundation** to uplift communities worldwide."

Behind Wang, a second figure waited in the shadows: a so-called "co-CEO," the public face of the **Experta** philanthropic venture. The real puppet-master behind them both—**Nicolás Tosh**—was not on stage. Instead, he monitored the entire scene from a remote terminal in the building's secure sublevel, using the same "identifier" device that let him read minds half a planet away.

From one vantage in the crowd, a bespectacled reporter leaned forward, furrowing her brow. She'd heard rumors of a hush-hush meltdown last year, and that Wang had quietly ceded operational control.

Where was the real power in this "new Lingtao"? She intended to find out.

Meanwhile, Tosh flicked through lines of code on his screen, verifying that Wang wasn't deviating from the script. In the months since Wang's plea deal, the White House had expanded coverage of the **Communicational Discrete Algorithms**, forcing thousands more government employees to come under discrete scrutiny. Now the President was nearing the end of his term, and the leading candidates—both from major parties—were jostling for the privilege of controlling (or harnessing) these invisible "weapons."

Yet even as Tosh ensured the stage event ran smoothly, a digital alert rattled the console: **UNAUTHORIZED NEURAL SCAN DETECTED**—source unknown. A cold spike of adrenaline shot through him. This was more than a simple infiltration. The encryption suggested quantum-level skill, reminiscent of his own codes.

"They might have a prototype," Tosh thought, swallowing hard. Did some rival group develop a brand-new system—**NeuraTech** or something equally potent—that bypassed his gating?

He tapped a mental command, connecting to **Rainer** at the Zermatt Data Center:

"Rainer, we have a breach attempt. I'm in Lingtao's basement facility. Are you seeing this?"

Rainer's voice crackled back in Tosh's head, tense: *"Yes. They're not just scanning. They're trying partial overwrites. People are losing short-term memory. We must mobilize."*

A chill ran down Tosh's spine. Overwrites? That was precisely the horrifying potential of the unreleased **CDA-325**—the power to plant or remove memories. He'd locked that research away, hoping never to use it. If an unknown faction had discovered a version of that algorithm, the entire world was at risk. This overshadowed any conspiracy they'd faced before.

Up on stage, Wang gestured to the crowd, announcing philanthropic grants and "ethical" AI expansions. The audience cheered. But down below, Tosh barely heard them. Another infiltration alert flashed. **He realized instantly**: The new threat wasn't a matter of blackmail or infiltration. It was a fundamental assault on free will—someone out there intended to rewrite minds.

His phone buzzed with a flurry of messages from White House channels. One read:

"All major intel agencies see a surge of bizarre memory-loss incidents. Possibly connected to advanced brain-tech." It ended with a single line of command: **"Stop them, or we do it ourselves. Deploy the next algorithm if needed."**

Tosh's heart hammered. The next algorithm—**Algorithm–325**—was the last measure to defend billions of unsuspecting minds. If they unleashed it, the world would never be the same. He forced a steadying breath and started up the service elevator. The event above still roared with applause for illusions of "hope," oblivious to the war for the human mind about to erupt.

High overhead, sleek monitors displayed a new slogan: **"LINGTAO & EXPERTA: Building a Tomorrow Without Boundaries."**

In Tosh's mind, ironically, those "boundaries" were all that prevented humanity from losing its soul. Because in the shadows, an unstoppable arms race was underway—one that would test every moral line he and his allies had ever drawn.

Welcome to **Algorithm–325**: the next step in rewriting the future.

About the Author,

Erasmus Cromwell-Smith is an American Writer, Playwright, Poet, and Pedagogue. He's published 32 books in the genres of self-help, poetry, young-adults, education, and sci-fi.